DEATH BY DEVIL'S FOOD

Also by Joanne Pence

Ancient Secrets Series

ANCIENT ECHOES - ANCIENT SHADOWS

ANCIENT ILLUSIONS - ANCIENT DECEPTIONS

ANCIENT PASSAGES

The Donnelly Cabin Inn

IF I LOVED YOU - THIS CAN'T BE LOVE

SENTIMENTAL JOURNEY - A CERTAIN SMILE

TIME AFTER TIME

The Rebecca Mayfield Mysteries

ONE O'CLOCK HUSTLE - TWO O'CLOCK HEIST

THREE O'CLOCK SÉANCE - FOUR O'CLOCK SIZZLE

FIVE O'CLOCK TWIST - SIX O'CLOCK SILENCE

SEVEN O'CLOCK TARGET - EIGHT O'CLOCK SPLIT

NINE O'CLOCK RETREAT - THE 13th SANTA (Novella)

The Cook and Inspector Mysteries

DEATH ON A SILVER PLATTER - A QUICHE BEFORE DYING -
THE MARINARA MURDERS -

CLOSE ENCOUNTERS OF THE DEADLY KIND

DEATH BY DEVIL'S FOOD

Others

SEEMS LIKE OLD TIMES - DANGEROUS JOURNEY

DANCE WITH A GUNFIGHTER - THE DRAGON'S LADY

THE GHOST OF SQUIRE HOUSE

DEATH BY DEVIL'S FOOD

THE COOK AND INSPECTOR MYSTERIES

JOANNE PENCE

QUAIL HILL PUBLISHING

Quail Hill Publishing

Eagle, ID 83616

Visit our website at www.quailhillpublishing.net

First Quail Hill Publishing E-book: September 2024

First Quail Hill Print Book: September 2024

DEATH BY DEVIL'S FOOD

CHAPTER ONE

L ittle did the people who walked the city streets know of the hidden life that teemed around them, a dark, deadly substratum that knew no compassion, generosity, or humanity. Humanity—hah! A weak, self-serving concept if he ever heard one.

Only an occasional noise in the darkness, a sudden shadow thrust across blood-filled cracks in a sidewalk lit by street lamps, gave unheeded warning that there was more to existence than they knew, those day-walkers, more than what they saw every day, what they felt. How surprised the blind would be if they could see as he did, all night, every night.

He was the Dark Lord, and he saw all.

A gray sewer rat slinked out from the shelter of a stone wall, raised its nose to sniff the night air. It froze as if paralyzed with fright. The Dark Lord smiled, his mouth wet with anticipation.

The rat's sharp claws dug hard against the sidewalk and its black eyes bulged. Abruptly, as if resurrected from its stupor, it scurried toward the gutter that ran under the old church of St. Michael the Archangel, its powerful hind legs pumping fast. But too late.

High, sharp squeals shredded the evening silence as it was captured and its neck snapped. Blood squirted from its twitching body and splattered on the demonic creature that fed on it.

Angie Amalfi looked back over her shoulder at her customer, flashed a big smile, and gave one last friendly wave. Barbara Knudsen, the wife of an assistant district attorney who had just been appointed to the bench, waved in return before stepping back inside and shutting the door. Mrs. Knudsen was throwing a celebration party for her husband the next afternoon. When she learned of Angie's brand-new "Comical Cakes" business, she asked if Angie could create and deliver a cake to her house that night, and she didn't care how late it would be.

Angie agreed and got her friend, Connie Rogers, to help her. An oversized smiley-faced gavel rapping down onto a replica of a Monopoly "Go Directly to Jail" card was difficult to pull off, and the cake didn't meet Angie's satisfaction until after nine o'clock. She and Connie didn't make it to the Knudsen home until nearly ten. But Angie received a generous bonus for her wonderful cake and late-night delivery.

"I can't believe how late it is. I've got to get up early to do some bookkeeping before I open my shop in the morning," Connie said as they hurried back to Angie's car, a Ferrari Portofino. In her thirties and divorced, Connie owned her own business, a gift shop called Everyone's Fancy.

"I'm sorry," Angie said. "I'm so new at this, I have no idea how long it takes to create what I think will be an easy 'comical' design. I really appreciate you helping and coming out here with me to deliver the cake."

"Well, a girl can't be too careful traveling around alone at night, especially going to strangers' houses," Connie said, as they continued toward the car, parked two blocks from the customer's house since every closer space was taken.

"Good point," Angie murmured, then looked down at her finger. "Darn! I got a paper cut from the invoice." She began fishing in her Coach tote for a tissue. "But when the customer said if I couldn't help her, she would see if Lolly Firenghetti was available, I knew I had to do something. Lolly is an awful baker. Her cakes should be used as doorstops, and her frosting can double as superglue!"

"I've heard she's not happy that you're cutting into her business," Connie added.

"I am?" Angie pressed the tissue to the small spot of blood on her finger. "I haven't even been at this a month."

"A long month!" Connie wailed.

"I know. And I really appreciate all you've done to help me get started."

"I'm sorry to say, I may have to cut back," Connie added. "Frankly, I never expected a business that began at a funeral would catch on this way."

They reached Angie's car. As Angie open the door, she shoved the tissue into her jacket pocket. It slipped out, caught by a breeze, and floated away so quickly she lost sight of it. It was late and dark, so she let it go, all the while feeling a bit hurt that what Connie had said about her business was true.

Her business began a month earlier when a friend's elderly grandmother passed away and the friend asked Angie to create a special cake for a post-funeral reception. Since the grandmother had loved chocolate to excess, the granddaughter wanted a chocolate cake. But then, to Angie's horror, she asked that the cake be covered with purple icing and trimmed with a macabre black border.

At first, Angie thought her friend was joking. Luckily, she didn't laugh, because the bereaved was deadly serious. She was catapulting her grandmother into eternity in the most questionable taste.

Much to her amazement, some members of the funeral party were deeply moved. Others commented that the black border added a bizarrely wry humor to it. Angie didn't know whether to be flattered, appalled, or to deny all responsibility.

A mourner asked if she'd be willing to create a truly comical sheet cake for an office party. A co-worker was retiring, and they wanted a cake that looked like a nursing home with the words "Not Long Now, Buddy," written in black.

Ha, ha.

Angie hadn't studied cooking and baking at the Cordon Bleu in Paris to come up with Metamucil Manor retirement cakes. She didn't want to simply refuse, so she quoted a high price. To her amazement, the woman agreed to pay what she'd asked.

That led to a cake for a baby shower. The parents' last name was Baer, and they asked for a bear cub in a baby blanket, which Angie happily provided. Two cakes later, she decided to regard her cakes not as mere confections, but as whimsical works of art, similar to ice sculptures at gala events. She drew up some business cards, and Comical Cakes was born.

"No matter how my business began," Angie said to Connie, "I couldn't have gotten it going without your help. But I understand your need to pull back. These cakes have taken on a life of their own."

"They have," Connie said, wriggling to make herself more comfortable in the car. "Now, let's get out of here. This place is pretty creepy. It feels like someone is watching us."

"We're in Pacific Heights, one of the city's best neighborhoods." Angie started the engine.

Connie pulled her python-print coat closer and latched the seat belt. "Yeah, beautiful except for that decaying church up ahead taking up most of a city block."

Down the street loomed a once beautiful old Catholic church that was now begrimed and foreboding. Built in the 1890s, the Church of St. Michael the Archangel had been one of the few structures that had survived the city's big 1906 earthquake and fire. After the not-quite-as-huge quake in 1989, however, the city's building inspectors wouldn't allow it to be reopened without earthquake retrofitting. Several years went by until, finally, the archdiocese decided against spending the money to shore up the structure. That caused the city's preservationists to campaign against the church being torn down. The disputes continued, in court and out, still unresolved.

So there the church stood, abandoned.

"It is kind of eerie out here," Angie agreed.

"Maybe delivering a cake to this spooky place is payback for your business's funereal beginnings," Connie said with a chuckle. "Anyway, I don't like it here."

With the engine purring, Angie took a moment to check her finger again under the interior car light. As much as she wanted to get away, she didn't want any bloody spots giving her car the look of a crime scene.

The finger was fine. As she shut the interior light, she noticed that no streetlights illuminated the area near the old church. As she looked at it, to her surprise, a chill ripple down her back. She reached over and hit the master door lock, and quickly pulled away from the curb.

The lacerated corpse of the rat dangled by its tail from his fingertips. Thirst and hunger satisfied for the moment, he tossed it into the gutter and wiped the back of his hand across his mouth as he slinked closer to the street. He had watched the two women in the luxurious car not only with interest, but with much attention judging from the effect one in particular had

had on his body. It had been a long time since simply looking at a woman could make his blood feel warmer, and flow more quickly through his body. Usually, he had to be doing much more than looking, even more than touching. He sucked the rat's blood slowly from each of his fingertips as the car disappeared into the distance.

A tissue fluttered to his feet; he bent over and picked it up. On it, he saw a spot of blood. A sign, he thought, and smiled.

I am Beast. I am Destroyer. I am where lust, terror, and death converge.

I am Nightmare.

CHAPTER TWO

San Francisco Homicide Inspector Paavo Smith sat at his desk in the Hall of Justice the next morning, lost in thought. He was a tall man with broad shoulders and a slim but powerful build. His short hair was dark brown, his high cheek-boned face hard and chiseled, the kind of face that crooks, thieves, and murderers might cower from.

From time to time, he would glance at the picture he'd pulled from his desk drawer. Angie Amalfi had given it to him some months before with the expectation that he'd keep it on the top of his desk, not tucked away inside. His fellow officers knew he and Angie had been dating, on and off, for nearly ten months. But to place her picture on his desk—a spot reserved for family members by every other detective in the bureau— well, they weren't there yet.

Still, whenever he looked at her smiling face framed by shiny brown hair with reddish-blond highlights, her soulful brown eyes, small nose and generous mouth, something inside him twisted. It was a good twist, he had to admit, but not one conducive to work. In fact, nothing about his current relation- ship with Angie helped his concentration in any area, and he had decided, finally, to put an end to this fish-or-cut-bait situation.

He returned the picture to his desk and shut the drawer. "The hell with it, Yosh," he said glumly to his partner. "I've got to do it. There's no getting around it anymore."

"Are you sure about this, Paav?" Toshiro Yoshwara gave him a piercing stare from the desk parked across from Paavo's. A big man, broad and muscular, with close-cropped black hair and a thick neck, Yosh stood only a couple of inches shorter than Paavo's six-foot-two-inch height, and just barely managed to squeeze into his swivel office chair.

"I know I can't keep on this way," Paavo admitted. Talking about his feelings to Yosh wasn't easy, but even a tough cop had to open up to someone, sometime.

Yosh had been his partner the past seven months or so. Before that, his longtime partner and best friend, Matt Kowalski, had been shot to death while investigating the case where Paavo met Angie.

Paavo never thought he'd be able to move past Matt's death. Maybe it was the reason he'd let down his defenses and allowed his own vulnerabilities show, the reason he'd let himself accept the warmth and love Angie offered.

And Yosh's friendship as well. That's what partners were all about.

But Paavo and Angie were so very different—and everyone, including the two of them, knew it—that a few months earlier he had tried to gently break up with her, to slowly fade away from her life, and to move on with his. It hadn't worked for one very obvious reason. Their relationship had moved beyond friendship, extreme liking, and even lust. They were in love.

But since admitting how they felt, their relationship had stopped moving forward. Paavo knew what the next step should be when two people were in love and wanted to be together. He knew exactly what was on Angie's mind, as well as her mother's and all four of her sisters'. But the thought scared him. Even the word... the "M" word... scared him. So, he stayed stuck.

Now, even he was sick of being stuck.

To tell the truth, amazingly soon after meeting Angie, he'd found himself drawn to her. It was as if she brought sunshine into his life, hokey as that seemed. Logically, they were completely wrong for each other. But the heart, he learned, wasn't logical. She was open, intuitive, and wore her heart on her sleeve. He was closed, logical, and kept his feelings bottled up. Trust was hard for him, but somehow, he had learned to trust Angie enough to be open with her, to be himself.

He treasured her for that.

Okay, Smith, he'd told himself that very morning, the time had come.

Yosh put down his pencil, turning away from the Form 10A9 he'd been typing, and swung his chair to face Paavo. "Good for you!" Yosh bellowed. "You two have been through a lot already. And you're both not kids." He paused, then added, "I think a man's gotta do what a man's gotta do."

"So, it seems." Paavo hated the trite phrase, one he'd heard too often used as an excuse for some of the most heinous acts imaginable.

"When will you do it?" Yosh asked, his face sympathetic.

"I'll have to wait until the time is exactly right. It isn't something to spring on her out of the blue."

"Hah! I don't think you need to worry about that," Yosh said, trying not to grin.

Paavo lifted his head as Homicide Inspector Rebecca Mayfield strode into the bureau. Homicide's newest and only female detective, her blond hair was pulled back in a ponytail, while her navy-blue sports jacket, starched white shirt and khaki slacks showed off a tall, well-toned figure. She moved with an unconsciously athletic, no-nonsense gait.

Rebecca's partner, Bill Sutter, dragged in about ten steps behind her. Sutter was the forgotten man of the Homicide bureau—non-descript, waiting for retirement, bland, and constantly wearing the expression of a person in need of a double dose of Pepto-Bismol.

"Don't say anything about this, okay?" Paavo said quietly to Yosh.

"My lips are sealed," Yosh answered. "But maybe you're feeling this way because we don't have a big case to work on. You might just be bored."

"I don't think I'm about to change my life out of boredom," Paavo said.

"I hope not."

"What's with you guys?" Rebecca asked. "You're sitting there like you just lost your best friends."

"Maybe so," Yosh said with a wry smile, glancing in Paavo's direction.

Paavo didn't answer, but walked to the window and stared out at the lights of the freeway snaking south and east, leading cars out of the bowels of a city where death occurred so quickly, so brutally, and so damned often it was becoming harder and harder to deal with. Was Yosh right, and his decision regarding Angie was part of the bigger picture, a much broader need for change?

No, that was too easy an explanation. This was about Angie and him, nothing more.

That same freeway also brought cars into the city, but Paavo didn't look at those lanes. He didn't want to think about them, only the ones leaving, the ones escaping.

As he studied the scene below, a chill struck him, one of those that Angie described as "someone walking over your grave." That was not at all the type of feeling he was expecting that morning. Not when, for the first time since forever—perhaps not since he was fourteen-years-old and found his much-loved sister dead from an overdose—he wanted to live life to the fullest. He felt as if he'd only been skimming the surface since then, year after year, and finally was ready for much more.

He spun away from the window and the eerie sensation it gave him to find Yosh staring at him, a quizzical look on his face.

Serafina Amalfi stormed into her youngest daughter's apartment like a running back for the Forty-Niners. "I'm so disappointed in you, Angelina!" Short, with a round body, round face and dyed black hair tightly pulled into a stylish bun, she plopped her boxy black purse on the coffee table and proceeded to remove her black scarf, overcoat and gloves. Even her dress was black. Not a good sign.

Angie still carried the dishrag she'd used to dry her hands after washing cake batter off them. "What did I do, Mamma?"

"Not what you did, what you haven't done. How did I raise such a *stupida!*"

Now what? Angie thought. "Would you like a cup of coffee?"

"Do you have any of your pecan shortbread cookies?" Serafina stopped her diatribe to ask, and joined Angie in the kitchen.

"No. I've been busy with my cakes. I haven't had time to bake cookies." Angie put on the coffee.

"You and your cakes! Who wants silly cakes?" The wooden chair squeaked as Serafina lowered herself into it. "Cakes are to eat, to melt in the mouth, not to look at and laugh!"

Biting her tongue so hard she feared permanent indentations, Angie opened the refrigerator. "I can offer you a sandwich. Or, how about a frittata?"

Serafina clasped her hands together. "I'm too upset to eat."

Angie seated herself at the table. "Okay, what's this about?"

"You. And Paavo."

Angie was shocked. "Paavo?"

"You've been through so much with him over the past ten months. You even lived with him for a while, Angelina, and what happened afterward? *Niente!*"

"Nothing?" What was her mother's problem? "What was supposed to happen?"

Serafina leaned toward her, eyeball to eyeball. "You were supposed to get him to propose!"

Angie could have shrieked. "With Paavo, one needs patience, mamma. When I was at his house, we'd both gone through a horrible situation. It wasn't a time to think about marriage. And besides, I wasn't there very long."

"*Testa dura!* Where have I failed as a mother? Marriage should have been the first thing on your mind. And his!" Serafina threw her head back, arms out, and announced to the ceiling, "*Madonna mia*, such a daughter I have, an embarrassment to Italian women *in tutto del mondo!*"

"I'm sure all the world's Italian women really don't care," Angie said as she placed a cup of coffee in front of her mother and plunked a bottle of brandy beside it. Serafina enjoyed her coffee royals, as she called them, and Angie was ready to join her. "As for me, I hope Paavo will propose when he's ready. I know his heart, and he knows mine. So, relax."

Pouring generously, Serafina instructed, "You have to help him get ready."

"No! No way will I push him. You know, whenever I try to force something to happen, it blows up in my face. I don't want anything to come between Paavo and me ever again. Right now, I'll concentrate on my new successful business, and that's all."

Serafina gave her a long-suffering look. "Angelina, you have a lot to learn."

CHAPTER THREE

Against the dark sky lit by a crescent moon, the run-down Victorian looked like a place the Addams family might have called home. Three stories tall, it had a steeply pitched roof and turret on the top floor. The paint had flaked off parts, and dirt rather than bright, contrasting colors, lined the gingerbread design of the house.

Scout Vannix followed the directions she'd been given to the west side of the building. Cracked cement steps led down to a heavy wooden basement door.

Should I knock? She didn't want to look like some dweeb. She turned the knob and, to her surprise, the latch slid open. She pushed the door wide and strode inside, a blasé, been-there-done-that expression on her face.

A big man with a shiny dome of a head, beer belly and black jacket buttoned tight against a bloated neck, caught the door and stared at her hard, then slowly lowered pit bull eyes to her extremely short black leather skirt and over-the-knee black leather boots. "Who do you think you are walking in here?" His voice was low and gravelly.

"Hey, there, my man." She tossed out the words in a fast,

urban clip. "I didn't know this little rendezvous spot was so classy it had someone just to open up the door. You know what I'm saying?" She put a fist on her hip and let it sway.

"You got an invitation?" he asked.

She rolled her eyes as if contemplating leaving. "Look, I heard this is a happening place and I'm new in town. Where was I supposed to get this invitation?"

"You got some I.D.?"

Scout blinked in astonishment. "You carding me?"

Uncle Fester's double gave her a leering smirk. "No. I just want to know your name. Let's see it."

She handed him a twenty-dollar bill. "Call me Andrea Jackson."

He eyed the money and smirked. "Now, you're catching on."

Once inside The Crypt Macabre, as the club was called, she felt she'd stepped into a Hollywood movie scene—a darkened room, crowded with dancers, thick with smoke from tobacco and the distinctive scent of weed. The raw, blaring sounds of electronic music with throbbing bass, reverberations, and distorted guitar riffs blocked out any other sounds, while pulsating strobe lights creating herky-jerky surreal images.

Shoulders back, Scout's white-powdered face slack as if world-weary, black-shadowed eyelids half closed, and plum-glossed lips arched in a slight sneer, she took leggy strides deep into the room. Halfway, she stopped, hips thrust forward, and ran her fingers through her thick, wavy, raven black hair, pushing it to the side in a way that made it flop over in greater disarray than it had been.

Her black blouse was only half buttoned, showing a considerable amount of cleavage, and a black, silver-studded dog collar was fastened to her neck.

If all this didn't get her noticed, she had no idea what more to do.

"Who are you?"

Scout lifted heavy eyes to the man who'd asked the question, slowly dropping her gaze over his black leather-clad body, then up again. He was tall and well-built, but his black hair was spiked, his eyes lined with red pencil, and three silver studs paraded along one ear lobe. But he'd made up his skin to look so pale and his lips so colorless, he looked like something out of Madame Tussaud's Wax Museum. She pouted sullenly. "Who wants to know?"

"They call me Rysk—that's like risky, but with a y."

An arrogant toss of her head caused her hair to fall onto her face. She raked it back as she spoke. "If you're trying to impress me, it's not happening. I know risky has a y in it."

He smirked and put his hands on narrow hips. "It's, like, two y's."

"I didn't come here for a spelling bee." She turned away. This punk was a waste of time.

"Who are you?" he repeated, stepping around her and blocking her path.

He stood too close. "Don't you get it? Or are you the I.D. police?"

He folded his arms and moved even closer, letting his elbow bump against her. "I ask the questions around here."

Nobody but nobody touched her. "Who the hell do you think you are!" She stepped back, her hands fisted.

"Relax," he said, reaching out to take her arm.

"Go to hell." Scout twisted away from him and eased into the crowd. Bastard, she thought, trying to calm herself. She needed to focus on the reason she was here, not to waste her time with jerks. One particular man's notice was what she was after.

Ear-splitting music, the constant white/black of the lights and the heavy, stale air made her head ache and her eyes sting. She tucked in her chin, her gaze moving slowly, carefully. The group was a mixture of races and genders, but most looked quite young. These were not the beautiful people of the city, despite the music and strobe lights, but appeared to be the troubled, society's rejects. Many of them still had remnants of teenage acne and the look of a teen not yet grown into an adult's body. Many had made up their faces garishly, funeral-parlor style, much like the obnoxious fellow who called himself Rysk. Most, either gangly or chubby, wore romanticized black or wine-colored velvet outfits, or went to the opposite extreme with black slacks and T-shirts with death or demonic symbols.

Most of their expressions were vacant or blandly happy, as if under the influence of drugs.

Scout wondered if any of this crowd had an idea, the way she did, of the danger they exposed themselves to by being here.

An almost overwhelming desire filled her to grip their shoulders and shake them, along with the firm knowledge that it wouldn't do one damn bit of good. Stupid, stupid children.

She clenched and unclenched her hands, breathing deeply as she willed her eyes not to tear up in anger and frustration.

Then she saw him lounging on a sofa, surrounded by the most beautiful women in the club. A ridiculously young platinum blond was receiving most of his attention.

Scout knew he called himself a baron—Baron Severus. *Baron, my ass,* she thought.

His hair, like almost everyone else's here, was black and combed straight back from a widow's peak in the center of his forehead—probably plucked into a perfect shape. His face appeared untouched by the sun, but despite that, he looked healthy and much more alive than the bloodless tone of most of his much younger cohorts.

Studying him before coming here to face him, taught her he was in his late thirties and had no family—at least none that he acknowledged. His shoulders were broad, and his arms and chest surprisingly muscular. His dark-brown eyes were deep set and soulful, and when he spoke to a woman, he would touch her face or hair with his long fingers and black-painted fingernails. Then he would smile as knowingly as a lover reliving intimacies. The women at his feet hung on his every word.

He made her sick.

Scout turned away, her head light. Before arriving here, the mere thought of the Baron had filled her with fury. Now, to see him, to be so close she could almost touch him, smell him, breathe the same air, made her physically ill. Her stomach roiling, she turned away and hurried to the exit, finding all this too much, too soon.

Someday, though, someday she was going to kill him. Of that, she had no doubt.

In bed that night, Paavo couldn't fall asleep. His chest was tight, and he gasped for breath. He checked through his small one-bedroom house for gas leaks, and finding no problem, opened the bedroom window wide even though the night temperature was in the forties, and the air heavy with ocean fog.

Earlier that evening he had phoned Angie, but he could hear in her voice the exhaustion from baking all day, on top of her late-night delivery the night before.

The situation with Angie had to be what was troubling him, causing this strange heaviness in his chest. He pulled a rocking chair up to the window and sat in front of it, rubbing his arms against the chill as he looked out at the night.

Angie awoke with a start. The clock by the bed showed three a.m. She listened, wondering what had caused her to wake.

The usual apartment sounds softly murmured in the background—the hum of the refrigerator, the ticking of a Georgian style wall clock in the dining room, the occasional rush of warm air pushing through heating vents.

A vague awareness of a troubling dream rattled in her head, but she pushed it away. Nightmares were the bane of solitary sleepers, and she didn't want to chance remembering it.

Her mind instantly went to the two Comical Cakes she needed to create the next day, and how she might make them, as well as concerns about how they'd be received.

She needed to stop this! If she didn't fall back to sleep, she would be unable to bake anything, let alone to cleverly decorated the cakes.

She turned over and tried to ignore the uneasiness that seeped into her bones for no reason she could discern. The clock's digital display showed four a.m. before sleep came to her again.

Night fell slowly in San Francisco, its ever-present fog carrying crystals of light long after the sun set beyond the rim of the ocean. Once the starless sky turned black, bright city lights illuminated the most populated areas, but the other streets were shrouded in darkness.

A few street lamps and a handful of patrol cars weren't enough, however, to keep the streets safe, to keep the monsters that lurked on them at bay. The creatures that preyed on the innocent were closer than anyone imagined.

Mason Markowitz knew that well. His body was gaunt from lack of food, but he could not eat. His hair had gone white from the things he'd seen and experienced, but he could not turn his eyes away.

His mind, others said, had been driven mad.

He knew it wasn't madness; it was reality.

He stood on a street corner in the plush Pacific Heights neighborhood, lured again to the deconsecrated church for reasons he could not rationally explain or justify. He'd witnessed strange things here, beasts, and the night before, two lovely women, too wrapped up in their worldly concerns to notice what was going on around them.

Coldness had descended on him as he'd watched them get into their fancy car. He feared what lay ahead for them and all that he must do. He'd been drawn to this place by evil, attracted here as he had been to other spots, but nowhere had he felt the dark forces as strong or as dangerous.

Beyond all doubt, here, the darklings of night roamed; the horrors of every nightmare walked. An army of exorcists laden with rituals and sacred chrisms should have been called upon to expel the possessing demons. But few believed in such ceremonies any longer.

Instead, he alone must cast them out. He dared not fail.

CHAPTER FOUR

wo days later, Angie was thrilled to be putting the finishing touches on a comical cake for a realtor. She was a neighbor of the new judge and had been so impressed by the judge's cake, she had immediately asked for a cake for a retirement party for a coworker named Marianne. The realtor wanted a cake to look like an ugly, run-down shack with a sign:

> For sale - Cheap.
> Cozy and quaint.
> Call Marianne.

Angie hoped this Marianne had a good sense of humor and didn't take it to mean she only sold dumps. But she could make the cake easily. One problem with comical cakes, however, was that they were oversized and delicate. If this one started to slide and the frosting smooshed together, she'd end up with what looked like a mud ball for sale.

For that reason, she once again asked Connie to help with

the delivery. Connie had promised to come by her apartment after closing her store, but hadn't yet arrived.

Angie waited for Connie as long as she dared, and then managed to carry her big cake to her car and head for her new customer's home, hoping Connie would be waiting outside the house to help her bring it inside. Angie circled the block, looking for Connie or her gray Toyota. But no luck.

The closest street parking to the realtor's home was in front of the same empty church she'd parked beside on her last visit. If she lived nearby, she would do all she could to get the city to resolve the situation—either tear the building down or use it. It seemed wrong to leave it vacant and subject to vandals or other intruders. The Catholic Church had a rite to desanctify a church when one had to be abandoned so that evil people could not misuse sacred ground. Angie hoped the archdiocese had already done that.

But the old building vanished from her mind as, alone, she lugged the big cake into the house and set it up, thankfully unharmed. Not-so-discreetly placing some of her business cards nearby to drum up more business, she left the home before the party began.

She probably should have asked Paavo to help her when he'd called and asked her to dinner that night. Instead, she had turned him down to make the delivery of the cake with Connie's help. She had even planned to take Connie to dinner as a thank you for helping her, but instead of all that happening, Connie was a no-show.

So frustrating!

As she walked back to the car, the sun was setting and the statue of St. Michael the Archangel at the top of the old church caught her eye. It was as if he was looking down at her and frowning. Connie had been terribly nervous here the other night. Maybe that was why she hadn't shown up this evening.

Angie would have laughed off Connie's fears except that her

superstitious Italian mother had raised her on stories filled with strange night creatures in closets, in basements, and in old churchyards. As much as her very-American practical self didn't want to believe in bogeymen, deep inside her, she couldn't quite shake the thought that they just might get you if you didn't watch out.

Were those footsteps behind her? Running footsteps?

Her senses sprang alert; a chill raced down her spine. She was almost at her car and began to run. Just as she reached it, hands grabbed her shoulders from behind.

Angie screamed.

Connie let go of her and laughed so hard tears came to her eyes. She doubled over, holding her stomach, unable to say a word.

Angie put her hand to her heart and collapsed back against her car. "Are you trying to kill me?" She didn't find Connie funny in the least.

"What a reaction! Were you scared or what!" Connie wiped her eyes, trying to control herself.

"I wasn't scared. You just startled me," Angie said, annoyed.

"With that scream? Every dog in the state heard you. You must have thought I was Lolly Firenghetti attacking you for starting up a rival Comical Cakes business." Connie started to laugh all over again.

"I'm glad you find it so funny!"

"I'm sorry." Connie tried to stop, but she wasn't very successful. "I drove here hoping to help, but I saw your car parked and realized I was too late. I parked and waited so I could apologize. But when you started to run, I realized you find this area every bit as creepy as I do."

"St. Michael's was once a venerable church. It's not creepy," Angie insisted, still irritated at how much Connie had scared her.

"Oh no? Didn't you see the sign that says 'graveyard?' Scary stuff."

Angie smoothed her hair. She was sure it was standing on end. "Old graveyards are interesting, not scary."

"I don't agree," Connie said. "And you're just saying that to be contrary."

Angie folded her arms, the idea for a little revenge forming. "Come to think of it, I'd like to go inside to check out some tombstones. They might make intriguing cake decorations."

Connie gawked at her. "You're kidding, right?"

"Not at all. Of course, if you're too scared to come with me..."

Connie blinked a couple of times, then resolutely raised her chin. "Lead the way."

Angie smiled to herself as she marched toward the iron gate. Connie stuck close behind.

"Maybe the gate will be locked." Connie sounded hopeful. "Or we could be arrested for trespassing."

Angie easily lifted the gate latch. "I guess nobody worries about grave robbers or trespassers anymore." The gate needed a hard shove to open, and its rusted hinges creaked in protest. She held the gate wide to let Connie enter. "After you."

"No," Connie drew back. "You can have the honor."

Grinning to herself, Angie walked into the garden. Since there were no streetlights on the sidewalk near the church, the area around the gate was quickly growing dark with the setting sun.

"I don't think this is such a good idea," Connie murmured.

"Sure it is." Angie followed a path deeper into the graveyard, then stopped. "Did you hear that sound?" she whispered.

Connie, quaking, grabbed her arm. "No."

Angie chuckled. "Me, neither."

"Darn you!" Connie lightly punched her in the arm. "That does it. Onward to the graves, Elvira, Mistress of the Night."

Angie suppressed her laughter as she walked faster and faster toward an area with overgrown bushes. The last hint of sunlight shone onto the ground marked with seven tombstones, all topped with crosses.

"I wonder if they were priests?" Angie whispered as she bent close to a stone. Although she'd been joking about little tombstone cakes, she had to admit the idea wasn't bad. But what occasion could they possibly be used for?

"Don't step there!" Angie said as Connie approached.

Connie jumped back. "Why not?"

"You were standing right on a grave. I wouldn't do that if I were you."

The wind whipped up and made a low, crooning sound. Connie shrank further to the side. "Angie, let's get out of here," Connie murmured.

"But this is so great! The atmosphere is wonderful. I should soak it in so I'll be ready when the time comes to make some comical cakes for a Halloween party." She moved to a larger tombstone and crouched down, but couldn't make out any of the letters.

The crooning sound grew louder, then suddenly stopped. All turned absolutely still.

"I can't take this, Angie," Connie said, whipping her head from graves to markers to rocks and trees. "Let's go."

Silence.

Connie turned back to the tombstone Angie had been looking at. She was gone. "Angie?" Connie's voice scarcely worked. "Where are you?"

"Angie?" Connie wailed, close to tears.

"Angie!" she shrieked at the top of her lungs. But then, she heard a rattling in a bush beside her and let out a terrified squawk.

"Boo!" Angie yelled, jumping out from behind the plant, laughing hard.

When Connie could breathe again, she glowered. "All right. You got even. Let's go."

Angie, well pleased with herself, was still chuckling when the iron gate suddenly clanged shut. The metallic echo danced down their spines.

"What was that?" Connie whimpered.

"I don't know."

"Did you do it?" Connie demanded. "Is this more of your idea of how to get even?"

"Believe me, I didn't do a thing."

Angie edged closer to Connie as Connie did the same.

"Probably just some pedestrian saw the gate open and decided to shut it," Angie said. "Being a good citizen and all."

"You're right." Connie didn't sound too convinced.

"Maybe we should leave now." Angie's mouth was dry.

"Good idea."

The two started walking toward the gate, clutching each other's hands.

From inside the church came a loud creaking sound followed by a hollow boom as, now, a door slammed shut.

"I... I thought the church was empty," Connie whispered, her hand tightening on Angie's.

"So did I. It must be the wind," Angie whispered back.

"But... there is no wind now."

They looked at each other, and then turned and began to run, hands still clutched, Connie in one direction and Angie in the other. Their arms out-stretched, their death grip unbroken as they pulled against each other which then caused their bodies to jerk back together and collide.

Not only had they stepped on graves, they now sprawled over them. Angie was chilled to the bone as she lifted her eyes. From this angle, she could read a gravestone's cheerful message. "All flesh is grass."

Connie was the first to her feet. She grabbed Angie's arm,

tugging wildly at her. The two plunged headlong through the churchyard, practically doing high jumps over anything that might trip them, hurtling down the garden path toward the gate.

The iron gate was shut. Connie pulled at it, but it didn't open. Angie reached for it as well, trying to help, slapping Connie's hands away from the latch until she could finally yank the latch back and pull the gate open.

Bouncing and jostling against each other, they squeezed through, ran to their respective cars and drove away in a mad dash.

CHAPTER FIVE

The Dark Lord couldn't help but chuckle to himself as he watched how easy it was to scare foolish women. They didn't, as yet, know real fright.

He never expected them to return to the old church, and then for them to go into its graveyard was beyond delectable. He drew the crumpled Kleenex from his pocket and carefully smoothed it out to view, once more, the speck of blood that had stained its white center. He shut his eyes as he rubbed it against his cheek, thinking of the two women, and in particular, *her*. The tissue felt soft... soft as a woman's skin. It was a sign, he thought, a sign for the convergence of lust, terror and death.

Folding the Kleenex, he tucked it safely away and then entered the old church, feeling the need to see, once more, the Book.

How long had the ancient text awaited him, knowing that he alone would be chosen to fulfill its prophecy? Once he felt isolated, a pariah. Soon, he would be all powerful, and those who scorned him would be sacrificed.

Now, as the darkness of night enveloped all, he opened the heavy, ancient volume of the *Ars Diabolus*. Just touching it caused fiery heat to flow through his body and he threw back his head in rapture.

Then, by candlelight in the basement of the church, a church soon to be reconsecrated to the night, he began to read the passage that always warmed his cold heart. His pathway, his inspiration:

You, Mortal, have received the call of the Infernal Prince and must now prepare your way to your Destiny.

Know you, Mortal, that as the Dark Lord you must assemble your Court of Five: the Four Dark Ladies and the one Queen. With them and through their Pentagram you shall be granted Power and shall Reign with the might of the Supreme upon this world forever.

Go, then, and gather your maidens...

It was nearly midnight when Scout Vannix entered the Goth club near the ugly old church. It took all the strength she could find deep within her to go there once more. But she needed answers, and this was the only way she knew to get them.

"I haven't seen you here before," said a pale young woman with hair so blond it was almost white. Her floor-length, gauzy white dress seemed more like a nightgown than something to wear to a drug-infused haven like this. Wine red lips provided her only color. She moved with a languid air, as if she'd taken too much of a narcotic.

Scout smiled. This was the woman who had received so much attention from the Baron the first time Scout came to this club. "Your outfit is out-of-sight," she said. "Quite hot."

"You like my dress?" the woman asked. "I'm glad somebody thinks it's pretty. I think it is."

"So, what do they call you?" Scout asked. "My name's Scout Vannix."

Heavy eyes, the pupils tiny pinpricks gazed up at her. "They call me Mina. Mina Harker."

"Mina Harker?" Scout's blood turned to ice. That was the name of one of Dracula's victims. Her study of the romanticized old-style Goth cultures was paying off, finally. She forced a smile. "That's cold-chill time. I like it! You must be a big *Dracula* fan, right? Me, too."

The woman looked puzzled. "*Dracula?* I don't care for it much. I'm not one for movies."

Scout swallowed her retort and forced her street-wise demeanor back again. "There I go, running off at the mouth when I don't have a clue what I'm talking about. My mistake."

Mina regarded her quizzically, then put her hand on Scout's arm and leaned into her. "You like my name, don't you? Most people tell me it's a pretty name."

"Sure, girl. It's real pretty." This woman was weird. Scout needed to get to the point fast. "Tell me, have you known the Baron long?"

"No, not very long. He's so cool. So sexy. So good-looking. Don't you think he's the coolest guy you've ever met?"

"Cool. Very cool."

"I think so, too." Mina sighed and batted her eyes at Scout. "I don't like his friend, though."

"Which friend is that?"

"You know, Wilbur Fieldren. You must know Wilbur?" Mina asked.

Fieldren... Renfield. Dracula's servant. Scout was tempted to say something, but if this woman didn't even know who her namesake, Mina Harker, was... "No. I haven't met him," she replied finally.

"He's kind of squishy and old. I don't like him but the Baron does. Fieldren lets me know when the Baron wants to see me, so I guess for that reason alone I should like him." Her giggle made Scout realize the woman was even younger than she'd thought—maybe only eighteen or so.

"Do you know what the Baron does?" Scout asked, changing the subject. "I mean, how can the Baron afford this big house? And this round-the-clock partying?"

Mina grinned. "Well, duh! He's a Baron. He doesn't have to *do* anything. How can you not know that?"

Good question. "I'm from Chicago."

"Oh," Mina said as if that explained everything.

"So, where is our dear Baron tonight?" Scout asked, looking around the room once again.

"I heard he's busy tonight." Mina's expression was odd, as if she was worried, or perhaps, jealous? "He's so cool." She forced a smile.

"So, I've heard," Scout said. "Tell me, do you live nearby?"

"Nearby?" Mina again looked worried. "These days, I live here."

Scout nodded, then excused herself and, since the Baron wasn't around, hurried from the club.

CHAPTER SIX

Paavo watched as two of his colleagues wearily returned to Homicide after an early morning wake-up call to a crime scene.

Luis Calderon was in his late forties, divorced, and bitter about it. The other homicide inspectors speculated that he, single-handedly, kept pomade manufacturers in business with his foot-tall pompadour. Calderon had liked it when he was a teenager, and he wasn't about to change his hair style now.

Different in every way from Calderon was his partner, Bo Benson—African-American, early thirties, streetwise, suave, and unabashedly single. He dressed like a Calvin Klein ad, went out with a new woman every week, and had a face and physique so appealing heads swiveled like turnstiles whenever he walked by.

"Look at you two playing on your computers like a couple of clueless college professors," Calderon said to Paavo and Yosh, who were catching up on paperwork in lieu of any interesting homicides to work. He dropped into his chair with a thud. "Don't you guys have anything to do?"

"Work? Hell, no." Yosh leaned back and put his feet up on

the desk, hands clasped behind his head. "We'd rather watch you two do it. Much more fun this way."

"Yeah, well I'm glad somebody's having fun here," Calderon said, half snarling as he threw his notebook onto his desk. "You wouldn't be having any if you saw what we did."

"It sucked, big time," Benson agreed. He took a bottle of Evian from his desk and opened it. "I'll be looking real hard to get my hands on the son-of-a-bitch."

"What've you got?" Paavo asked, interested.

Calderon took off his jacket and rolled up his sleeves. "A teenager, Native American, Lucy Whitefeather. Only nineteen years old. She was real pretty, long, black hair. Shit!"

Paavo was surprised at Calderon's tone. It wasn't like him to sound so personal about a victim.

"Yeah, I know," Calderon said as if reading Paavo's mind. "But there are some things you just don't get used to."

"She was last seen waiting for the bus to take her home from a City College night course," Benson added, explaining the situation. "Everyone said she was a good kid. Going to school at night, working days. And then some bastard killed her. She'd been missing all night, but her folks thought she was with her boyfriend. Her body was found this morning by garbage men in an alley just off Lobos, across from Ocean View Playground."

"Sexual assault?" Yosh asked, sitting upright, feet on the floor as the seriousness and tragic nature of the young woman's murder filled him.

"All we know so far is that she was strangled to death. But that wasn't the weird part. She was surrounded by burning candles—little votive candles like you see in church."

"Weird," Yosh agreed.

"No," Calderon chimed in. "The weird part was that her heart was cut out."

"Cut out? You mean it's gone?" Paavo looked from him to Benson.

"You got it," Benson said. "It was like something you'd see in one of those old horror movies, the ones with demons and witches and Christopher Walken."

"My favorites," Yosh said.

"Not mine," Benson admitted, head shaking. "Gave me goosebumps."

"Hell, now I gotta deal with chicken partner," Calderon grumped, pouring himself a cup of strong, black coffee. "He's probably going to be seeing Freddie Kruger in every closet."

"It was spooky, man." Benson shuddered. "Her laying there, naked, that candle wax around her, and all that blood.... At least, the M.E. said she was dead before her heart was removed."

"Bawk, bawk, bawk!" Calderon flapped his elbows.

Benson shook his head.

"Sounds like some kind of ritual," Paavo said. "Do you think that's what you're dealing with?"

"That's what I don't like about this," Benson replied, lifting his dark eyes. "Still, to kill the woman and then set up all those candles... It makes me wonder if the killer didn't have others helping him, others as sick as he is."

"Let me know if I can help," Paavo said.

"Not you, Paav," Yosh said. "You've got other things on your plate right now."

"Such as?" Calderon asked, looking curious.

"Angie." Yosh winked, then glanced at Paavo and began to hum the tune "Tonight" from *West Side Story*.

Paavo didn't say a word. Yosh cackled then made a gesture as if he were zipping his mouth shut.

Real helpful, Yosh, Paavo thought, the urge to strangle suddenly strong. He had tried to see Angie the last few evenings, but she was always creating a cake, delivering a cake, or was so exhausted from baking and delivering she could hardly keep her eyes open.

Calderon lifted his eyebrows and faced Paavo. "What's the problem?"

"No problem." He turned toward his desk and began pushing papers around as if he was looking for something important. He knew he wasn't fooling anyone.

Calderon and Benson continued to look at him expectantly. Suddenly, he couldn't handle the closeness of the Bureau, and walked out without another word.

Stanfield Bonnette leaned his slim body casually against the kitchen counter and watched Angie with puppy-dog eyes as she switched on her KitchenAid. Her neighbor from across the hall worked in a bank where his father happened to be the bank's president. "I hate to say anything, Angie, but I don't think I'd want to eat a cake that reminds me of a dentist's office."

"Good, because if you touch this, you die." Angie had gotten a request that morning from a dentist's wife for a Comical Cake for her husband's retirement. She came up with a set of dentures with the words "Bite Into A Happy Retirement." But Angie had to figure out how to shape a cake to look like dentures, and at the moment was in no mood to put up with Stan's suggestions.

At her fierce expression, he backed up. "What are those big, round cake pans for?"

"Those are for Saturday's project—a wedding cake." Serafina's nagging visit came to mind. *Nothing like adding insult to injury,* Angie thought, as she scraped the batter from the sides of the bowl. She stood back, hands on hips of her peach-colored jumpsuit as she watched the mixer do its job.

"Since when does a company called Comical Cakes do

wedding cakes?" He sidled toward the cake batter and stretched a forefinger toward it. Angie slapped his hand away.

"Apparently, it's the third marriage for each so they went for a cake that said in iridescent colors: Remarriage—the Triumph of Optimism over Experience."

"Hah! Not a bad line," Stan said.

"It's a gloss on a saying by Dr. Johnson or somebody like that," she added. "Traditional bakers weren't interested in the job."

"They do have reputations to maintain," Stan said, pushing back the silky light-brown hair that had flopped onto his forehead.

"As if I don't?"

He didn't answer, but reached in the cookie jar for some sustenance. It was empty. "Have you given up baking for yourself because of your business?"

"It's taking up all my time, in case you haven't noticed." She turned off the mixer and poured the dentist's cake into two round pans. She would attempt to cut the cake into the right shape after it was baked and then cooled.

"I'm starving," Stan said as he opened the refrigerator door. "I didn't eat yet today." Halfway inside, his voice echoed as he said, "Doesn't seem to me that baking ugly cakes should take up all your time this way."

"That's just what I needed to hear!"

"It's true, though." Since no interesting leftovers beckoned, he shut the door, folded his arms and stared glumly at the cookie jar.

Yes, she had to admit, it was true. Her fledgling business was taking up her time, but wasn't that the way with any start-up? You devoted your life, heart and soul, to the enterprise, whatever it was. Well, she was doing that now, whether Stan or Serafina or Connie or anyone else liked it or not. At least Paavo stood by her.

"You know what, Stan, I'd have time to bake for me—and you—if each cake didn't take so long. For example, when I bake the wedding cake, I'll need three ovens. And I only have two"—she pointed to her fire engine red, professional-size Viking range—"but if I could use your oven, the baking would go that much faster."

He snorted. "I hate to be petty about this, Angie, but I don't see how letting you use my oven would help at all. Look at the time you spend doing this. How much are you making from it? Sixty cents an hour? Not to mention the danger."

"What danger?"

"Didn't you hear about the strangler?" At Angie's questioning look, he continued. "It was in this morning's news! Really creepy. They found the body of a woman, a young woman, and—here's the really scary part—her heart had been cut out."

"How awful!" Angie was shocked, but not surprised she hadn't heard about it. She'd slept poorly last night, probably caused by her adventure in the graveyard, and hadn't even put on the TV or radio, let alone looked at online news, yet that day. All her time seemed to be taken up either baking, delivering, or designing cakes.

"I've heard that with some of these satanic cults, they keep people alive while they do horrible things to them," Stan added. "What if she was alive when they started to cut out the heart? *Tha-thump, tha-thump.*"

"Will you stop!" She threw a potholder at him.

"I can imagine ugly, evil people in robes standing around some poor young woman. It must have been so terrible for her—"

"Enough already! You're scaring me now!" Her escapade in the creepy churchyard must have jangled her nerves more than she'd realized.

"Why didn't your boyfriend tell you about it?" Stan plucked

an apple from a ceramic bowl on the counter. "Shouldn't he warn you of such things?"

"I haven't talked to him yet today." Angie hoped the conversation was closed.

He took a big bite, chewed and swallowed. "If I was your boyfriend, I wouldn't let you go out late at night delivering cakes to strange people unless I was with you. It's too scary out there right now. Stay home, Angie, give this up." He glanced woefully at the apple, then back at the refrigerator. She could almost hear his unspoken plea, *Cook!*

"I can't stay home hiding under the bed every time someone is killed in a city this size." She said this as much to convince herself as Stan. "Things like that happen, unfortunately."

"You could stay in my bed... anytime, Angie." He grinned.

She rolled her eyes and opened a box of confectioner's sugar for the icing.

Loud staccato raps sounded at the door. Her heart leaped. Paavo had come to call.

Angie greeted him with a kiss but then he kept his hands on her shoulders as his pale blue eyes studied her a long moment, his expression serious.

"Is something wrong?" she asked, wondering why he was looking at her so intensely.

"I just wanted to see you." He began to draw her closer when Stan appeared in the doorway to the kitchen.

"My, my, look at what turned up," Stan said, slouching against the doorjamb, a half-eaten apple in hand.

Angie knew her neighbor's mere existence was enough to put Paavo's teeth on edge.

"If it isn't Bonnet," Paavo said. He didn't sound happy.

"You might want to call me *Mister* Bonnette since I'm going to be Angie's partner."

"What?" Angie gawked at him.

"Oh?" Paavo said, looking quizzically from Stan to Angie.

Stan strolled further into the living room. "She'll be using my oven, and I'll be seeing that she's all right when she goes out at night." He cocked an eyebrow. "She didn't even know about the strangler."

"It just happened last night," Paavo said to Angie.

"There's a strangler who cuts out hearts loose in the city?" She looked horrified. "Stan's right?"

Paavo grimaced, but nodded. "We don't yet know what we're dealing with. But you should be careful, just as always."

"So, maybe Stan should go with me at night?" she suggested. "At least until you catch this guy."

Paavo's mouth tightened even further. "If there's no one else around, including me, he's better than you going out alone, I suppose."

A bell chimed and Stan scooted away from Paavo's glare, hurrying into the kitchen. "*Our* cake is ready, Angie," he chirped. "Come help me test it. I'll find a toothpick for us."

"Don't touch it, Stan!" she cried, ready to run after him, but hesitated, glancing at Paavo.

"It's okay, you're busy," he said. "I'll get going. But we are still on for dinner tonight, right?"

Oh my God, she thought. It had slipped her mind with all these cakes, timing them, scheduling them, not to mention delivering them. "That's right! Yes, I'm looking forward to it."

A clatter of dishes sounded in the kitchen. *Stan!* Angie turned to run in there, but stopped to face Paavo. She felt torn. He'd come to see her for some reason, but all she had done was to fuss about murder and cakes.

He gave her a quick kiss. "Go!"

With a nod, she ran into the kitchen to see Stan trying to remove the cake layer from its pan and making a mess of it.

"*What are you doing?*" she screeched. In Stan's frozen silence, she heard Paavo shut the apartment door as he left.

Connie Rogers sat at Angie's dining room table later that same afternoon, discretely yawned, and forced her eyes to focus on the papers in front of her.

Earlier, Angie had put in an emergency call to Connie. Even if Stan hadn't ruined the test cakes trying to remove them while hot from their pans, her idea of a set of dentures just wasn't a good one. They were simply too ugly. While waiting for Connie, she printed out a bunch of computer graphics and sketched her own pictures of teeth—lots and lots of smiling mouths filled with brightly whitened teeth.

"When you think about it," Connie said, after going through the printouts and drawings several times, "teeth are really kind of ugly. Big, white, hard-shell things protruding from shiny pink gums. Yech."

"If the dentist's wife wants teeth, she gets teeth," Angie said, her nose deep in magazine ads for toothpaste and denture adhesives. "Judging from her house, they've been good to her."

"I can imagine. I think I've paid for at least three rooms of my dentist's home all by myself."

"What about fangs?" Angie mused.

"I don't see your Dr. Pain as having fangs," Connie replied. "Maybe you should settle for a set of choppers with 'Eat Me' across the top."

Tossing the magazines aside, Angie put her head in her hands. "I give up!"

"You'll come up with something," Connie said. "You always do. It'll be fine."

"I always do? I'm the one with so many failed businesses I'm the family joke! Daffy Duck gets more respect."

"You just haven't hit the right business yet."

"I'm running out of ideas," Angie said wearily.

Connie nodded. "I can imagine."

The two studied the pictures a while longer. "You know what," Angie said, lifting a computer graphic from the stack. "I like this single tooth best of all. He's kind of cute, and he's got a nice smiling face."

"The boxy looking molar?" Connie asked. She bent close to study the drawing. "How do you know it's a *he*?"

Angie pushed her out of the way. "Look, we can kind of curve the roots so it looks like he's jumping for joy."

"A jumping tooth. Now why didn't I think of that?" Connie said straight-faced.

"I like it! Just think what a cute cake it'll be for a dentist."

Connie scrunched up her mouth. "I hate to tell you, Angie, but I don't think there is such a thing."

CHAPTER SEVEN

Finally, Paavo's time of waiting and anxiety was coming to an end.

He even left work a bit early to get ready. Now, in his bedroom, he buttoned up his dress shirt, lifted the collar, and slid his necktie over it. Just a couple more hours, he told himself.

Before starting the knot, he reached into his pocket one more time to make sure the jewelry box was still in there, a handkerchief stuffed on top of it to prevent it from slipping out.

After reaching his decision the other day, he'd gone to see Yosh's brother-in-law, who owned a jewelry shop. He knew Tadeo, or Tad, as he liked to be called, would give him a fine ring at a good price. Even at a discount, he was appalled at how expensive diamond rings were. Still, he couldn't give Angie anything cheap.

Tad had heard a lot about Angie from Yosh, and so suggested a smaller diamond that was colorless and all but flawless to the naked eye would be more to her liking than one larger but flawed. After learning about diamonds and looking over the rings, Paavo chose one he thought was perfect for

Angie—classic and sophisticated—an emerald-cut diamond in a platinum solitaire setting. Tad nodded his approval.

Paavo bought it, and had been praying ever since that she'd like it.

Touching it made his heart beat quicken and caused a dryness in his throat that not even a hard swallow could alleviate. He wanted to get this over with. Ever since deciding to propose, he hadn't slept a wink, but would spend each night thinking about what to say, where to go, and how to actually ask her. Did he stand? Sit? Get down on one knee? Hell, he had no idea.

He'd shown up at her apartment that afternoon with the hope of finding the mood right to propose then and there. In the end, he was glad Stan's presence had ruined his plan. Angie deserved better than to get a marriage proposal while half-covered with powdered sugar and flour.

The ends of his tie in hand, he watched himself in the bath-room mirror as he crossed one length over the other to begin a Windsor knot.

If was up to him, he'd simply say, "Angie, want to go to Reno?" They could buy a license in Reno and be married in ten minutes. No waiting period, no tests, no relatives, wedding showers, bachelor parties, or gift registrations. No hurt feeling over bridal party choices, no rehearsals, no decisions on church, day, time, reception, honeymoon or clothes to wear to any of them. All in all, a very reasonable way to get hitched.

He let go of the tie. Why was he doing this? He pulled the skewed knot apart and started over.

The truth was, Angie wouldn't want to elope. She and her mother would be in seventh heaven planning her wedding. The whole idea was overwhelming, but somehow he'd get through it. Other men had. He could as well. He hoped.

But just thinking about a big wedding was enough to make

him consider taking the ring back to the jeweler and to forget the whole thing.

He looked at his tie. The back side was half again as long as the front. He pulled it apart and pressed a cold washcloth against his forehead. *Get over it,* he ordered himself. *You've faced gun-toting crazed killers. You can ask one little woman to marry you and cope with her mother's wedding plans.*

He drew in his breath and began the knot again.

He decided to order crepes Suzette for dessert, so that when Angie's eyes were on the flambé, he'd put the ring on her dessert plate. The waiters were told that as soon as she noticed, they were to immediately disappear and not return until he gave the nod that she'd said yes.

Of course, if she said no, he wouldn't want dessert anyway.

The knot ended up so lopsided that no matter how much he pulled and tugged, it wouldn't straighten out. He yanked it off his neck.

No need to worry so much. She wouldn't say no. Would she?

But Angie was nothing if not unpredictable.

She wanted him to propose. No doubt about it. This nervousness was part of the ritual, that's all. He would survive it.

Somehow.

As he worked on the knot once more, out of the corner of his eye he noticed that his cat had joined him. Hercules sat on the bathroom floor, his tail curled around him, whiskers twitching as he looked up at Paavo.

Paavo was sure the cat was laughing at him.

* * *

Angie and Connie stopped talking when they heard a knock on the door. A loud knock. A cop kind of knock.

"That can't be Paavo," Angie said as she got up. "He's never on time for a simple dinner date. It practically takes an act of Congress to have him show up when he's supposed to for an important function."

She opened the door and gasped. It was him.

"What are you doing here?" she asked, and peeked around him to check the hallway. "Is anything wrong?"

"Why do you always think there's something wrong when I come to see you?" He walked in and noticed Connie at the table with papers spread all over. They exchanged greetings, then he turned back to Angie with a frown. "We're supposed to go to dinner now."

"I know, but you're on time." He was wearing one of his nicest sports jackets, a Ralph Lauren she'd bought for him at Saks. His shirt was new and his tie had a crisp, full Windsor. What, she wondered, was going on?

"I made reservations for us at Les Fleurs," he said.

"Les Fleurs?" It was expensive and elegant. "I had no idea. I thought we were just going somewhere casual. Is tonight something special?"

"No. No, not at all. You've always liked it there," was his only response.

Her brow furrowed. "I'm so sorry. I assumed you'd be all wrapped up in that young woman's murder. I honestly thought you would either cancel or get here quite late, as usual."

His frown deepened. "Do I do that? Anyway, it's Calderon's case."

Angie took a deep breath. *Les Fleurs...* She was wearing slacks and a short-sleeve pullover. As one who loved to dress up and used any opportunity to do so, she needed to change, to put on something elegant. And that would take a bit of time, and Connie was still here, and her project still needed help...

"What's going on?" he asked.

She shook her head. "I'm sorry. I invited Connie to come over after work to help me with a dentist's cake."

His jaw seemed to tighten, and she had no idea why.

"How close are you to being done?" he asked.

"An hour, maybe."

"An hour?"

"Hey, you two," Connie said as she joined them. Her eyes widened as she took in Paavo's clothes, his nervous expression, and his choice for a restaurant. Then her eyebrows rose. "Say, Angie, why don't I leave now? You'll be fine with the tooth thing. Change your clothes and go out with Paavo. We can finish up everything else tomorrow."

"But tomorrow morning you'll be at work," Angie said walking in circles as a twinge of hysteria began to form. "How can I go anywhere now? Stan wrecked the cake, so I had to bake it again, and then my tooth design is ugly, not comical. And I need to find a new design, figure out how to ice it, and deliver it by noon tomorrow! But I don't know what it's supposed to even look like!"

"It's okay, honey," Connie said, her voice soothing and warm. "Go get ready for your dinner. I'll come over early before my shop opens. I never get customers first thing in the morning, anyway."

Angie looked at her friend and then at Paavo, and tears filled her eyes. "Thanks, but I can't let you do that. I know I'm tired and I'm frazzled and probably being a bitch. But my business is important to me. I think I should just call and cancel the order."

"No," Paavo said, then wrapped Angie in his arms. "Dry your eyes and finish what you were doing. We'll go later, or another day, okay?"

"Are you sure?" she asked. "You look so nice and I... I'm just messing everything up for everyone."

Connie and Paavo exchanged glances. He nodded, then

Connie shrugged and returned to the dining room table to look again at comical teeth designs. Angie's gaze leaped in confusion from one to the other.

"I'll call the restaurant and cancel the reservation," Paavo said. "If you finish early enough, we'll go out for a late dinner."

Angie cheered up at those words and went to join Connie. "Thank you, that sounds great. I'll try to make this quick."

Baron Severus's basement seemed different, Scout thought as she entered The Crypt Macabre a little after eleven that night. She wore a studded black leather jacket and slacks, and black patent Doc Martens. The bouncer had given her a leering smile, and when she handed him twenty dollars, he didn't question her being there. She guessed that meant she now belonged.

Candles lit the room and instead of loud, pulsating dance music, this night, the soft, haunting sound of Peruvian wind instruments played in the background. Costumed Goths in black leather, or flowing velvets and brocades, seemed more drugged-out than usual as Scout made her way across the dark room, searching for the Baron.

A hand took hold of her arm. "The ice princess returns."

She spun around to see the same tall man, Rysk, who'd been so obnoxious to her. "And you, the Frog Prince."

"You've cut me to my slimy green quick," he responded with a good-natured smile.

"Good. You can hop away and lick your wounds." Their eyes caught a moment before she jerked her arm free.

"Why so unfriendly?" he asked, hurrying after her.

Tonight, he wore a deep red poet's shirt with flowing sleeves, a black velvet vest, black slacks and boots. If he had a sword, she thought, he'd look like a swashbuckler. And if he'd wash that red crap off his eyes and get some sun, he might even be halfway decent looking. "Don't you have someone else to annoy?"

She reached the far wall, but hadn't yet seen the Baron anywhere. She regretted having dashed out so suddenly the first time she'd visited, but coming face to face with the man—or monster—of her nightmares had shaken her so much she'd had to leave. She believed she would have plenty of other chances to see him and learn about him and the people around him since this was his club.

"He's not here yet." Rysk folded his arms, his mouth down turned. It bothered her that he was able to guess who she was looking for. "All the babes zero in on him. They like to say he's a cool dude. I'd hate him if he wasn't."

"Like he'd care, I'm sure." She backed up to the wall and faced the crowd. As much as she should be alone to find a way to get close to the Baron, Rysk's nearness made her feel a little bolder, a little more self-assured.

"Forget about him." Rysk put his hand against the wall beside her head and leaned closer. "For one thing, you're not his type."

She was forced to make eye contact again. His eyes were hazel, deep and intense, and she found she liked looking into them. "Oh? What is his type?"

He smirked. "Gorgeous. And rich."

She whirled away from him, her cheeks fiery. "Thanks loads! Why don't you go play in a shooting gallery? You can be the duck."

"Don't worry about it." He followed close, his breath tickling her ear as he said, "You're gorgeous enough for me."

"Stuff it!"

Rysk laughed, but before he had a chance to reply, a teenager ran up to them. He was dressed in the Goth-as-vampire costume—a white ruffled shirt and black-with-red-lining opera cape. The overall effect was spoiled, however, by the gold ring on his right eyebrow and a circle of bleached blond hair looking like a raw pancake sitting atop his head. "Where's the Baron?" His face was drenched in perspiration.

Before they could answer, the boy lunged at a pasty white, bulbous man walking by. His brown hair was so short it was a mere stumble, and his ears protruded, as did his two front teeth. If not for his white skin, black lipstick and black fingernail polish, he would look like a boring, overweight neighbor whose main activity was to spend weekends drenched in sweat mowing his lawn.

"I've got to see the Baron," the teen cried, loud enough for Scout to hear. "I've got to give him this." He held up a paper bag. The man took it, looked inside, and led the boy away.

"Who are they?" Scout whispered to Rysk.

"The big one is the Baron's assistant, Wilbur Fieldren. I don't know who the kid is." They followed Fieldren and the boy to the back of the club.

Scout remembered Mina Harker mentioning Fieldren to her. She watched as Fieldren knocked on a door. The Baron came out and spoke with the boy who was shaking and animated as if badly frightened.

Finally, the Baron patted his shoulder and walked to the center of the room. Tonight, his hair wasn't slicked back, but fell in clean, thick waves to his shoulders. He wore a traditionally cut black suit, and with it, a blue shirt with a round collar and no tie. He was the antithesis of the young, motley crowd before him, yet he commanded their complete attention.

The only time Scout had ever witnessed a group of people fall silent so quickly was in a church, and even there, she could usually hear a baby cry or a toddler whine during the service.

"My friends," the Baron began. Piercing brown eyes gazed out at the crowd, capturing people one-by-one with their intensity. "I'm sorry to interrupt your time of play, your time to feel free of the torments and troubles of the world outside, but I bring you grave news. Terrible news that you must pay close attention to. It is a matter of life... and death."

A buzz began in the room, followed by shushing sounds.

"Look carefully." He nodded, and the boy held up a thick white candle in one hand, and a small glass bottle filled with clear liquid in the other. "This candle and this flask filled with holy water were left at the door of my young friend's home."

Audible gasps filled the room.

"A religious fanatic has targeted us," the Baron shouted, his arms spread wide. "Whoever did this thought we would sizzle when we touched the water, and would burn from the light of the candle. We're only missing a Bible and the tolling bell of the sacrament to have the symbols of excommunication. They snuff the candle, muffle the bell, and slam shut the book when they cast us from their feeble churches." He then positioned his hands as if in prayer.

The crowd laughed nervously.

The Baron dropped his hands to his side. "I wish it were a laughing matter," he said solemnly. Scout felt his rumbling, stentorian voice deep in the pit of her stomach, and experienced the pull of his seductive manner, of the power that radiated from him to the others, drawing them into his fold.

"The madman hunts those he regards as evil. He believes in vampires and witches and," he paused, "in demons. I fear he regards us as demons."

Any vestige of party-going had disappeared, and the people stared in stunned silence.

He bowed his head as if all their worry was borne on his shoulders. "The sad part is that this man is dangerous. He believes people who feel alive at night, who live in the shadows as we do, who like our music, our way of escaping the ugliness and bitterness of this world, are possessed. He will seek us out.

He will try to harm us, to drive evil from our souls. He thinks that we must be destroyed!"

Together, the crowd moved closer to the Baron, as if seeking his protection.

He gazed sadly at them. "You may need to fight for your very lives if he accosts you!"

"What does he look like?" a young woman asked.

"My friend here saw him. Taylor, what can you tell these people?"

Scout took a step forward, her hands unconsciously clenched. She didn't pay attention to the sharp look Rysk gave her.

"I'm not sure," Taylor said. "He's a white guy, ugly." The group softly laughed, and the boy chuckled self-consciously. "He wore a hat, an old man's hat, with a brim all the way around. He was kinda old. Fifties or sixties, maybe. He was skinny, maybe six feet tall. I don't remember his face—just his eyes. But he knows me, man, and it kinda freaked me out." Taylor glanced up at the Baron. "That's all I know."

"That's helpful, my friend." The Baron patted the boy's shoulder and then stepped toward the people, his arms outstretched as if he would shelter them all.

"The man's name," the Baron waited to be sure he had everyone's complete attention, "his name is Mason Markowitz. Remember that, for it may save your lives. I am his prime target, my friends, but he hates all of us." His voice boomed. "He thinks our kind are outcasts, freaks and monsters! He wants to take away our freedom, to make us cower like the nine-to-five slaves in the rat race they call modern life!"

Cries of "No!" and "He can't do that!" echoed through the room.

"We won't let him!" the Baron roared. The crowd cheered, ready to do his bidding. Rather than incite them further, as Scout expected he could do, he dropped his pitch almost to a whisper. "Markowitz is crazy, and therefore dangerous. Together, our love, our strength will shield us." His voice grew louder. "Together, we will be victorious over everyone who wishes us harm!"

People cheered.

"If he comes after us, we will crush him!"

Shouts of "Yes! Yes!" were deafening. But as they quieted, Scout's voice rang out. "What do we do if he comes after us?"

The Baron stood very still, and the full force of his eyes struck her like a body blow. Silence reigned, the room mesmerized by what might follow.

"Come to me if you see him," he said, and she felt as if he were speaking to her alone. "Come to me if he is near. Come to me if you are afraid." Slowly, carefully and loudly he enunciated his last words. "I will not let him harm you!"

The room erupted, and the entire crowd surged toward the Baron. Hands, men's and women's, outstretched to touch him, to thank him for caring for them, for loving and protecting them. As the music began, a raucous Grave Pleasures tune, he smiled and seemed to grow even larger in stature. He touched and hugged and patted his people, relishing this love fest as they danced wildly around him.

Scout backed away, scarcely able to believe what she had witnessed. She'd thought tales of the Baron were bizarre and exaggerated, some out-and-out lies. Now, she wondered if she was the one who had been naïve.

CHAPTER EIGHT

A hand shook his shoulder. With a start, Paavo opened his eyes and blinked, momentarily confused. Angie's living room... her sofa... her. He sat up and saw that she'd draped a blanket over him. "I must have dozed."

"Four hours' worth," she said, her brow filled with concern that he'd been so tired.

"Four?" He looked at his watch. "It's past eleven?"

"I hated waking you. You were sleeping so soundly. You seemed exhausted."

"I haven't been sleeping well lately." He rubbed his eyes. Angie was in her nightgown and fluffy pink robe. Disappointment filled him. No candlelight dinner for them tonight. He blinked a couple of times, trying to get his brain to function. "You should have woken me up."

She sat beside him on the sofa. "By the time Connie and I finished with everything for tomorrow's cake, I realized our dinner would have been too rushed to enjoy it fully. And you really did look so peaceful, and cute, curled up here, I didn't have the heart to wake you. They'll be other nights for us— ones I haven't ruined by letting a dental cake drive me crazy."

"Is it, at least, finished now?"

"Not hardly. I still have to get the pieces to fit together properly. I'll get up early tomorrow, seven or so. That way, if I mess up, I'll have time to try again, before the noon delivery."

He shook his head and yawned. "This business of yours is amazing. I had no idea so much time went into baking cakes."

"Me neither! This was supposed to be a fun job," she said with a woeful gaze. "Would you like to stay? I know a spot far more comfortable than the sofa, if you would."

The idea was tempting, but she looked tired, and he realized that getting a seven a.m. wake-up call was not a normal part of Angie's routine. One benefit of not having a regular nine-to-five job, along with a wealthy and generous father to support her, was that she could sleep in while trying to come up with something innovative, exciting and lucrative to do with her life. Until this cake business turned up, her poor choices in career planning had resulted in lots of beauty sleep.

The ring he'd bought for her was burning a hole in his pocket. He could ask her, get this over with...

But, no. Tonight was not the night. And particularly not after she'd worked all evening on her new business and he'd fallen asleep waiting for her. No, he needed to do this thing properly.

"I'll head for home." He stood. "Seven o'clock will be here before you know it."

"I'm sorry about the way the evening turned out," she said as they walked toward the door.

"It's okay. As you said, we'll have plenty of other evenings together." He kissed her, more of a to-be-continued than a goodbye kiss. "What about tomorrow night?" he asked as he opened the door.

"That won't work. Connie will help me deliver a big cake that looks like a garbage truck to a Sanitation Workers Conference. Then I'm taking her to dinner as a thank you for all her help."

He nodded. "It's good you're not going out alone. I'll call you."

"Okay."

As he walked toward the elevator, he wondered when he'd ever get a chance to pop the question.

Paavo walked into Homicide a little after six a.m. Having fallen asleep at Angie's for so many hours, he'd spent the rest of the night lying awake thinking about her.

Ironically, whenever he had pondered his future, which wasn't often, he had never imagined himself married. Instead, he'd envisioned a life that was short and lived as a loner. Now, that image had changed, or so he hoped.

It was almost as if fate, or karma, was making his desire for change become frustratingly difficult. The kind of cold, lonely life he'd been living was no longer enough for him. He wanted more in his life. But taking the next step was proving to be a lot more difficult than he'd ever imagined. Yet, the thought of being with Angie all the time, feeling her warmth, her smile, her trust... her love... she made it all worthwhile.

Soon, the two of them would have their dinner date. He'd propose, she'd consent, and everything would be fine once more.

He turned to the paperwork on his desk, each item more boring than the next. They weren't really dull. It was just that he had something so much bigger on his mind—something about life, not death.

He picked up the first file. Focus, he told himself.

For whatever reason, his mind drifted to the first time he met Angie. He'd been investigating a murder that had occurred near her apartment when she received a ticking package at work. She'd put it in a dishwasher. A strange thing to do, but when the package exploded, it being in the dishwasher had saved her life. That should have told him something about her. Warned him? No, intrigued him. As his murder investigation and the threats against Angie's life intertwined, he soon came to see beyond the rich, pampered and beautiful woman he'd thought she was, to the warm, loyal, generous—and, yes, beautiful—woman he fell in love with.

Nothing about the way she thought or acted was as he'd come to expect based on his own life experience; nothing was as harsh or cruel or selfish. She was just...

He forced himself back to his notes concerning a gunshot victim. The perp had been arrested, and a plea-bargain was in the works. Case closed, except for writing out a long, tedious report.

A smile touched his lips as he imagined how Angie would tussle with an attorney at a plea-bargaining. The guy wouldn't know what hit him.

He shook the image away. *Concentrate!*

The bureau was empty, and he stood up and paced, trying to work off his distraction. The other inspectors hadn't arrived yet, and once they did, they'd soon head out to interview witnesses, track down leads, testify (or more likely, sit around a courtroom waiting to testify), while he was supposed to finish up paperwork.

The unfortunate part was that even though he had no difficult murders to solve at the moment, it wasn't because people had decided to love their neighbors. They still killed each other, but they weren't bright about it, leaving a trail of witnesses and evidence that practically begged the police to find them. Dumb killer; easy arrest; case closed.

He shut the folder with photos from a murder scene and again took out Angie's picture from his top drawer. She'd given

it to him after visiting Homicide and noticing that other inspectors had pictures of wives, kids, friends, or even a beloved pet
on their desks, while his was empty. It was just one of the
numerous small presents she'd given him. Generous to a fault,
loving...

Stop this! He was driving himself crazy. He shoved the photo
back in the drawer and slammed it shut.

He had to do something work-related or he would go nuts.

Turning to his computer, he began to search through old
records and computer files of unsolved murders looking for
one with a similar modus operandi to Calderon and Benson's
Lucy Whitefeather murder case. First, he queried murders that
had candles at the murder scene. Big mistake. The numbers of
murders and the strange uses candles had been put to was
overwhelming. He narrowed the search by adding the words
votive and ritual.

It worked.

A month earlier, a body had been found in Marin County,
north of San Francisco, in an empty lot near Sausalito's yacht
harbor.

The victim, a woman, been strangled. A paper bag filled
with votive candles was at the side of her naked body, leading
to speculation about some sort of ritual involved with the
killing. The case got very little publicity for two reasons. One,
the woman was thought to be homeless, and two, most of
Sausalito's income came from tourists. No one wanted to rock
that particular boat by advertising anything as distasteful as a
grisly murder.

When Paavo entered the Sausalito Police Department and told
the desk sergeant who he was and why he was there, he was
directed to Sergeant Trent Bowdin.

Bowdin was in his late twenties, about six-four, with a blond crew cut, wide blue eyes, and a missionary-like squeaky clean demeanor that made him appear completely out of his element handling a grisly murder case. Sausalito was the kind of town where the worst crimes were souvenir rip-offs, pickpockets, and drugs. Bowdin probably charmed the tourists, especially the female ones.

As soon as he realized Paavo was interested in his murder case, he was ecstatic. San Francisco's police department was organized differently from many cities. All homicides were handled by officers in the Bureau of Inspection, not by cops in the precinct stations. Homicide was a specialty, and its inspectors had been specially trained.

Bowdin had been floundering with the case and it was clear he wanted to pick Paavo's brain. That was fine with Paavo. He wasn't using it for much at the moment, anyway.

Bowdin immediately drove Paavo to the spot where the body had been found, a vacant lot near the bay. The lot had been excavated and, once the review process was completed and permits granted, would be built into a bank of townhouses.

"She was lying right there," Bowdin said. "Candles—the short ones like you see in church—were in a bag next to her. We figured they were going to be used somehow, so maybe the killer got spooked and ran off."

As Paavo studied the scene, the feeling of evil was palpable. He didn't like it, and backed away as he buttoned his jacket and raised the collar. He guessed the iciness that suddenly enveloped him was cold air from the bay. He was surprised Bowdin wasn't bothered by it.

Looking over the nearby area, he saw warehouses, a restaurant, a couple of businesses, and other lots being readied for construction, but no homes. It was the sort of place that would be empty in the middle of the night.

Bowdin admitted that he had no suspects yet. The only lead

was an old man who was seen hanging around. "One of the shopkeepers said they thought his name was Mac or Marx or something like that," Bowdin said. "But we haven't been able to find him. He was probably just some old drifter."

"Could be, but if people noticed him enough to mention him to you, there was something unusual about the guy."

"That's what we thought. We haven't given up on him altogether. The only other lead was a shoe print. A clear one."

Paavo glanced at him, interested.

"A cheap sneaker, available all over the place. Turned out one of the medical examiner's team wore the same shoe. He swore he never stepped in that spot, but who knows?"

"True." It sounded like another dead end. Few would admit to stomping over a crime scene. Trained investigators and medics should know better, but those in Sausalito wouldn't have had much practice.

"One more question," Paavo said. "Was the victim's heart cut out?"

The sergeant looked stricken. "Where the hell did you hear that? Goddamn! We were trying to keep that detail under wraps. It was our way to make sure we had the right perp once we found him."

"No one talked; just a guess."

As they headed back to the station, Paavo told him about the Lucy Whitefeather murder. Bowdin shuddered, then added, "The only other info I can give you is that we think her name might be Mina Harker."

Something about the name resonated with Paavo, something in the far reaches of his memory, but it didn't want to move forward. "How did you find that out?"

"Well, her prints weren't on file, and although a few people thought they'd seen her hanging out on the streets, no one had a name. But then we received a missing person's report from the county office in San Rafael that fit our victim to a T, even down to a chipped front tooth," Bowdin said. "The problem was, when we went to talk to the girl who filed the report, she was gone. Judging from the address she gave, a vacant lot in Marin City, she was another transient. So we still have no confirmed identity of the victim."

"What was the reporter's name?" Paavo asked.

"No idea. She signed the form Taylor Swift with a fake phone number."

"Thanks. Can you tell me anything else about Mina Harker?"

"She was young—seventeen, eighteen or so, blond, blue eyes, five seven. She looked like any runaway living on the streets. We put out a report on her, but came up empty. It wouldn't be the first time a runaway changed her name. Last time I checked, there were about a hundred thousand runaways who fit her general description."

"I'm not surprised," Paavo said. It was time for him to leave. "Could you send copies of the autopsy report and the missing person's report to Inspectors Calderon and Benson? They're the lead detectives on the Lucy Whitefeather investigation." He handed Bowdin a card with Homicide's email.

"Will do. Good luck, Inspector," Bowdin said.

"Thanks. You, too."

CHAPTER NINE

"I'm exhausted, Angie," Connie whispered out of the side of her mouth as she sliced another piece of the latest Comical Cake and served it to a guest. They were in a modern redwood and glass building overlooking the Sandpoint Golf Course, an exclusive, private club. A group of golfers surrounded them, admiring the gigantic cake Angie had created for the club's tenth anniversary.

It was a sheet cake, or actually, four sheet cakes cobbled together to recreate a golf course, complete with hills, sand traps, water hazards and bunkers. Along the lower edge of the cake, Angie had drawn a cartoon strip. The first pane showed a golfer hitting his ball into a pond. The next had him so enraged that he threw his club in fury. The following pane showed him looking up in bewilderment as the club caught high on a tree limb. The last pane showed the chagrined golfer climbing up the tree.

At the bottom were the words: "Golf—evolution in reverse."

"I can't take another minute of this," Connie continued. A dab of frosting stuck to her finger, and she wiped it onto the full apron she wore over her ruffled mauve blouse and hip-hugging purple skirt. At Angie's prompting, Connie had taken extra care with her clothes and hair, but so far the rich male party-goers were more interested in cake than the woman serving it.

"You're doing just fine," Angie murmured, scarcely paying attention. Her mind was on Paavo.

He'd called and asked if she'd be free for dinner that night. He'd spent the prior day in Sausalito and wondered if she'd like to go there for dinner on the bay. She would have loved that except she'd already agreed to stay at the golf club and serve. He seemed surprisingly disappointed, as she was. It was maddening. Lately, whenever they tried to get together, something would come up, and it usually had to do with her business, not his. That was a complete turn-about from the past.

Something seemed to be troubling him as well, but whenever she asked, he'd denied it.

And now, instead of going to dinner with him and wheedling out of him what, if anything, was bothering him, she was stuck here serving cake to golfers who weren't even paying attention to Connie who was looking quite lovely in hopes of catching the eye of a single, widowed, or divorced—she wasn't fussy—golfer.

"I've used muscles I didn't know I had," Connie admitted. "In fact, I never knew cake decorating and serving was so strenuous."

"Think of how strong your hands will become from squeezing those pastry bags filled with icing, and also the muscles you'll build on your arms from carrying around huge amounts of cake mix, not to mention the cakes themselves. It's better than most exercises."

"Only if I want huge shoulder and back muscles on skinny legs atrophying from standing still," Connie groused. "I'll end up shaped like a dolphin! What about the way my feet hurt from hours of standing? And my back from bending over the cakes? And my neck from hunching—"

"Stop! Okay. You're right. We'll serve a few more pieces, and then we'll be out of here."

"Your cakes are very clever," an elderly woman in a lacy, beige Chanel suit said to both Angie and Connie. "I believe my club might be interested in having the two of you make some cakes for us."

Angie immediately began her rapid-fire speech about the benefits of buying a Comical Cake.

Connie rolled her eyes and turned away from watching Angie trying to convince the Chanel-wearing patron to become a customer.

Just then, Angie's neighbor, Stan, showed up. Ever since he decided he was a "partner" in Angie's enterprise, he would pop up unexpectedly at parties, usually near the end, in time to sample any food the party served, as well as to take leftovers back to his apartment.

"Why don't you grab a knife and help me serve?" Connie said.

"I'm a silent partner." Stan waited until Connie dished up three pieces of cake then took one for himself. "It's pretty nice of you to help this way," he said before filling his mouth with frosting-laden chocolate cake.

Connie glared at him, then glanced over at Angie, who was still talking with the member of the blue-haired set. Didn't Angie ever take a breath? She certainly didn't bother to see how Connie was doing. For all Angie knew, she could have dropped dead face down in the frosting.

As if Angie would care. The two of them used to have fun together—they would go shopping, to the movies, to street fairs, or just to coffee shops to talk. But since Angie's business took off, Connie felt as if she'd ceased to exist for anything but slapping cake slices onto dishes. And Connie had her own ten-to-six, six days a week business to run. She had a part-time clerk, but the girl was fairly young and inexperienced, so needed a lot of oversight.

"Do you close your gift shop while you're helping Angie?" Stan asked. "I heard it doesn't do all that much business."

Connie whirled at him, hurt vying with anger at his words. "Where did you hear such a thing? Did Angie tell you that?"

Stan's eyes widened. "Oh... well, um, I'm sure I misunderstood. You're a real sport about this, that's what I meant to say."

With each utterance he made, Connie felt her fury at the entire situation grow. "A *sport?*"

Stan backed up a step and then found a way to move Connie attention off of him to someone else. "Oh, look, that man wants a piece of cake."

Connie served the customer and sent him off with a pasted-on smile. Then she frowned. "Oh, Angie," she called.

Angie didn't even look her way as she wrote down the phone number of the woman she was talking with.

"Angie!" Connie called again, louder.

"One minute, Connie," Angie replied, then quickly turned away again.

"It's not that she's ignoring you, Connie," Stan said out of the side of his mouth. "She's busy."

"Busy like a fox. Seems to me she's having a good time chatting with these party-goers while I do all the work."

"It's her job."

"I think she's taking advantage of my good nature." Connie put down the cake knife and folded her arms.

"Don't be so uptight," Stan continued around a mouthful of cake. "It's okay."

"I doubt it." Hands on hips, she glared at Angie's back.

"Well, I'm outta here," Stan said, grabbing a glass of punch in one hand and another piece of cake in the other. "The last place I want to be is in the middle of a cat fight."

Connie ignored him. "Angie!" Her voice was a little more strident. "I need to talk to you."

"In a minute," Angie said quickly.

Connie grew more irritated. "Angie, I mean it!"

"Excuse me," Angie said sweetly to the woman she'd been talking with. She grabbed Connie's arm and dragged her a few steps away from the cake. "What is it? I'm talking to a potential customer—a potentially huge customer!"

"I'm feeling used." Connie folded her arms. "You aren't giving me proper recognition for the work I'm doing."

Angie stared at her. "I offered to pay you, and you said no way. Have you changed your mind?"

"Of course not!" Connie said. She tried to find the words to explain more, but couldn't. Stan's ugly comments that still filled her head were too hurtful.

"Of course, I value you, Connie," Angie said. "I couldn't do half of all this without you." But then her gaze wandered back to the old biddy. "Please, would you mind going back to serving the cake?"

Connie suddenly felt weepy. How could she admit to feeling ignored, taken advantage of... and jealous that Angie was very likely soon to become engaged while she couldn't even find a halfway interesting guy to date? She had seen Paavo's expression when he showed up the other night to take Angie to a fancy restaurant. She'd understood, even if Angie was to obsessed with cakes to recognize what was right under her nose. But instead of saying any of that, she simply jutted out her bottom lip. "I don't think so."

"I give up." Angie waved her arms in exasperation. "The woman I was with runs a huge non-profit organization. If I can get them to use my cakes for a charity function, I'd be set for life!"

Hearing that, Connie's cheeks grew fiery red. "Well, bully for you!" She then took off her apron, shoved it in Angie's hands and marched out of the room.

***

Surrounded by brightly burning candles and incense, the Dark Lord stood before the altar with his eyes shut, his hands clasped and pressed against his breastbone. The filth was all around him. Vomit. Excrement. Urine. Blood. The desire to destroy raged within him. To kill, to stomp out the whores and harlots with their lies and their phony smiles.

Only his Queen stood above the others, perfect and divine. He'd followed her today, watched her with her cakes, serving others, working to ingratiate herself to the swine.

Soon, my Queen, they will all bow to you.

He quaked with the need to act. Taking deep breaths, he waited until he was filled with visions of darkness and of hell. Only then did he turn to the Book to read a favorite passage.

You, Mortal, shall not be alone, for a Queen awaits you, and she will reign with you as Consort and Mistress. Her Dark Ladies, the Four chosen as the Night's Concubines, will do her biding. As your Power is perfected, all will tremble, Queen and Concubines, in Your Presence as you lead them from Darkness to Deepest Night. Perfection is summoned from the Undead Pentagram: the Five that you have called to you.

From the Four Corners of the Earth, they will come to you, bringing you Power and Strength and Secrets of their Lands. Your Queen alone must be of the True West, a Place of Gold...

CHAPTER TEN

"Good morning, Connie," Angie said as she burst into Everyone's Fancy. Connie was whisking a feather duster over the store's many knickknacks. No customers were in the shop. "We need to talk."

Angie headed straight for the back room where Connie had a small office crammed tight with a desk, table, two chairs, shelves and many boxes of stored merchandise. Angie placed two non-fat lattes and the white-and-green Victoria pastry box on the table. Inside were cream puffs, lemon bars, and the custard napoleons that Connie particularly loved.

Connie remained in the shop dusting, as if she couldn't care less about Angie or the box of goodies.

"Could you take a moment to come in here and talk to me?" Angie called.

Connie sighed heavily. "I guess I can do that." She entered the office and dragged her desk chair to the table where Angie sat.

"Coffee?" Angie gave Connie a latte and then lifted a napoleon out of the box for her.

"Thank you for the coffee." Connie slid the pastry back, her lips pursed. "I'm dieting."

Connie was always dieting, but that hadn't stopped her before.

Angie wasn't one to beat around the bush. "I was wondering about yesterday, and why you were so upset."

"Why shouldn't I be? You schmooze while I stand around working, and I'm the one with a store to run."

"But I've got to find new customers," Angie explained logically.

"You and me both!" Connie shouted. "I've got bills to pay, I have no idea what's happening with my inventory, and you expected me to serve cake? The heck with that. Let them eat bread!" With that, she stood up, duster in hand, marched out into the shop, and began furiously dusting once more.

Angie hurried after her.

"Those people see how cute your cakes are and it helps your business grow," Connie continued, a cloud of dust wafting around her head, "but it isn't doing my business any good at all. I can't do it anymore."

"It's only been three or four weeks."

"Five weeks. And that's four too many."

"But Connie, I need your help." Angie was on one side of a display table, Connie on the other. "That's why I came here. Please, let's try to work it out, okay? Something that works for both of us."

"I just wasn't cut out for this, Angie. Helping you after I'm here all day is physically exhausting. I'm too tired when I'm in my shop. I'll lose all my customers if I keep this up."

Angie looked around the empty shop, but immediately realized that was a BIG mistake.

Connie's mouth dropped open, and she put down the duster. "Well! So that's how you feel!" She headed for the sales counter and the too-silent cash register.

Angie pressed her hand to her mouth. "I didn't mean anything. It's early. I know your customers come in later in the day."

"Oh no!" Connie cried out and jumped back, ignoring Angie's latest words. "How did that get here?"

Angie hurried to her side. A dead mouse lay on the floor behind a couple of yet-two-be-unpacked boxes. "You have mice?" she asked.

"I never have before!" Angry tears filled Connie's eyes. "Maybe if I were here more, I'd have noticed!"

"Connie, tell me what's wrong? Please, tell me." Worried, she reached for Connie's hands, but was rebuffed.

"Nothing! I told you! Will you just leave?"

"Why?"

"First you insult me, then you ask why I want you gone?"

"I didn't mean any insults. I guess I just thought your customers come to your store when they need a cute gift whether you or your clerk is here."

"So I'm not needed here either, is that what you're saying?" Connie was so angry she could scarcely spit out her words.

"No! Okay, I'm saying this all wrong. Your customers love your store and they always come here when they need a special gift. But I'm trying to build a business. To do that, I need loyal customers like you've got. I have no choice but to talk to people, to schmooze with them, as you call it."

"Everyone has a choice, Angie," Connie said with a frown. "Even you!"

"Okay," Angie said, giving up. "I get it. I'll leave."

"Looks like we got a friggin' serial killer on our hands," Calderon said as he wandered through aging steel desks, file cabinets, stacks of folders, books, and papers to drop a sheaf of email attachments he'd printed out onto Benson's desk. "These are from the Sausalito P.D."

Paavo stood up and looked over Benson's shoulder. "It's the same M.O., then?" he asked as Benson began reading through the material.

"Sure is," Calderon replied. "Good work, Paavo. It was a help, a big help. We're going over to Sausalito, checking out the crime scene, maybe even having some fish for lunch. Let's go, Benson."

Benson shoved the boring police reports into a folder, glad to leave them aside and do some first-hand viewing and discussion. The two inspectors swaggered out the door.

Paavo dropped back in his chair and watched them go. What he wouldn't give for an interesting case right now. The temptation to sneak a glance at the Sausalito file was great.

"Well, did you do the dirty deed yet?" Yosh asked.

Paavo jerked himself upright and then glanced around to see if the inspectors and secretary still in the room were listening. He shook his head. "Not yet," he answered softly.

"Why not?" Yosh's voice carried like a megaphone.

Rebecca Mayfield lifted her head from her computer and glanced their way. Paavo lowered his voice even more. "She's been too busy."

"Too busy? Is that a joke? What does she have to be busy about? You don't have a big case for her to stick her nose into."

Paavo tried to whisper his response. "She bakes cakes."

Yosh burst into a loud laugh. He now definitely had everyone's attention, including Lt. Hollins, head of the Homicide Bureau, who was talking to Inspector Bill Sutter. "So she's pushed you aside for Duncan Hines, huh? What a gal!"

"No, that's not it," Paavo said, glaring at the others until they turned back to their work.

Just then, the sound of high heels on the outer office's scruffy linoleum floor was heard. Very high heels. Against the drabness of Homicide, Angie appeared in the doorway, an almost other-world vision in a smart rose tweed suit over a trim and petite body, four-inch high heels, matching lipstick and long, manicured fingernails. She carried a bakery box.

"Here's your chance," Yosh said. "Not an oven or egg beater in sight. Go for it, pal."

Paavo hurried toward her. She said hello to the others in the room, all of whom she'd met since dating Paavo. "What are you doing here?" he asked.

"I'm sorry to bother you, but I need to talk." She saw that everyone was watching, so she gave them all a half-hearted smile. She handed Paavo the box filled with homemade chocolate cupcakes piled high with mint frosting. "Do you think your friends would like these?"

She hadn't finished the questions when Elizabeth Havlin, the lieutenant's administrative aide, offered to help. Paavo handed Elizabeth the cupcakes.

Oohs and aahs and thank yous followed as Paavo led Angie to his desk.

"Are you terribly busy?" she asked.

Paavo pushed the paperwork to one side. "This can wait. Nothing more is going to come of it."

"What is it?"

He wondered if she were stalling. It wasn't like her to want to know about homicides. "Drug overdose," he answered. "Seems there's some heavy-duty stuff going around. The guy was one of those Goth types."

"That's the long black trench coat set right?"

"Pretty much." He studied her a moment, noticing the dark smudges under her eyes and a pinched look to her face that wasn't there a couple of days ago. The uneasiness he'd been feeling came back to him, along with his morose thoughts of never being able to propose. "Is something wrong?"

She studied him a long moment, then, with her sad gaze meeting his, she nodded.

His breath caught. Had she figured out what he wanted to ask her? Was she here to tell him not to bother? His stomach twisted, and he all but broke out in a cold sweat. "You want to tell me about it?" He managed to speak with some modicum of calm, while inside, some raving lunatic was screaming that he didn't want to hear it.

She bit her bottom lip, and then blurted out, "Connie hates me."

Connie? This is about Connie? Relief hit him so hard he was almost giddy. "I'm sure she doesn't. We all know that you're best of friends."

"No. She really does." Angie placed her hand on his as tears filled her eyes, and in a voice little too loud confessed, "She wouldn't even eat a napoleon with me!"

He could feel the silent chuckles of every eavesdropping inspector in the bureau. He stood and shrugged on his sports jacket. "Let's go." As they walked out the door, he glanced back at the others. "Break time."

They went to a Starbucks around the corner. Police inspectors, assistant DAs, and even judges could be found dropping by there all hours of the day.

Paavo ordered Angie a non-fat latte, and himself an Americano. "Now, tell me about you and Connie," he said as they settled into a small, dark nook.

She presented her sad story as best she understood it.

"Maybe you are being too hard on her," he said after picking up their coffee orders. "She does have a business to run."

"Hard? I wasn't. I tried to explain—"

"I suspect you hurt her feelings."

She was stunned. "I didn't mean to! I tried to apologize." Elbows on the table, she propped her chin in her hands. "I was trying to help. But no matter what I do, it seems I push people away. And I don't know why."

He gazed at her, surprised to hear this self-doubt coming from Angie who usually was remarkably self-assured—sometimes, a bit annoyingly so. "Has this sort of thing happened to you before?"

"Maybe." She grabbed a napkin and dabbed her eyes.

"Do you want to tell me about it?" Paavo asked.

Angie straightened. "Well, there was the time my sister Frannie wouldn't talk to me for months when she and her boyfriend were having troubles and I told her I thought she'd be better off dropping a loser like him. He *is* a loser, too."

"Is that the guy she married?"

"Yes, but this was before they were engaged. I thought she'd want to hear my opinion. I was wrong."

He didn't reply. He'd seen homicides resulting from one person's desire to inflict their opinion on others in matters of the heart. "But you realize your mistake."

"I guess." She took a sip of her latte, then blurted out, "Although I still don't see why my cousin Richie got mad at me a couple years back when I gave him a copy of a good diet."

Paavo nearly lost the mouthful of coffee he was sipping. "Oh? And how would you feel if someone did that to you?"

"This was different. He was going through a rough patch after his fiancée was killed in an auto accident. He was drinking too much, and putting on weight. That put his health at risk."

"And you don't think he knew that?"

"I was just trying to get him to take care of himself. He didn't let me explain."

Paavo nodded as he was starting to see a pattern here.

"Then," Angie began, but when she caught Paavo's eye, she clamped her lips together.

"Then?" He was almost afraid to ask.

"I don't—"

"Come on."

She sighed. "It has to do with my former friend, Nona Farraday."

"The restaurant reviewer?"

"That's right. On occasion, I'd make a suggestion about a review, especially if she had something wrong. Like once, she confused *roulade*, which are beef rolls, with *rouleaux,* which are cream rolls. I would have died of embarrassment if it had been me. I called her and told her she should demand an immediate retraction of her magazine article. Instead of doing that, she got mad at me! She told me to keep my nose out of her business. Can you imagine?"

"Well..."

"I don't get it. I was trying to be helpful, and they got mad at me. Maybe I just don't know how to be a good friend."

He took a sip of coffee and then chose his words carefully. "Sometimes, when people ask your opinion, what they really want is help deciding what they should do. They're not asking for your opinion, but for you to help them draw their *own* conclusions."

She nodded. "You think?"

"Trust me on that," he said. "Your friends and relatives know you; they know you can be a bit... outspoken. But Frannie and your Cousin Richie still love you, Nona Farraday still talks to you about restaurants, and I'm sure Connie has a reason for acting the way she is, which has nothing to do with hating you."

Angie rubbed her temples. "Connie said I don't value her. It makes me wonder if I've been so busy with my business I haven't paid enough attention to those around me. And that includes you." She clutched his hand with her silky smooth one. "I'm so sorry I keep having to turn down our dinner dates."

"I can't argue with that," he said.

"That settles it!" She withdrew her hand. "I'm going to turn over a new leaf. I'm going to talk to my sisters."

He hoped he hadn't heard right. "Your sisters?" Angie had four older sisters. Nice women, but fonts of enlightenment they were not.

"They can help me," she said. "I'll ask them what it takes to be a friend."

He rubbed his chin. "I don't know about that. Well, maybe Bianca, but..."

"But what?"

"I'm sure you can think of a way to take care of this yourself. Go to Connie. Try to work it out."

"I tried that this morning and failed miserably. My sisters are older and wiser. I'm sure they'll have good advice for me. I'll talk to them and then work it out with Connie." She glanced at her watch and jumped to her feet. "My God, I had no idea it was so late. I've got an appointment with a new customer, and then I've got to get home and bake. I've got a special cake—a huge wedding cake—to deliver to Fugazzi Hall tomorrow! I'd better run." She gave him a quick kiss and a big hug. "I feel so much better now. Thank you so much for putting up with me and being so helpful!" Then she dashed out the door.

He stood and put on his jacket. And once he was sure she was gone and couldn't see him, he just shook his head, a wry smile on his lips.

CHAPTER ELEVEN

Angie didn't like the appearance of the house of her latest customer. What should have been a beautiful Victorian home in the Pacific Heights neighborhood where her cakes were becoming increasingly popular, the house's peeling paint and grimy façade made it look as if it had been taken over by a devotee of grunge.

Strangely, it was right next door to the old church graveyard that so freaked out Connie.

She shook away the thought. It hurt too much to think about Connie now.

Angie stepped up to the front door and rang the bell, reminding herself that despite the state of the house, anyone who could afford a home in this neighborhood, could certainly afford a Comical Cake.

After a while, she rang the bell again, and then knocked on the door.

Finally, she heard footsteps in the hall. The door was opened by a hefty man with very short brown hair, wearing a floor-length black velvet bathrobe and black satin slippers. His eyes were dark-rimmed, as if he'd just woken up.

"Baron Severus?" She extended her hand. "I'm Angie Amalfi."

His puffy eyes opened wider. "Miss Amalfi, whatever are you doing here so early?" He took her hand and shook it. To her surprise, his fingernails were round and high and painted black, making them look like black parrot seeds. She didn't give in to the desire to wipe her hand against her rose-colored Prada suit, tempting though it was.

"I thought we had an appointment," she said. "Am I early?"

"Er... yes, about twelve hours. You see, when the Baron said he wanted to meet you between eleven and twelve, he meant at night. Not"—he shuddered—"in the morning."

Was this a joke, she wondered. "And you are?"

"I'm his assistant, Wilbur Fieldren. Oh my, whatever shall we do? The Baron is most anxious to meet you, but right now... Come in, come in. Excuse my dress, or lack of. We're all late sleepers here."

The house was an assault of mahogany Victorian antiques, with heavy drapery and table scarves in dark reds and greens. Fieldren led her down a hall lined with overlapping Persian carpets, with sideboards and armoires filling every available inch of wall space and crammed with figurines and knick-knacks. Multicolored Tiffany-style lamps with low-watt bulbs dimly lit the way, and she found herself clutching Fieldren's arm more than once to avoid stumbling on the carpet or bumping into a piece of furniture.

He led her into a study which was also stuffed with furniture, and had a strange, almost medicinal smell to it. Two brown-leather chairs were against one wall, a window behind them, but the heavy purple brocade drapes were closed so no sunlight entered the room. A small drum table sat between the chairs. He led her to one, and she sat.

Small round candles burning on wrought iron candlesticks emitted the offensive odor, almost like camphor. She wondered if the house had some kind of bugs he was trying to get rid of. "Those are interesting smelling candles," she said, hoping the assistant would take it as a cue to extinguish them.

Instead, he took a deep breath. "The Baron finds the scent most stimulating, don't you?"

Reminding herself he was a potential client, she murmured, "Very."

"Now, about the Baron's club," he began. He told her that there was dancing, liquor for those over age twenty-one, but mostly it was filled with young people who liked to dress up in dark, mysterious, romantic ways, as if they were little Lord Byrons and such. The owner being a European baron lent it an air of validity.

The club sounded very strange. Angie couldn't quite imagine it, and also wondered how much scrutiny this so-called baron's pedigree could stand up to. But, she kept her mouth shut and nodded.

"If your cakes have the look the Baron wishes, he might make numerous special occasion orders for his club. So why don't you bring us a cake to see how the Baron likes it? Many of the members here have sweet tooths, as I do, I'm afraid." He smiled and patted his generous stomach.

Angie's own stomach somersaulted at the sight of his fingernails, not to mention his suggestion that she 'bring' them a cake to try. That was presumptuous. It's not as if he was holding a wedding and she needed to provide selections for tasting.

"You'll come at night—after eleven is best—so the Baron will be sure to meet you and have time to devote to you alone."

She stood. "I'm afraid I'm rather busy at the moment. I'll call you when I have more time so we can talk about the type of cake you'd like and *my cake prices*."

"Of course."

Saying goodbye quickly, she hurried to the door.

"We look forward to you coming back soon!" he called after her.

Once outside, she let the warmth of the bright sunlight fill her, and took a deep, cleansing breath. *I'll be back,* she thought, *when hell freezes over.*

The Dark Lord skulked toward the street, eyes searching for prey, his mind elsewhere, wrapped around the one above all others who would be his, the one he would love for all eternity.

To have someone to love...

Didn't all beings, great and small, want that? He'd never given it much consideration in the past, but merely went about his way, doing what he must, what he'd learned he must. But then, he saw *her,* watched her time and again, and his heart changed. He felt the ache and the joy of love. True love.

He heard a noise behind him.

Slouching into the shadows, he found an opening between two buildings, and eased into it, listening. The footfalls were distinct, yet soft, as if someone were purposefully trying to remain hidden.

He grabbed hold of the bottom of a fire escape, and he pulled himself up onto it, then scurried onto the roof as quietly as he could. He waited, watching the street below.

Before long, a man appeared. He was tall but gaunt, his shoulders stooped as if from age and the weight of worry. In the lamplight, the man's face was drawn, his cheeks sunken, his hair only a few, gray wisps, yet his eyes were resolute as he vigilantly searched the darkness for neither man nor beast.

Mason Markowitz.

The Dark Lord watched as Markowitz sprinkled holy water on the grounds of St. Michael the Archangel's church. The fool. Why put holy water on a deconsecrated church? It would do no good. The church belonged to him and his people. This clown was wasting his time.

He remembered how frightened of Markowitz the teenager, Taylor Walters, had been. Of course, Walters was just a boy and a nervous sort at that, so afraid of his own shadow that if anyone said "boo" he would run crying to his mother. Or the police.

The thought jarred him. What if Taylor went to the police and told them everything? That would never do.

His eyes zeroed in on the old man, and an idea came to mind. A devilishly clever idea. He was well pleased.

CHAPTER TWELVE

"Bianca, it's so terrible." Angie reached for one of her sister's butter cookies. That morning, she had gotten up early, baked and decorated the wedding cake, and decided to make an emergency visit to her eldest sister before the time came to deliver it. "I desperately need your help." She bit into the cookie and chewed woefully.

"What's wrong, Angie?" Bianca poured them each some coffee before joining her at the kitchen table. She was the most down to earth of Angie's four sisters. With a husband and two sons, she was content to raise her family and do a number of things the "old" way that their mother, Serafina, had taught them. Strangely, from time-to-time Serafina grew irritated by Bianca's lack of adventure and her innate conservatism toward just about everything.

"Paavo said…" Angie felt tears well up in her eyes.

Bianca placed her hand on Angie's arm. "Paavo? I thought everything was fine between you two. What's wrong?"

"No. I mean, yes. I mean, he's not the problem. It's everything else." Her tearful sniffles stopped her from being able to say more.

"Blow your nose and tell me!" Bianca ordered, handing her a Kleenex.

Angie did as told, then said, "Connie got mad at me, and as I was trying to explain to Paavo all about what happened between us, I mentioned a couple of others who also got a tad irritated at me. I feel like I don't know how to be a proper friend. Or that I, somehow, push people away. Even Paavo said I'm a... a tad outspoken. But he also mentioned your name, that you might be able to help me."

"Oh?" Bianca sat a little straighter in her chair. Obviously, she took this as a compliment. "I suppose I've had more years of experience in being a friend to people than you have." She stroked the front of her neck as if trying to smooth out some wrinkles.

"So what's the secret?" Angie wiped her tears then took the compact mirror from her purse to make sure her mascara hadn't run.

Bianca thought a moment. "Be nice and be honest."

"Oh, puh-lease! Those are platitudes. I need details. You have lots of old friends, right?"

"Well, I would have lots if I wasn't so busy." Bianca sighed and grabbed a cookie for herself. "I have to cook, and wash, and run the house and take care of the kids and listen to family."

"Family--"

"That's what I said. Always family!" She waved the cookie. "Between older parents, and all of you younger sisters, not to mention my own husband and sons, and I'm not counting all our cousins, all of you take so much time, I just don't have any left for myself."

"You don't?" Angie was shocked. Bianca complaining?

"It's not that I'm complaining. I love my family." She dunked the cookie into her coffee and watched it as she spoke. "And family should come first. But sometimes, sometimes I'd like to be able to see people and do things just for me, you know?"

"Yes, I never dreamed--"

"Why should you? Why should you think about your big sister? My hopes, my dreams, my way of having fun? I've always been here for you, for Peter, for the boys, for our other sisters, our cousins, their kids. Sometimes I feel as if all of you take more and more pieces of me until there's just nothing left for my own use." As she lifted out her cookie, the part in the coffee had grown so soggy it broke off and sank to the bottom of the cup. She put the remainder on her plate.

To Angie's horror, tears filled her sister's eyes. "Bianca, I'm so sorry."

"Don't be sorry. It's not you. I'm just feeling sorry for myself, I guess. And to think that you—with all you have going for you—are feeling bad? I can't believe you! I just don't know what to do anymore. I try and try but I can't make everybody happy all the time."

"No one expects you to!" Angie said, patting Bianca's hand.

"Yes, everyone does. That's just the problem."

Angie jumped up and gave her big sister a hug, holding her close. "I didn't mean to upset you."

"I know. No one ever does." As Angie sat back down, Bianca dried her eyes with a napkin and then scrunched it in her hand. "It's all right. I'm used to being ignored."

Angie didn't know what to say. "I never meant to ignore you. I don't think any of us realized how you're feeling."

"It's okay." But then her face brightened. "Ah, I've just thought of something that will help you." Bianca rushed off and soon, she was back with a compact disc in hand. "You should listen to this. It's old, but it might help."

"Great." Angie looked down at the CD and her face fell. It was Dale Carnegie's *How to Win Friends and Influence People*.

Mason Markowitz huddled on the side of a building and watched the dark-haired woman park a Ferrari Portofino outside Fugazzi Hall, a reception hall and night club in the North Beach district. On his bony frame, his skin sagged, as if he'd recently lost a lot of weight. He wore a baggy, wrinkled brown suit with a belt whose buckle bore a new, tighter hole. On his head sat a battered brown fedora.

Angie got out of the car, walked around to the passenger seat and opened the door, then lifted out a bright red wedding cake. The cake rested on the edge of the car as she scanned the area, as if searching for someone or something. It was afternoon, and the sun shone brightly.

The cake tottered, in danger of sliding off its base before the little brunette righted it. It was so huge it could have weighed as much as she did. She was quite pretty—beautiful in fact, with a healthy vibrancy about her. Even across the street he could feel the strong life force within her.

He had to talk to her. How skittish would she be if he approached her? Perhaps as a customer? He could always ask about her cake business. It had been a long time since he'd eaten cake. Three years, in fact. They didn't serve cakes where he'd been lately.

If he could get inside Fugazzi Hall, he could talk to her there, but it was probably a private party.

He needed to make contact soon. Things were growing worse much more rapidly than he'd expected. Time was speeding up. *Ars Diabolus* told of grave changes in the future. But the future, he believed, was now.

She continued to stand there waiting for someone or something. It was his chance. He hurried across the street toward her. "I need to talk to you."

She seemed alarmed at his appearance. He should have realized that, with a woman like her. His hair, he knew, was so long it hung in wild tufts of white below his hat, and the remnants of two weeks' worth of meals stained his shirt and tie. "I'm sorry, I'm in a hurry," she said, trying to pick up the cake.

"It's terribly important!" he yelled.

"Go away or I'll call the police." He noticed her grip the cake's wooden base tighter, as if ready to bop him with it if need be.

Across the street, a tall, dark-haired man got out of an older, blue Mustang. The man had ice-blue eyes and a hard, chiseled face. She didn't have to call the police; that fellow looked intimidating enough.

"Oh... sorry, you're not the person I thought you were. Sorry!" he said again as he backed up. The woman looked at him quizzically as he headed off, and hid behind a nearby delivery truck.

She wouldn't talk to him now, Markowitz thought. It was all right, though. He had another idea.

Paavo walked up to Angie just in time to prevent the cake from slipping off the board she'd put it on. "Are you all right?" he asked, grabbing hold of the board. "You look upset."

"Maybe because there's no Connie, no Stan, and I had to ask you to take time away from your day off to help me." She sighed. "Other than that, all is fine. At least you're here. Thank you for that."

"I guess I'm a little late."

"It's okay. You made it and apparently scared off a panhandler."

He looked around. "You mean that old man? Where did he go?"

"Who knows? Let's go inside."

By the time they'd entered the Hall she was feeling guilty for having been short with Paavo, even momentarily. After she'd struggled to carry the wedding cake down the elevator and into her car, she'd called him and asked if he could help her get it into Fugazzi Hall. She hadn't wanted to disturb his day off for her business, but she was desperate. He hadn't even complained, but instead came right over.

Her guilt grew as he not only carried the cake into the Hall for her, he even helped set it up, and stayed to serve it.

But soon, as much as she appreciated his help, she quickly decided to never again let him help serve. The number of women who flocked to the cake, asking him for seconds, and in a few cases thirds, made her blood boil. More than half of them stood around and made small talk with him about cakes and baking—as if he cared—as they nibbled at her creation, scarcely tasting it.

A couple of them even threw one piece away, just so they could chat with Paavo while he gave them another. They had their nerve!

Once she and Chef Gordon Ramsey, there, finished this Fugazzi Hall stint, they would go to her apartment and order a pizza. She was far too tired to cook. Maybe afterward, a nice soothing soak in a tub filled with some Dior's bath gel... and Paavo... might be exactly what was needed before worrying about tomorrow's cake, or about hiring someone to help her with her business. It was well past time for that.

The Dark Lord watched Julie Sung wave goodbye and hurry away from the others. Friends, he guessed. Who else would be in this desolate area at this hour? The others went to a parking lot, and she crossed the street to a bus stop. As she passed under the streetlamp, he saw her face, her beautiful face, and the words of *Ars Diabolus* heartened him.

She appeared almost happy. And she should be. Tonight she would achieve immortality. Too bad she didn't know it.

Once, just once, he'd like to be able to tell one of his consorts what awaited her and not have her scream and try to get away. He was used to that reaction now. The first time, across the Bay, it had caught him by surprise, and he'd had to kill her quickly to shut her up.

Now, he knew to expect it.

That was why he carried a syringe filled with sodium thiopental.

The street was empty except for the woman. In the distance, he saw the approaching bus. He'd have to act quickly.

As he walked toward the bus stop, he tripped. Arms flailing wildly, he stumbled toward her. Amusement filled her face and she put her hands out to help steady him, even though he was easily twice her size.

Her expression turned to alarm as he grabbed her arm with one hand while with the other, he plunged a needle through her light wool jacket to her skin and emptied the syringe. "What are you—"

He pulled her close, holding her head, her face, against his broad chest as if they were lovers, muffling her cries. In seconds, the sodium thiopental did its work, and she slumped. With her tucked firmly against his side, he led her to his car and placed her in the passenger seat. He gently brushed her long, black hair back off her face. She was so very beautiful, so very exotic. He fastened the seat belt around her, placed a kiss on her forehead, then got into the driver's seat. A quick check all around told him no one was watching, and he drove away.

In the back seat were candles, rope, a knife, and a heavy plastic bag.

CHAPTER THIRTEEN

Angie felt she was finally getting the hang of this cake business. It helped that after yesterday's wedding at Fugazzi Hall, Paavo had returned to her apartment with her where they relaxed and eventually fell asleep in each other's arms. She hadn't slept that well in weeks.

She had spent this morning and afternoon baking, and tonight, she had a spring to her step as she walked out of the restaurant where she had delivered a cake to a small party for a couple celebrating their fortieth wedding anniversary. It was a simple cake in the shape of a big nose with a cobalt blue bird sitting on top of it. Around the edges of the nose was the phrase, "May the bird of happiness fly up your..."

Apparently, for many years the couple had gotten a chuckle out of a country-western song with those lyrics. It wasn't one Angie was at all familiar with.

Except for Connie running out and leaving her high and dry, she liked her business. Her customers were usually festive and good-natured. What surprised her was that they were often also quite nervous waiting for a gala to begin, even those who entertained regularly. About half of her set-up time was spent calming down her customers.

She loved doing that, which she thought of as the psychological side of her job. Maybe she should have gone into psychology instead of cooking. The thought of being a psychologist, using a keen insight to help soothe troubled souls, was a heartening one.

Now, if only she could figure out why Connie had ditched her and her business, she'd be even happier.

She needed Connie's help. Stan and nothing were the same thing, and she didn't want Paavo to feel obligated to help. He was far too busy with his own challenging job, anyway. For the first time in her life, she had a business that was poised to really take off. She had to be sure not to blow this opportunity.

As she neared her Ferrari, the same old man who had approached her outside Fugazzi Hall came up to her again. She backed up. "Who are you?" she yelled, looking around for help. "What do you want?"

"There's great danger," he said.

"From you?" she cried. Her breathing quickened and thoughts of the ritual killing she'd finally read all about in the news sprang into her head. She didn't know if she should try to outrun him, despite her high-heeled platform shoes, or stay and stare him down, like she'd been told to do with a mad dog.

Self-defense classes cautioned her not to show fear. That was easy to do in a gym with an instructor and a bunch of determined woman, but not so simple out here on the sidewalk facing a possibly deranged man.

He moved even closer. She was ready to turn and run, when a young woman stepped out of the shadows. "You're messing with the wrong chick this time, old man," she yelled. Her voice was loud and sharp, and her words spoken fast. "Get the hell out of here if you want to see another birthday!"

He looked from one to the other, then turned and hurried down the street.

Angie stared at the woman in shock before she remembered her manners. "Thank you."

"Damned creeps going around bothering women. This girl's had enough of it." The woman's breathing seemed suddenly labored.

"You did good," Angie said, studying the woman with increasing concern.

She swayed a bit and stumbled toward Angie's car, then turned and leaned against the fender, bending forward at the waist. "Whoa, I guess my blood's gone supersonic on me. I got to rest a minute." She was about Angie's age with shoulder-length, wildly disarrayed dyed-black hair. She wore a cheap beige jacket with a hood, and old blue jeans covered long, thin legs and slim hips. Her shoes were inexpensive white sneakers.

"What's wrong?" Angie asked, lightly touching her shoulders.

The woman tried to stand, but dizziness must have overtaken her, because she slumped back against the car once more. "God, I hate this," she murmured, rubbing her stomach.

"Does your stomach hurt? "

"Not. It's just…" The woman put her hand to her temple and studied Angie a long moment. "I felt dizzy. That's all. I'll be fine in a second."

"Maybe an adrenalin rush, as you said?" Angie suggested.

The woman seemed to smirk at the words. "Maybe."

"Or maybe you're a bit hungry?" Angie asked cautiously, afraid the woman might take her words as an insult.

The woman didn't respond for a long while. "I'm okay."

"Here." Angie reached into her purse and pulled out a twenty. "There's a store on the corner that has sandwiches and stuff. You might just need some carbs or protein."

The woman hesitated, but then her shoulders sagged and

she took the money. "I'll pay you back," she said, making sure the money was pushed deep into her pocket. "I'm not broke because I want to be; I had a job but lost it."

Angie nodded; she'd heard that before. "I'm sure you'll find another job soon."

"I don't know. I was a pastry chef, but nobody wants us anymore. Too many fast-food places and grocers mass producing sweets, and the old places priced themselves right out of business."

Angie couldn't believe her ears. Were her prayers being answered? "A pastry chef? Are you kidding me?"

The woman shook her head, then fixed her gaze on the grocery store and its promise of food as she murmured, "Scout Vannix doesn't kid. No way."

"Excuse me, is Homicide in there?" A nervous teenager who'd been pacing the Hall of Justice corridor asked Paavo as he reached the door to Room 450. The boy had dyed the top of his hair blond, wore a gold ring in one eyebrow, baggy jeans and a tee shirt.

"This is it," Paavo said. "I'm Inspector Smith. Can I help you?"

The boy turned his head from side to side. "I need to talk to someone. I... I think I saw..." He swallowed then ran his tongue over his lips. "It's about Julie Sung."

Julie Sung was Calderon and Benson's latest murder victim. Another strangulation, heart removed, and the body found in an alley surrounded by burning candles. The two inspectors had finally headed for home for some sleep after working over twenty-four hours straight on the case.

"You can talk to me," Paavo said, not wanting to tell the kid to come back later, or even to leave his name and number and wait for a call back. Nervous witnesses tended to get cold feet, which often led to a bout of forgetfulness.

Paavo led the boy to his desk and gave him a seat. "Can I get you coffee or a Coke? Water, maybe?"

The teen shook his head.

"What's your name?"

He had to clear his throat before he could speak. "Taylor Walters."

"Taylor, thanks for coming down here to talk to us," Paavo said, trying to make him feel more at ease. He didn't look like the type who would normally give the police the time of day. Paavo quickly took down his address and phone number. "Were you a friend of Julie's?"

"Yeah, kind of. She was nice." His eyes widened as the shock of her recent murder hit him again. "That's why." He stopped, suddenly unsure.

"It's all right," Paavo urged, his voice calm and soothing. "Go on."

The teen was so thin and pale a stiff breeze could blow him away. "I'm worried," he whispered.

"Why?" Paavo would have liked to turn on a tape recorder, or at least take notes, but the kid was already having a hard time talking, and the chance of him freezing up was high.

"I was with a friend. He drives, I don't. We thought we'd go by and like, you know, pick up Julie after work. She worked late —I guess you know that, too. We thought she'd be at the bus stop, but we didn't see her. Instead, we saw an old man. He was like, just standing there staring; standing where she should have been. I think... I think he might have had something to do with her murder."

"An old man?" Paavo tensed. Officer Bowdin had talked about an old panhandler hanging around the Sausalito crime scene—Mac or Marx. But there were lots of old, homeless people in the Bay Area. It might not mean a thing. "Why do you think he might have been involved?"

The boy's blue eyes were stark. "He's followed me. He hates us—people who live like we do—the whole scene. Some old-timers call us Goths. I prefer Vampyre Community. He even came to my house and left some holy water and a candle. The guy's a freak, and I've heard he's dangerous."

"Do you know his name?"

"Yeah. It's Markowitz. Mason Markowitz."

Yes! Paavo thought. "You're sure of that?"

Walters suddenly seemed to grow panicky and gave a quick nod.

"Good, that's very helpful," Paavo said encouragingly. He didn't want to lose Walters, and a lot depended on the answer to the next question. "How did you learn his name?"

Walters chewed his bottom lip thoughtfully. A sheen of sweat beaded on his forehead. "I just heard it. I'm not sure where." He suddenly stood up as if ready to bolt. "Look, it's just an idea. I mean, like, I didn't see this guy kill her or anything, but if he was involved, and if he's hanging around my house, I want some protection."

"Don't worry," Paavo said, also standing. "Inspector Calderon or Inspector Benson will be in touch with you very soon."

"They'll take care of my protection?"

"They'll do everything they can. Try to think of anything else that might help them. But tell me, where did you know Julie from?"

He backed up, his eyes darting. "I, uh, go to school with her sister. I got to go now." He turned and hurried out the door.

Paavo suspected the last answer was a lie, and wondered why the boy chose not to answer truthfully.

He quickly wrote out a report of Walters' interview, along

with the teen's address and phone number. One copy each went to Calderon and Benson, and one, he kept for himself.

Neither lead inspector had yet returned to the bureau. Paavo opened the Sausalito report on Mina Harker's death to see what had been written about "Mac" or "Marx." Scanning it, he found nothing more than he'd been told, but something unrelated caught his eye—the answer to another of his questions.

The friend of Mina Harker who had filed the missing person's report was a young woman, probably around twenty, light brown skin, long black hair, about five-foot-five, and estimated at a hundred twenty-five or so pounds. A ripple went down his back. Although the description fit many, many young women, it also fit that of the first San Francisco victim—Lucy Whitefeather.

CHAPTER FOURTEEN

"Frannie," Angie said, her head swiveling from side to side as she followed her sister's pacing as she rocked and patted her baby to get him to stop crying. "I need to talk to you about a couple of things. Did you know Bianca often feels put upon by all of us going to her with our problems?" She'd left her endless stream of comical cakes to pay a visit to her sister's small city house.

"Nonsense. She loves it. She's told me so whenever I've talked to her. Ignore her. What else is bothering you?"

Seth Junior's head bobbed on Frannie's shoulder, his face beet red and contorted from crying. Frannie was the sister closest to Angie in age. She was the tallest of them and had a bulimic's thinness, even during her pregnancy. Her hair was light brown, chin length, and permed into ringlets. Angie would have preferred an inch-long surfer clip to that mess. Frannie's blue denim housedress hung shapeless and her Birkenstocks looked ready to fall off.

Angie swallowed hard at Frannie's reaction to Bianca's woes, and then moved on to her next issue. "I need some advice on being a better friend."

"A friend to who?" Frannie rubbed the baby's back, hoping a loud belch would stop his distress.

"No one in particular, just in general," Angie explained. She made a funny face at her nephew and nearly had her eardrums explode with his next cry. "How do you keep your friends?"

"What are you talking about?" Frannie had to shout to be heard.

"You must have someone to talk to, don't you?" Angie shouted back.

Frannie turned the baby sideways in her arms and rocked him from side to side, which he hated even more than being on her shoulder. His tones were earsplitting. She rocked harder. "Of course, when I so choose, which isn't often." She flopped into a chair and began bouncing her son on her lap to see if that would stop him. It didn't. "I'm self-contained, a fine-tuned machine. I don't dawdle."

"That's good. And little Seth doesn't interfere with that?" Angie tried to hide how appalled she was at how loud Baby Seth's shrieks were.

"He'll learn. I have no patience with a brat."

"But, at times, I suspect you want adult company, besides your husband, of course."

The baby's cry turned strident. "Not me." Frannie yelled to be heard over him. "Before Seth Junior, I was busy with my new job, then my new husband, then my new apartment, then my new car. When I got pregnant, I was always sick. The last thing I want is other people, including my husband, telling me their woes. As if I care!" Her eyes narrowed. "Why are you asking me all this?"

Angie trailed after her into the kitchen where Frannie used a warmer for the bottle of formula. Angie didn't bother to give her any of the gory details. To say that Frannie was a bit self-centered and lacking compassion was like saying the moon was round. "I'm having trouble with a friend, and I wanted to talk to someone about it."

"You? Nonsense. If you ask me, you need to be choosier about who you associate with and talk to, the way I am." With the bottle finally warm, she crammed the nipple into the baby's mouth. "I can't believe you, Angie. You just don't know how to deal with people. They'll bleed you dry if you let them."

Angie bit her tongue. "I don't think so."

"I *know* so," Frannie insisted. "Precision and organization, those are the keys."

I'm out of here, Angie thought. She should have known better than to visit Frannie. She got up to leave when Frannie suddenly handled her Baby Seth, who promptly spit a mouthful of formula onto her favorite Dolce and Gabbana dress.

"Before you go," Frannie called from the bedroom, "I've got a book you need. It should help you straighten up and fly right."

With little Seth hanging over her arm, Angie dabbed at her dress with a clean diaper. "What book is it?"

Frannie could have written the book in the time it took her to find it, but eventually she returned and handed it to Angie. *Time Management.*

Paavo drove to Lucy Whitefeather's address, a flat in a three-story building in the Ingleside district. She had been living with her parents when she was killed. An idea had come to him, a long shot, but he needed to check it out.

Squaring his shoulders, he steadied himself before facing the girl's parents and rang the doorbell.

Ruth Whitefeather answered. The ravages of losing a daughter showed in her lined and haggard expression.

Paavo introduced himself, gave his condolences, and talked a little about the investigation, all that the police were doing, and so on, before he showed her a picture of Mina Harker. He didn't hand it to her. It was a death photo, and many people were squeamish about even touching such a thing. Ruth White-feather was one of them. Her whole body jerked as she realized why the eyes were shut.

"Have you ever seen this woman?" he asked. "I'm trying to find out if she and Lucy knew each other. Her name was Mina Harker."

"She's dead, too?" Ruth asked, horrified yet unable to avert her gaze.

He nodded. "We think the same man may have killed them both."

Ruth's eyes filled with tears. "I'm sorry. I've never seen her. Not many of Lucy's friends came to the house. Maybe her boyfriend knows this girl. He's a good man. Hard working, with no airs. I'll give you Ernie's address."

Paavo tried Ernie Pierson's home phone, and when no one answered, he drove to Pierson's work address, C&Y Pipe Fitters, in the southeast part of the city. It was an area where an increasing number of industrial buildings were being converted into yuppie offices and lofts. Pierson was back in the shop, and Paavo waited at the front desk for him.

A tall, barrel-chested young man, with a scar over his right eye, greeted Paavo with a string of expletives. "Why are you here?" Ernie Pierson demanded. "Another woman was just killed, and you waste time asking me more questions? I told those other two assholes I don't know nothing about it. Lucy's killer is out there, not here!"

"I know that," Paavo said calmly. "I'm here to ask about this woman." He showed Pierson the Harker photo.

The man settled down immediately. "Is she another victim?" His voice was choked.

"She was killed in Sausalito about a month ago. A friend reported her missing, a young woman who meets Lucy's description."

His gaze lifted to Paavo's at the name of the town. "Sausalito, yeah. Lucy liked it there. But that woman, she don't look familiar."

"We believe her name is Mina Harker. Does that sound at all familiar?"

Pierson's head rolled from side to side. "I don't know. I don't think so. Lucy and me, we had troubles. She was going to school, to college. Look at me—a pipe fitter. We split up for a while. She got into some bad shit with some crazy group. One night, about two weeks ago, she came back to me, crying. She said she was sorry. Called them evil. She wanted us to be together again."

"Did she tell you where she'd been? Who she'd been seeing?"

He shook his head. "She didn't want to say, and I didn't want to ask." The big man's eyes turned inward and hollow. "She was back with me again, and that was all that mattered."

Paavo left. There was nothing more to say.

His last stop was a complete Hail Mary, but worth the trip to San Rafael if it panned out. He was directed to Officer Kimura, who handled most of Marin County's missing person reports, including the one on Mina Harker.

Paavo introduced himself. "The Harker report was given to you by a young woman," he said.

Kimura nodded. "Yeah, I remember her. Young, real pretty."

"Is this her?" Paavo handed him a photo of Lucy Whitefeather. To aid in the investigation, her mother had given Paavo one of Lucy's high school graduation photos. It hadn't even had time to yellow with age.

Kimura didn't need to study it. "That's her."

Finally a connection, Paavo thought. The killings weren't completely random. A solid lead.

"But she's a lot more 'cool' looking now," Kimura quickly added as he handed back the photo. "So, is she giving you any more information about Mina Harker?"

Paavo drew in his breath. "Not exactly."

Know your Queen, Mortal, by her connection to the Earth, Fire, Ice, and the Heavens.

Through the Heavens, you shall know her. Beware the Moon in Void of Course, for only in its Fullness, in the House of Aquarius, when Pluto is in retreat, shall you rise to the Power that is yours. Strong forces are aligned to stop you, and your Struggles will be fierce.

At such alignment, Mortal, shall your transformation to Dark Lord be complete. The Queen and her Consorts will be yours.

Time was speeding, hurtling him through the continuum toward Eternity. The Dark Lord was high, higher than he'd ever been. Mission three accomplished, and not only for his Queen, but also to rid the world of his enemy. He could have danced for joy. If only his Queen were here to dance with him.

He turned to his astrological tables. Did he have to worry that he would be an old man before the moon and planets aligned properly for his Queen?

He studied the planetary charts. Pluto had gone from stationary to retrograde six weeks earlier. Could it be? The date was just a bit before the voice had directed him across the bay to his Queen's first consort.

Excitement bubbled within him.

Pluto would remain in retrograde for four more months. A lunar calendar presented the cycles of the moon during this period. When he found the next full moon, he stared at the chart, awed and shaken and, yes, humbled by what he was seeing.

This very month, this exact month, the full moon would occur in the house of Aquarius at the same time as Pluto was in retrograde, precisely as demanded by the thousand year old text.

Sweat broke out on his forehead. Could this conjuncture be one that happened regularly, and he'd never before realized it? He continued to search for the same three elements to conjoin throughout the year, and then on to the next year, and the next. All three did not occur again simultaneously until the year 2047.

There was much work to be done, and forces, as the Book warned, were trying to stop him. He must eliminate them, all of them. Could he meet the challenge?

He remembered the *Ars Diabolus* final warning—beware the moon in void of course.

Studying the star and planetary charts, he determined the day he must be ready to claim his Queen.

When he looked at the calendar, he laughed out loud, something he almost never did. This very month. Friday the thirteenth. How perfect!

CHAPTER FIFTEEN

Angie sat on the sofa in ivory lounging pajamas and matching mules, her feet up, a wake-up cup of coffee on the end table, and her computer tablet on her lap open to the morning *Chronicle*. From the picture window, a million-dollar view of the Bay stretched from Oakland and the Bay Bridge in the East, to the Golden Gate in the West.

She was startled to read that there had been another murder in the city. A woman had been strangled, a Korean woman named Julie Sung. She was only twenty-one years old, and had been last seen at a bus stop in the south of Market area.

Her body was found in an alley, just as the last woman's had been.

The newspaper alluded to it being another "ritualistic" murder scene. Angie stopped reading. The story was enough to give her nightmares. She didn't want any gory details.

At the sound of a soft tapping at her door, she looked through her peek-hole to see Scout Vannix in the doorway. In a momentary flash of enthusiasm at Scout being a pastry chef,

Angie had given the young woman her business card and suggested she might have a job opening. Only later, her more rational self figured she would never hear from her again. Angie had always heard there was a shortage of good pastry chefs. Scout's employment story had to have been made up. The woman had surely laughed all the way to the nearest bar or crack dealer.

Her irritation flared. She yanked the door open hard, ready to run her off.

"Here you go," Scout said, her hand outstretched. "Your change." She handed Angie four dollar bills, two quarters and a dime. "I bought myself some big old sacks of dried beans and rice. I'll be eating fine for a while."

Stunned, Angie gazed from the money in her hand to Scout. Her throat tightened as she realized what the pittance might mean to Scout. She handed the money back. "No, it's for you. Won't you come in?"

Scout's eyes widened as she entered the fancy apartment with the delicate antiques, the small Cézanne watercolor over the state-of-the-art entertainment system, the beautiful view. "Since I'm here," Scout said hesitantly, "you seemed interested, yesterday, when I said I'd been a pastry chef."

"I did," Angie said, cautiously.

Scout reached into her back jeans pocket and pulled out a piece of white paper. Unfolding it, she said, "In case that means you might have a job available, I brought some references."

Angie gazed at the list of several top chefs. She was stunned. "These are your references?"

Scout shrugged.

"And they can vouch for you?" Angie asked incredulously.

"I believe they will. Call and ask them about Honest Scout Vannix. See what they tell you."

Scout looked a lot healthier today, although her skin looked too pale against such jet black hair.

Angie made a quick decision. Refolding the list, she placed it on the coffee table. "I'll call them another time. I'm sure everything will be just fine. In fact, if you'd like a job, I have to bake a cake this morning for a surprise party for a"—she coughed delicately—"proctologist. It's obviously the type of profession people love to joke about. This is the third request I've received in as many weeks. The other two I refused, but since this one wanted a cake in the shape of a rubber glove, I accepted."

Scout grinned. "So you really are a baker?"

"A cook, actually. But I fell into a cake business, so I'm learning a lot about professional baking. It's not easy."

Scout studied her. "You're seriously offering me a job? Are you sure you don't want to contact the people on that list first? Because I don't want to get grief about what chef so-and-so says later on."

"I feel comfortable about hiring you," Angie said with grave sincerity. "Your ability to help with the baking will determine whether you keep the job or not."

Scout gazed at her a moment, then dropped her eyes. "You're a nice person." Her voice was quiet.

Given the way her so-called friend had been treating her lately, those words touched Angie's heart. "Let me show you what I need you to do. You can get started while I dress. You might not think of me as so nice once I put you to work. I'm pretty fussy."

In the kitchen, cake pans in a variety of shapes were stacked on the counter.

Scout stood in the doorway. "That's how you make your cakes?"

"The trick, you'll find, is in the decoration. How's your handwriting, by the way?"

"My teachers told me I should become a doctor. But I'm a whiz at fancy designs."

"Oh, dear. Well, I learned penmanship from Sister Mary Ignatius, so it looks like that'll continue to be my job."

"We've got the name of the killer," Calderon said as he strutted into the bureau.

Paavo stood at the coffee pot, filled his cup, then faced his fellow inspector. Only moments earlier he'd walked in and noticed the Taylor Walters report untouched on Calderon and Benson's desks.

Yosh, who'd been writing the conclusion to an investigation on a multi-millionaire who'd died while jogging on his honeymoon with a wife forty years his junior, shoved aside his paperwork, put down his pen, and swiveled in his chair to face Calderon.

"He left fingerprints at the scene," Calderon said smugly. He sat at his desk, feet up, and stretched his arms high as if to get the kinks out after a hard day's work.

Calderon was clearly enjoying the fact that he and Benson had the only interesting case in Homicide at the moment—and that it was driving the other inspectors nuts. He played up every news flash with all the drama of a Shakespearean tragedy.

"His name's Mason Markowitz and he's an interesting case, if you believe in spirits." He paused dramatically. "Markowitz was, from all we're hearing, just a normal guy, an insurance agent in a small town in Illinois until about three years ago when he was in an auto accident."

Paavo moved closer, eager to hear more. Bo Benson sat on the edge of his desk, clearly enjoying Calderon's verbal swagger. "It wasn't even much of an accident, but Markowitz hit his head against the windshield and was knocked unconscious. He was in a coma for two months. When he woke up, he was a changed man."

Calderon stopped, looking like the cat who ate the canary.

"I give up," Yosh said. "What was changed?"

"He claimed he could see people on the 'other' side."

"Other side? You mean dead?" Paavo asked.

"I saw that movie," Yosh said skeptically. "But wasn't it about a little kid?"

"One big difference. Markowitz didn't say he could see dead people—he said he could see *devilish* people."

Paavo and Yosh exchanged glances. "What the hell does that mean?" Yosh asked.

"What am I talking here? Swahili?" Calderon's voice boomed. "It means what I just said. Markowitz thinks he can recognize when people aren't people at all, but those who are really demons, devils, witches, and warlocks."

"Sounds like the Salem witch trials or something." Yosh picked his pen back up and began flicking the top so that the ballpoint bounced in and out.

"I'll admit, it's all garbage that I never paid attention to in Catechism classes," Calderon said, starting to grow annoyed with Yosh's dismissive attitude. "Anyway, this guy thought it was his duty to expose evil, to warn good people about staying away from the bad ones, but now it looks like he's gone a step further. Now, if he thinks some people are evil, he just kills them."

"You're saying he's some kind of killer-exorcist?" Yosh flipped his pen onto his papers. "Are you kidding us?"

"I wish we were," Benson interrupted. "Markowitz apparently hunts demons, vampires, and werewolves. He goes after all of them and 'roots out' or kills the evil entities."

"A night stalker," Paavo said.

"Exactly. The shrinks who worked with him swore he wasn't dangerous, that all he was doing was seeking 'monsters.' So even though his wife—now, ex-wife—had him picked up by the police several times when he'd head for a big city to hunt evil, he'd always be let go after a seventy-two-hour hold."

"Claiming he could see demons wasn't a good enough reason to hold him longer?" Yosh asked.

"If it was, the loony bins would be all filled up." Calderon answered for Benson. "His old lady couldn't handle worrying about him and what he might do to other people or to her, plus fighting with authorities who refused to lock him away until he got over his crazy ideas. She left him and moved to Florida."

"So you're saying he killed three women because he thought they were demons?" Paavo asked.

"Who knows what a guy like that would think?" Calderon replied. "It doesn't matter, anyway. We know who he is. We'll nail his ass in no time now."

"We figured the candles were his idea of how to cleanse their bodies or something," Benson said. "Maybe he cut out the hearts instead of driving a stake through them."

"Isn't that just for vampires?" Yosh asked.

"Shit! How the hell are we supposed to know about all that crap!" Calderon growled. "It's all mumbo-jumbo. The guy's a frickin' murderer. I don't care why, and I don't care how."

"What about the fingerprints?" Paavo asked. "Where did you find them?"

Calderon suddenly grinned. "He messed up big time. Everything else had no prints. He must have used gloves. But we fresh fingerprints on the pole holding the bus stop sign— the bus stop where Julie Sung's friends left her after class. The print were Markowitz's. It looked like he took hold of the pole for some reason. Maybe while waiting for her. Who knows?"

"Interesting," Paavo murmured. He quickly told them about the connection he discovered between Lucy Whitefeather and Mina Harker, and about the visit from Taylor Walters. Paavo remembered that Taylor seemed to think he saw Markowitz at the bus stop after Julie had left it. But maybe he had the time wrong, or Markowitz returned there for some reason.

"Whoa-ho-ho!" Calderon shouted, and high-fived Paavo. "Fingerprints and an eyewitness. We got him now, bro!"

Before Paavo went to Angie's apartment that evening, he'd called to make sure Connie wasn't there and that they would be on time for his reservation at Les Fleurs.

She was dressed beautifully in a shimmering royal blue low-cut dress with a silvery sparkle as she walked. It showed off a nice amount of cleavage and clung to every delicious curve. His heart was in his throat as he looked at how beautiful she was. Finally everything was falling into place just as he had hoped.

She handed him the keys to her Ferrari, and soon they were at the restaurant, on time. His mood was good, and despite his nervousness, he ordered for them both an appetizer of calamari stuffed with salmon, a warm spinach salad with smoked duck breast, followed by filet mignon *en croute*, and crepes suzette for dessert, with a paired wine for each course. It was one of the most elegant meals he'd ever ordered. Angie looked at him as if he'd taken leave of his senses. It was clear to him that she wanted to ask what was going on, but somehow she managed not to. They both enjoyed every last bite.

They made small talk through the dinner, with Angie chatting about her business, as well as her troubling talk with Bianca and irritating talk with Frannie, her concerns about Connie, and the new helper she'd hired. As he waited for the dessert to be served—the staff queued to his plans to propose —Angie went to the ladies' room.

He expected she was also going to check her telephone messages. Being a businesswoman agreed with her. Although tired, she seemed happier and more self-satisfied than she'd been in quite some time.

The waiter came out and asked when "monsieur" was ready to have the crepes suzette served. He said as soon as his date joined him. The restaurant made a wonderful presentation of the flambé at the table, and Angie needed to be with him, especially since he'd arranged to surprise her with the engagement ring.

For the umpteenth time, he reached into his pocket to be sure it was still there. It was. Fifteen minutes had gone by since Angie left. She should return any moment, and then....

After another five minutes, he beckoned a waitress to check on her in the women's room. She might be sick.

The waitress came by and announced, "Mademoiselle is on her cell phone. She said she will join you in another minute."

He nodded, glancing at his watch once more.

The waiter came by again five minutes later, and Paavo waved him away.

Twenty additional minutes passed before Angie returned.

"I'm so sorry. I didn't mean to take so long," she said, fairly bursting with enthusiasm. "I had a couple of messages, one for an appointment with the owner of a dot-com company." She leaned forward in her chair. "He throws a little party for the staff every month, business is apparently quite good, and would like me to provide interesting novelty desserts on an ongoing basis. It could mean a lot for my business." Her face positively glowed. Unfortunately, it wasn't for the food. Or him.

"I see."

"I'm so excited! I've got to get ready for tomorrow's meeting. He wants me to bring in a number of ideas. It's an online lingerie business catering to young businesswomen. It and should be a lot of fun..." When her eyes met his, she stopped talking. "Oh, dear! I'd forgotten all about dessert."

"Yes," he said through gritted teeth. "Do you want it now? The waiter has been hovering over our table. I think he'd like to serve us and get us out of here."

She barely glanced at the waiter. "I'm so stuffed, Paavo. I love crepes suzette, but I think I'll pass. My head is so filled with ideas for lingerie cakes, I can't think of anything else!"

He froze. "Oh?"

"I guess you don't really want to hear about it."

He couldn't seem to find any words to say.

"Well, shall we leave?" she suggested brightly.

"Fine."

Though he thought he had hidden his dismay and frustration, she must have sensed his unhappiness. Maybe it was his lack of response. "I'm sorry," she said. "I know I get overly excited about my new business. I don't mean to, but it is nice to feel successful at something. Still, on second thought, let's stay here. Dessert would be lovely. Call the waiter back, please."

With that, he sighed. She couldn't read his mind about wanting to propose, and he certainly didn't want his engagement to come at a time when her mind was filled with cakes that looked like bras, panties and camisoles. He'd waited this long. He could wait until the time was perfect. "It's okay. Your business is doing well. That's fantastic, and I'm really glad for you. I'll ask for the check."

"Are you sure?" Her brow was wrinkled with concern.

Despite himself, his lips formed a rueful smile. If he thought back on his time with Angie, nothing had ever come easy for them. Why should this be any different? "Yes. I'm quite sure."

"It was a wonderful dinner, Paavo. Absolutely wonderful— almost as if this were a special occasion or something." She peered at him curiously.

"It was time for us to have a really good meal," he murmured, and then added, "to celebrate your business success."

"Thank you for saying that. I needed to hear it." The smile she gave him was worth the night's disappointment. Somehow, he promised himself, he would come up with a time and place that would work for them both.

CHAPTER SIXTEEN

A pale young man, dressed in baggy black pants, a classic Siouxsie and the Banshees tee-shirt, black spiked hair, black eyeliner, and three silver studs in one ear walked up to Angie as she and Scout handed out pieces of cake at an Elks Club meeting the next evening. The cake was an elk's head, complete with antlers created by a judicious use of cake, frosting and toothpicks.

"Where's the punch bowl?" He carried a large sack of ice on his shoulders. To say he looked out of place at this meeting hall was an understatement.

Before Angie could answer, Scout marched up to him, her arms folded. "This is a nice place. What's the trash doing in here?"

Angie gawked in astonishment at Scout's uncharacteristic rudeness.

"If you mean me," the fellow said, eying her frilly blue apron with a smirk, "I'm delivering ice. What does it look like?" He shifted the ice to rest on one hip.

"Go deliver it someplace else," Scout ordered. "This is the cake area, in case you haven't noticed."

"You're doing your job, I can't do mine?" he asked petulantly.

"If it is your job!"

"Hold it." Angie's head swiveled from one to the other, the tension so thick she could almost taste it. "What's going on here?"

"This creep seems to have lost his way." Scout flicked her thumb at him.

"Don't listen to her." He put the ice at his feet and smirked, surprisingly at ease despite the venom Scout was hurling at him.

Scout's eyes narrowed to anger. "How did you end up here? Are you following me?"

"Don't you wish, sweetheart." The man grinned, a straight, shiny-toothed smile that reached his eyes, quite at odds with his otherwise dark, punkish looks. "I will admit, though, when I saw you with a beautiful woman, I decided I'd come here to look for the punch bowl instead of asking one of the fat old dudes who runs this place."

He turned to Angie and extended his hand. "My name's Rysk, with a y."

"Angie Amalfi." She shook his hand. His grip was much stronger than she'd expected. "Rysk is an interesting name. Are you one?"

"Nope. I'm as dependable as they come."

"Don't listen to him," Scout warned, hands on hips.

"Looks like my friend here's hustled you for a job," Rysk said. "What's the matter, Scout? Afraid I'll cut in on the action?"

Angie was all ears and eyes watching these two, and she was interested to meet someone who might shed some light on Scout. Where could Scout have met Rysk? The bristling hostility between them intrigued her. She wanted to know more.

"I don't know which I'm more pissed off at," Scout said. "You calling me a friend or your delusions that Angie would want to hire you for anything!"

Rysk turned to Angie. "I saw you two lugging around those cakes. I can do that for you easy. What if you dropped it? I'd save you time and worry. I'll work for only thirty bucks an hour, and I'm an independent contractor, so you don't have to worry about payroll taxes or anything."

Angie knew what he meant. He wanted to get paid under the table.

Nearly spitting, Scout glared at Rysk. "Nobody needs to pay anyone to carry a cake! I carried all kinds of cakes when I worked for Cocolat. They aren't exactly heavy as stones, you know."

Rysk ignored her and faced Angie. "I could use part-time work," he said. "How about twenty-five dollars an hour? And if Scout ever stopped being so angry, she'd tell you I can be trusted."

"Right, about as far as you can throw him," Scout commented before Angie could reply. "Ignore him, Angie. He's bad news."

"Don't listen to her, Angie. She hardly knows me... yet." He winked at Scout, and as she sputtered in outrage, he gave Angie a boyish grin.

Amused, Angie was now aware that the sparks flying between those two had nothing to do with hostility. And she had to admit, it was getting more and more difficult for her to deliver cakes, especially big ones, and at the same time to take new orders and prepare the cakes already scheduled.

"Give me your phone number and a couple references and I'll keep you in mind," she said. "Now, you'd better take that ice to the table at our right before it all melts."

The web was being woven tighter. Alone, in the dead of night, a crescent moon overhead, he felt at peace. He had moved a step closer.

First Mina. Dear, sweet Mina. She had wanted a new persona, a new name, and she'd trusted him to choose a special name for her. As he got to know her better, he realized why the conjunction between them had been so strong. That was when his path, his life, first became clear.

He could have cried for himself, for his loneliness as a child, when others had called him a monster, a freak, and a lunatic. In time, he began to understand who and what he truly was. As he learned to accept the forces of darkness, to revel in their blasphemy and his own contentment, others stopped regarding him strangely, and instead looked up to him.

He'd never forget the day Lucy came to him. Dear Lucy. He had almost laughed aloud. Mina and Lucy, both his for the taking. That was when all doubt left his mind.

The little Korean girl fell into his arms next. So gentle, so sweet. He sighed as the memory of her warmed his cold heart.

Joy filled him then, and for a moment he was tempted to reveal to *her,* the one who would be his Queen, who he was and all that he planned. But that would be unfocused, and dangerous. She wasn't ready yet to give him the answer he deserved.

There was much more to do and so little time to do it. By the astrological calendar, the most propitious time would be the coming Friday the thirteenth. Only nine more days.

But first, he had a couple more... loose ends... to take care of. He picked up the phone.

CHAPTER SEVENTEEN

Yosh shut his notebook and put it in his breast pocket. "Well, I'm convinced. It looks like suicide to me."

It was five a.m. Paavo and Yosh stood in an alley off Sansome Street, peering up at the three-story high glass tube-like walkway that linked two Financial District office buildings. They'd gotten a call from Homicide's dispatch that a young man had fallen from the walkway onto the street below and was killed.

Paavo felt bone-chilling cold and for some reason and even found it hard to breathe, as if the air had been drained of oxygen. Yosh seemed to feel none of that, and Paavo wondered if he'd caught a flu bug.

When they arrived, Paavo was saddened and dismayed to discover that he recognized the victim—Taylor Walters. The boy had practically begged for protection, and all Paavo had done was to take a report for Calderon and Benson. Although Taylor Walters had been frightened and nervous, he hadn't seemed in the least suicidal. Quite the contrary.

Paavo studied the bridge between the buildings. What had happened here in the early hours of the morning? All the windows were sealed, which meant Walters must have fallen from the top of the walkway, not from inside it. Walters had to have gone to the floor above, lowered himself to the top of the structure, crawled to the middle, and then either jumped, or fell, or was pushed by someone out there with him.

Walters was dressed in a black opera cape with red lining, black slacks, and a white ruffled shirt. On his cape was a patch with Germanic lettering that said "Nosferatu Rules."

"What's Nosferatu?" Yosh had asked. "Some rock group?"

"It's the name of a vampire," Paavo had responded. At his partner's look, he explained. "Angie likes old classics. We went to a film festival to see it. It was pretty grotesque. The guy was rotten, not your friendly Bela Lugosi-playing-Dracula type."

They had carefully checked for any sign that the boy had been forced onto the top of the bridge. Crime scene investigators had dusted for prints other than his on both the window that had been pried open, as well as the fourth-floor ledge he'd climbed onto before lowering himself to the bridge.

Eyeballing it, only one clear set of prints was found. The CSI would have better information after running their tests.

Officer Varney, who had called in the homicide report and secured the crime scene, walked over to Paavo. "I just remembered something." He hesitated. "It's probably nothing, but thought I'd mention it."

"What is it?" Paavo asked.

"Well, this alley is part of my normal patrol. I pass by, two, three or more times each night, depending on what's going on."

Paavo nodded; he knew the routine.

"The time before finding the kid, I saw an old man in the alley. A street bum. You know the type."

"What did he look like?"

"Tall, shaggy white hair, skinny. I rolled down my window and called him, told him to get on home. He never even glanced my way. It must have been because of him that I paid close attention to the alley on my next drive by. That must be what caused me to decide to investigate what looked like a mound of black cloth on the ground. I just don't know."

Mason Markowitz, Paavo thought, heartsick that he hadn't taken Walters' fears more seriously. He shivered.

"Are you all right, Inspector?" Varney asked, alarmed at Paavo's expression.

He didn't answer, but instead asked, "Have you ever seen the old man before this morning?"

Varney shook his head. "Never."

***

"Taylor simply wouldn't listen to me," Geraldine Walters said, trying to control her tears. She lit another cigarette. Her hair was short, straight, and dirty blond, her face tanned and lined with dryness, the area above her upper lip yellow-tinged from tobacco.

Yosh handed her yet another tissue. He and Paavo sat in the living room of the two-bedroom apartment. The furniture was worn and old TV Guides were the only visible reading material.

The dead boy's mother was coping with the news better than Paavo had imagined she would, almost as if she had expected it.

Taylor Walters was only seventeen years old. He rarely bothered to go to school, preferring to sleep most of the day. A loner, he had few friends, and his relationship with his divorced parents was sullen and hostile.

At home, he would spend all of his time on his computer in his room, a sanctum his mother never entered.

"I'd make him go to visit his father," she said. "I'd tell his father to do something with him, but he couldn't. Taylor seemed to hate us, hate everything we ever tried to do for him. All he wanted to do was play video games and listen to crappy music. I told him to stop it, to clean himself up and to stop wearing black. You know what he said to me?"

Paavo and Yosh shook their heads. They sat quietly with the woman and let her speak, let her pour out her anger and resentment and deep, deep hurt.

"He said he was a vampire. A vampire! The damned fool idiot. I wanted to wring his neck. Or laugh." Her tears turned to sobs. "Instead, I slapped him. Nothing, nothing got through to him. Nothing. And now..."

The two detectives waited until she gained some control.

"Had he ever been in trouble with the law?" Paavo asked.

"Never."

"No record of any kind? Tickets?"

"He didn't have a driver's license. I didn't want him to drive until he showed he was more responsible." She shut her eyes and shook her head.

Paavo again waited. "Do you know where he spent his evenings, or the names of some friends, Mrs. Walters?"

She stared at the wet tissue as if it might hold answers that had eluded her for years. "I suppose I should, shouldn't I? I tried to give him everything he could want. Why wasn't he happy?"

"Did he talk about the places he went?"

She sucked hard on the cigarette, then crushed it. "He'd talk about a club sometimes. A place he and his friends hung out. I had the impression, though, that it wasn't a club at all, but someone's home. Maybe some kid's garage or something. I just don't know. There was one kid who would come by the house. Fred. I don't know his last name."

Paavo and Yosh glanced at each other. They had Taylor's phone and would look for Fred on it.

"Did he ever mention an old man watching him? Or the name Mason Markowitz?"

She seemed puzzled by the question. "No. Why? What's this about?"

Paavo thought about his conversation with the boy. "What about a flask of holy water?"

"Holy water?" Her expression told him he could have been speaking in tongues.

Just then, the doorbell rang.

"That must be my husband. I mean, my ex. Taylor's dad. Excuse me." She hurried to the door.

"I'm Inspector Calderon." The voice carried into the house. "And this is my partner, Inspector Benson. We'd like to talk to Taylor Walters."

Geraldine Walters glanced in confusion back to Paavo and Yosh, then spun on Calderon. "Is this a joke? Get out of here! All of you!" She screamed at Paavo and Yosh as well. "Get out!"

Calderon gawked in confusion at Paavo and Yosh, and quickly yanked a photo out of a folder he carried. "Wait, Mrs. Walters. We just need to ask if Taylor—or you—recognize this picture? His name is Mason Markowitz."

She slammed the door on them all.

Paavo stared, unbelieving, at the photo Calderon held. He recognized the old man in the picture. He was the panhandler who had approached Angie outside Fugazzi Hall.

CHAPTER EIGHTEEN

After having been ordered out of Geraldine Walters' home, Paavo had spent the rest of the day checking school records and talking to Taylor's teachers. He also discussed preliminary findings with the medical examiner, who hadn't yet performed the autopsy. Paavo also ran searches for any prior offenses, and just before dawn went back to Sansome Alley and talk to people who worked night shifts to see if anyone had noticed Taylor or an old man.

Nothing new resulted.

Paavo then spent the rest of the night stewing about the botched visit with Geraldine Walters. It was bad enough to tell her that her son was found dead, but then to have the supposed investigators tripping over each other was beyond upsetting for the poor woman.

The investigation as to whether Taylor Walter's death was a homicide, suicide, or accident, fell to him and Yoshiwara. The fact that it seemed to align somehow with Calderon and Benson's ritual killings was a situation that they, in Homicide, needed to work out on their own. Not in front of the victim's mother.

The next morning, Paavo, alone, went back to see Mrs. Walters. He offered his sincere apology for the mix up that caused four homicide inspectors to visit her the day before. "If I could take a look at Taylor's computer, it might give us answers," Paavo said.

Mrs. Walters led him to Taylor's bedroom and switched on the lights. "There it is. You can take it. I don't think I could ever touch it."

"Thanks." He stepped into the bedroom and stopped short, as if he'd hit a wall. The smell of damp earth and decay turned his stomach. Morbid was the only word Paavo could think of to describe the room.

"I wouldn't let him paint the walls black," Mrs. Walters said, oblivious to the stench. "He did this instead."

Every inch of open space, including the ceiling and the windows, were covered with posters from *The Crow*, *The Lost Boys*, *Vampyre*, *The Matrix*, the bands Twin Tribes, Bauhaus, She Past Away, and other venues. All were so filled with blood, death and dying, it was a room made for nightmares.

Paavo turned on the computer. It had no password protection. Taylor had either trusted his mother, had nothing to hide, didn't care if she looked at his computer, or knew she didn't care enough to bother.

Mrs. Walters left Paavo alone as he read through the e-mails and perused the history file of internet visits.

Most of the e-mails were between Taylor and a friend named Fred Limore. They showed Walters to be a lonely boy living in delusions of a world filled with evil, a boy expressing a dangerous interest in Satanic cults, crypts, the causes of the murders from Columbine High to the present, and even the demons behind the Son of Sam.

It was sickening but also very sad reading.

Suddenly, Paavo sat up, and reread an e-mail to Fred, in

which Taylor feared he was in danger. The e-mail had been written a week earlier.

There were no e-mails after that.

Paavo looked around one last time, getting ready to leave, when he noticed a small flask with a gold cross on it under the bed. He dropped it into an evidence bag. Before leaving the home, he asked Mrs. Walters if she knew what it was. She didn't.

He would have it checked for fingerprints.

Before returning to homicide, Paavo decided to make one more stop. Limore wasn't a common name, and he found a Jason Limore family living less than a mile from the Walters residence. Paavo went there and knocked on the door.

Cautiously, it opened and a dark brown eye appeared. Paavo flashed his badge. "Are you Fredrick Limore?"

The young man pulled the door wide enough so Paavo could see most of his face, pale with sleepy eyes. He had on a loose gray sweatshirt and brown cords. "Yeah, that's me." His words were heavy and slurred.

"Did you know Taylor Walters?"

"Yeah." Limore's voice turned soft. "I heard he bought it."

"I'd like to ask you a few questions."

He stiffened. "I don't know nothing."

"You might know more than you think. First, how old are you?"

"Nineteen. Why?"

"In that case, your parents don't need to be here while we talk. Can I come in?"

"You have a search warrant?"

Paavo stared coldly at him. "I'm not here to search, just to ask a few questions. You can handle this however you'd like, but we will talk either here or downtown."

The teenager opened the door wide to let Paavo enter. "My Mom's at work. So's my Dad."

Paavo entered the upper middle-class home. The spotless living room was furnished in yellow gingham, with ruffles and frills galore, and yet had a strangely staged feel to it, as if, despite the hominess of the décor, there was little warmth in this household.

He began by taking down basic information about Limore, who he soon learned worked as a bicycle messenger. "Tell me about Taylor Walters," Paavo said. "Had he talked about killing himself?"

Limore had hopped onto the sofa, skinny legs crossed under him. "It's not unheard of these days."

"So he talked about it?"

"We all do, man. Life isn't worth much, you know. Not the way things are." Limore brushed a lock of purple hair aside. It was the only long lock of hair on his head. The rest was about a half inch long, dyed black, and had a fuzzy look to it. His bare feet were almost as black as his hair. His hands, as he pushed aside his hair, were equally filthy, with dirt under the nails. Paavo couldn't help but wonder what a woman who would furnish her home this way thought of her son's appearance.

"Many people think life is bad, but don't kill themselves," Paavo stated. "What do you think drove him to it?"

"I don't know. Maybe he was scared," Limore offered.

"Scared of what?"

"That he'd be found out."

"Tell me."

"He was... a vampire." Limore stopped talking, obviously waiting for Paavo's reaction to this so-called revelation.

"I thought vampires were supposed to live forever, and that

they killed others, not themselves," Paavo said with as little emotion or cynicism in his voice as he could muster. No one had ever told him how much of an actor he needed to be in this job.

"Yeah, but it's a crappy life," Limore said.

"Are you one as well?" Paavo asked.

Limore smirked. "If I was, I sure wouldn't admit it to a cop."

From what Paavo had seen of young people who lived the way Taylor Walters and Fred Limore did, the danger came from drugs, not vampires. And if drugs were involved with Walters, delusions and paranoia could easily have followed. The tests from the autopsy would tell him a lot.

"What's your opinion? Do you think Taylor killed himself?"

"He was wigged out, man. Probably got some bad... uh... liquor."

"Where do you and your friends meet?"

"Nowhere special. We go to each other's places, that's all."

"Tell me some of their names."

"I can't do that, man. I can't rat on my friends to the cops. They'd never talk to me again."

"Look, a teenager is dead. We want to make sure he wasn't given an assist off that building, understand?"

"Well, if he was, it wouldn't have been from any of us." Limore abruptly broke off his words, his gaze shifted to a wall.

"Yes?" Paavo asked.

Limore again faced Paavo. "I did hear there's some weird old dude in town. He's some kind of vampire slayer or something. We were warned to watch out for him. I thought it was just a kind of joke, you know. Just some rumor going around about a killer to make things a little exciting for us, make things a little different. It gets kind of dull sometimes. Life sucks, then you die, you know?"

Paavo waited.

Limore began to play with his thumb nail. "But what if it's

not a rumor?" he said quietly. "What if it's true and a vampire killer found Taylor? That could be what happened!"

Paavo knew the kid was acting. He was willing to go along, up to a point. "Do you know his name?"

"No."

"Have you ever heard of Mason Markowitz?"

"I heard it."

"Do you know how to find him?"

"I heard he hangs out near some old Catholic Church nobody uses. Near Pacific Heights. A nice area, but it's got a halfway house or something like that nearby."

Paavo nodded, then drew in his breath. "If Markowitz believed one friend was a vampire, what about the others? Aren't you all in danger?"

"Holy shit, man, I hadn't thought of that. I'm really scared now." Limore's voice, despite his words, was flat.

"Knock it off, Limore."

The kid stared at him. Paavo returned the look, and before long Limore dropped his eyes.

"What's really going on?" Paavo said. "This isn't a game."

Limore continued to worry the thumbnail, as if looking for guidance on how much he should or shouldn't tell. Finally, he shrugged. "The hell with it. The closest me and Walters came to being vampires was eating raw meat from Albertson's. We once got our hands on a bottle of human blood from a blood bank and tried to drink it. Do you know what that shit tastes like?"

Finally, Paavo thought, Limore was giving an honest answer. "Where did you hear about this vampire killer?"

"I'm not sure. A bunch of people were talking about him."

"What else did you hear?'

"He left some holy water outside Taylor's house. That's all I know, I swear it."

"Taylor said he knew Julie Sung. You, too?"

"She was Taylor's friend, not mine."

"Didn't you drive Taylor to the bus stop to pick her up the night she was killed?"

"Yeah." Limore paled. "We but we never saw her. We didn't do anything."

"You saw an old man there." Paavo remembered Taylor's statement.

"No. There was no one. The bus stop was empty."

"Are you sure?"

Limore shrugged. "I didn't see anyone, that's all I can tell you."

"I'd like a list of people who knew both you and Taylor."

"I can't do that man," Limore whined.

"You just said there might be some guy who thinks he's a vampire slayer out looking for them. And probably you, as well." It was all Paavo could do to keep some semblance of patience with this fellow. "It might not be play-acting this time, Limore. They might all be in danger—or even dead. One of them might know something to stop whoever is behind this. You owe it to them to tell me."

"I should call them first."

"Do you want to call them from the police station, or right now, quickly, from your home?"

Limore picked up his phone.

CHAPTER NINETEEN

"Paavo, is everything okay?" Angie clutched the phone tight. She was in her apartment. It was midday and, despite everything, when she saw Paavo's name on her phone's display, she picked up. When he was at work, Paavo never called just to chat. "I'm in the middle of a mess here. I've got a kitchen filled with flies. Flies! I don't believe it. It's crazy!"

"Flies?" he asked.

"It's an infestation! They've destroyed my cake!"

"Okay one quick question. Do you know Catholic Church in Pacific Heights that is no longer used as a church?"

She was surprised by the question, and pleased she could immediately be helpful to him. "As a matter fact, I just delivered two cakes near it. St. Michael the Archangel."

"Great. Thanks."

"Oh, my God! A fly is headed for the living room. Can I call you back?"

"It's okay. That's all I need to know for now. Thanks. And go!"

She immediately put down the phone and picked up the bed sheet she'd pulled from the linen closet.

Unfolding it and holding the ends, her arms wide, she crept into the kitchen, step by quiet step, careful not to tread on the part of the sheet that dragged on the floor. She'd never tried to sneak up on a mass of flies before.

Early in the morning, a woman had phoned asking if Angie could bake and bring her a cake of a devil's head that evening at nine o'clock. It was a "surprise," she'd explained. She wanted the cake to be scary, not humorous, and offered to pay Angie quite well. Angie found a scary devil's head online, texted it to the customer and got the okay. She and Scout had quickly baked and frosted it, along with finishing up other orders she'd had. Then, they headed off to deliver the cakes they'd already promised for the afternoon. When the job ended, Angie let Scout go home, their work done for the day. Or so she had thought.

When she reached her apartment and went into the kitchen, she froze in the doorway and shrieked.

Her devil's head cake was covered with flies. How had they entered a twelfth-story apartment? The doors were all shut, and the windows rarely opened. If she ever went out and left any windows open, the wind up here would blow her belongings from one side of the apartment to the other.

The sheet, she hoped, would now help her capture most of the little beasties. That was when Paavo had called, actually asking for her help. She was thrilled to be of service to him for once, and sorry she had to cut the conversation short.

Now, she inched closer to the cake with the sheet, not wanting to disturb them as they munched and pranced on her once-beautiful albeit scary devil's head frosting. They'd ruined one cake, and the last thing she wanted was to have them fly all over her apartment, hide, and then attack another cake behind her back. Finally close enough, she raised her arms and heaved the sheet over both cake and flies. Quickly grabbing the edges, she swirled it so that the flies couldn't escape. A few did, but she'd deal with them soon enough.

Rolling the whole mess together, she carried it to the garbage chute.

"Mrs. Calamatti, are you down there?" she called, sticking her head inside the chute. Her elderly, and somewhat addled neighbor, spent much of her time poking through garbage bins looking for treasures. Not that she needed the money—she had plenty of it, but couldn't remember that she did.

Angie didn't want to bean the old lady with her cake, even though it probably wouldn't do much damage, considering the state of poor Mrs. Calamatti's mind.

When Mrs. Calamatti didn't respond, Angie dropped the cake, then went on a search-and-destroy mission through her apartment, meticulously checking all doors and windows. How had those flies gotten in? A couple of them could have been in a sack of groceries, she supposed, though that didn't seem very likely. Or maybe one very pregnant fly had somehow snuck indoors, multiplied, and then the whole family hid until they had a Comical Cake to attack.

How long was the lifespan of a fly, anyway?

No, that didn't make sense. At the moment, she had no time to ponder the great fly mystery. She had another devil's head cake to create. Somehow, she'd managed.

Comical Cakes had never failed anyone yet.

After talking to Angie, Paavo found the Catholic Church she'd mentioned. He knew she'd be familiar with the Pacific Heights area, and with a huge Catholic family constantly going to churches for weddings, funerals, baptisms, first communions, confirmations, and even Bingo nights, he expected she was probably also familiar with most of the churches in the city.

In no time, he learned of one halfway house near the church. It was near, but not in, the Pacific Heights area. If Fred Limore's words were accurate, it could be where Mason Markowitz lived. Paavo and Yosh went there to pay Markowitz a visit.

The house had been built in the nineteen-twenties, and that might have been the last time it had been painted. The entryway was so dank and sunless it looked like a cave.

"This is creepsville," Yosh said as he and Paavo entered. The door off the entry was open, and inside a tiny, middle-aged Hispanic woman sat on a floral wingback armchair facing a tabletop television.

She turned off the set as the two detectives faced her, showing their badges. "We're looking for the manager," Yosh said.

Standing ramrod straight, she replied, "That's me, Mrs. Garcia."

"We're looking for this man," Paavo said, handing her a photo of Markowitz. "We were told he's staying here."

The landlady nodded, her eyes questioning. "Milt Mason does live here, but he's not home now."

"We need to see his room," Paavo added, noting the change in name.

Mrs. Garcia didn't ask for a search warrant or anything else, but simply led them to the second floor, which had four bedrooms and a shared bath. She unlocked the second door on the right and pushed it open.

A hawk, stuffed and mounted with his wings spread wide, stood on a bookshelf just inside the door.

"'Quoth the raven,'" Yosh said, facing Paavo. "Why do I feel as if I just walked into a Halloween set-up?"

"Except this is no play," Paavo said grimly.

Large and small candles formed a circle on the floor. Others stood on the bookshelf, windowsill and dresser top. Newspaper clippings and computer printouts from vampire-like and supposed Satanic cult slayings throughout the country hung by thumbtacks on the walls.

A pillow with a grimy pillowcase and a rumpled blanket lay on the floor. Although the wall held a Murphy bed, a table butting up against it overflowed with papers and pharmacy bottles. "Look at this," Yosh said. "Clozapine. Thorazine. Aren't they used for schizophrenia? If he's actually taking these meds, the guy shouldn't be able to walk, let alone kill people."

The landlady gasped and hurried from the room.

On a table were newspapers stories about the two San Francisco ritual murders, plus a small clipping about Mina Harker's murder in Sausalito. "I thought this place was creepy," Yosh murmured. "It's just gone into over-the-top sick."

Paavo walked over to a small table with a tray with bathroom supplies. The toothbrush was damp, as was a glob of shaving soap that clung to a Gillette razor. "Someone was here not long ago," Paavo said. He opened the closet door. Instead of a pole for hanging clothes, it had shelves. "Whoa!"

Row after row of bats, each with a tiny wooden dowel stuck into their midsections, had been pinned onto wooden boards and lined up on the shelves.

"That's gross," Yosh said with a shudder. "I don't like bats, but they deserve better than to fall into the hands of the Marquis de Sade."

Paavo studied the displays. "Time to call Calderon and Benson. Looks like we found their night stalker."

Night had fallen when the time came for Angie to drive to the Haight-Ashbury district to deliver the devil's head cake. Her customer had claimed she wouldn't be home until eight-thirty that evening, and needed the cake delivered at nine on the dot.

Since she'd offered to pay extra, Angie agreed to the late night delivery.

Still, as Angie drove to the address given, she was so tired, she ached in places she never even knew existed. The red devil cake rested snugly in the passenger seat of the Ferrari. She had barely finished it in time—a couple of flies she'd missed in the kitchen had led her on a merry chase.

She didn't like the district she was going to. It had a high crime rate and was the part of the city most "into" witches and warlocks. No wonder this was where a devil cake was wanted. If demons and their minions had a favorite city, it was surely San Francisco. Still, a job was a job, and Comical Cakes never disappointed.

What had her especially upset was that she'd hoped to get together with Paavo that evening. She sensed something was troubling him, despite his denials. He wasn't acting quite like himself and she needed to find out why. Maybe tomorrow... she sincerely hoped.

The deliveries she'd made earlier in the day with Scout had been for "routine" comical cakes. The fun-type she enjoyed making. One was for a baby shower, and the other a promotion in a lawyer's office. For that one she'd been asked to design a smiling barracuda. *Oooh-kay.*

But having to remake the devil's head, decorate and now deliver it, was exhausting. Maybe it was time to contact that fellow named Rysk and have him take over her cake deliveries. Doing so much herself was simply too much. Scout spoke terribly about Rysk, yet Angie had noticed a look in her eye when she gazed at him that wasn't hate-filled in the least, and he'd been out-and-out flirtatious with Scout. Well, Angie would give hiring him more thought when she was less exhausted.

Whether she hired Rysk or not, she definitely would lease a minivan to help with deliveries. A Ferrari simply wasn't a cake delivery vehicle.

She found the street number she sought, parked, and lifted out her cake. At least it wasn't huge or heavy. A dimly lit walkway led to the end of the building, on the ground floor.

Steeling herself, she inched along in the dark and knocked on the door.

A thin little man opened it. His nose was hawk-like, his thick glasses grossly magnified his eyes, and his face was crisscrossed with lines. "Who are you?" he asked, hugging the door.

"I'm from Comical Cakes," Angie said brightly. "I brought the cake you ordered."

"Me?"

"Yes. Here it is." To the man's astonishment, she elbowed the door wider and put the cake in his arms.

He gaped at the box he held. "A cake?"

Looking at the man's home, at the man himself, she couldn't imagine why he had ordered such an expensive cake from her. "That'll be ninety dollars."

"Ninety dollars for a cake?" he shrieked with outrage.

"Hey, you ordered it. Or your wife. I spoke with a woman. And the ninety is because she asked for this late-night delivery. And if you think this is high, I hope you never need a plumber at night." She gave a little laugh, hoping that would ease the financial blow a bit.

"You're crazy!" He pushed the cake back into her arms.

She shoved it back at him. She couldn't believe this. She'd worked all afternoon and evening to make this cake and frosted just right, drove out to this odd neighborhood to deliver it on time, and even gave up an evening with the only person she really wanted to see that night, only to have her cake rejected? Like hell! "You can at least look at it. It's exactly what your wife said she wanted! Why isn't she home? She said she'd be here by eight-thirty, told me to arrive at nine, and that this cake would be a surprise for someone. All I can say is, I kept my part of the bargain, and you need to keep yours!"

"I don't even have a wife!" he shrieked, and gave her the cake again, then put his arms behind his back so she couldn't return it.

"Your lady friend, maybe? Or a sister?"

"I live alone!" he raged.

"Won't you even look at it?" she asked.

"I'm busy, lady. Go away! I know nothing about you or your cake."

"What are you talking about?" She marched past him, right into the apartment, placed the cake on the coffee table and lifted the box lid.

He peered into the box. The red devil cake leered back at him. His eyes widened, and he screamed. "You are evil!" he yelled.

"Me? This is what was ordered!"

"Get out!" He lunged toward a chest of drawers and pulled one open. She was afraid he was going after a gun and began backpedaling.

"All right, I'm going!" she cried, stumbling over her feet in her attempt to get away from him.

"Evil one!" he yelled, pulling out a crucifix and brandishing it at her.

"It's just a cake!"

He raised his fist.

Scared, upset, and angry... but mostly scared... Angie turned and ran, leaving her cake behind. As she lurched down the dark pathway, something hit her head, nearly knocking her over. Luckily, the man didn't follow her out to the street. She jumped in her car and locked the doors.

Tentatively, she touched the back of her head. At first she thought she was bleeding, and then she realized the red coloring wasn't blood.

It was frosting.

Paavo shut the lamp on the nightstand, pulled the quilted comforter over his shoulders, then, careful not to disturb Hercules, who had curled up asleep at the foot of the bed, rolled onto his left side and shut his eyes. Although it was ridiculously early for him to be in bed, he'd spent most of last night on his case, so he was tired. Taking a deep breath, he waited for sleep to envelope him.

He'd called Angie earlier to ask about her flies but also hoping to see her that night. He didn't even ask after hearing her tale of baking all day, plus having to go out and deliver some cake this evening. Damn, but he was sick to death of being understanding. Still, he didn't want to pop the question when she was too tired to keep her eyes open.

Soon, things should settle down and she'd be available again. She couldn't keep up this pace forever. Of course, she'd never had such a successful business before. Was this her future? Their future?

He didn't want to think about that. He didn't want to think about anything but going to sleep, which hadn't been easy to do for well over a week now. He rolled over and shut his eyes again.

But then, his mind turned toward the material he'd read earlier that Calderon and Benson had collected on Mason Markowitz. Markowitz had arrest records and psychiatric holds from five other jurisdictions, and in every one he'd been convinced he was going after demons or vampires, stopping them, and breaking up their "nests" before they hurt anyone.

Each time before, the police had arrested Markowitz for disturbing the peace or on similar charges based on the crazy ideas he had spouted. Always, he'd been let go because the cases were weak. He'd never been connected to any crime, although strange deaths and missing persons had happened in each of the locales he'd visited.

That's what made this case different. Markowitz's fingerprints had been found on the holy water flask from Taylor Walters' bedroom and on the pole where Julie Sung was last seen.

It was odd that a man who could manage to leave no clues whatsoever around three murder victims, would leave his fingerprints on a pole or flask of holy water.

Of course, no one ever accused most criminals of being Mensa candidates. That was why they were caught. The smart ones gave the cops fits.

Paavo rolled over once more, reminding himself it wasn't his case.

Taylor Walters was his case, and Walters had believed in much of the same stuff as Markowitz.

Fred Limore had eventually coughed up the names of two other friends, but they'd had even less information about Taylor than Limore had. All three implied Taylor's beliefs had caused him to take his own life. None would admit to having known Julie Sung, or could name any place that Taylor hung out. They made it sound as if Taylor had led the life of a hermit, yet he'd gotten Markowitz's name from someone. Who that was just might be the key to this whole investigation—both his and Calderon's.

More and more his instincts told him Taylor hadn't killed himself, but that another person caused him to go out onto that bridge and jump, leaving no prints or evidence of having been there.

He flopped onto his stomach, putting the pillow over his head. Hercules mewled in annoyance.

When he rolled over in bed once more, Hercules bounded onto the floor with a squawk, and stalked out of the room, his tail flicking with indignation.

Paavo couldn't explain what it was about the Markowitz evidence or Walters' suicide that bothered him; all he knew was that something did. Eleven years of experience rarely lied.

But he had to get some sleep and tried counting sheep.

He was somewhere around the eighty-seventh sheep when the doorbell buzzed.

Grabbing his Glock, he walked to the door and checked the peephole.

Angie stood on the front porch, pale and wide-eyed. And there were strange red blobs on her hair.

CHAPTER TWENTY

"This has been the suckiest day of my entire life," Angie muttered as she snuggled closer to Paavo on the couch. Her hair was damp from a quick shower, and she was wrapped in his big blue terrycloth robe. "The thought of those toads in my apartment still gives me cold chills. They were so ugly! And when I walked in, I'm sure I felt one slither over my foot before I turned on the light." She began to shiver again.

"Take it easy," he said for at least the twentieth time. "Toads won't hurt you as long as you don't lick them." He stroked her soothingly on the back.

"Not to worry," she muttered. "But don't toads give you warts? What if I get warts on my feet? What if they leave wart germs on my clothes? Who's doing this to me?"

"We'll find out, Angie," he said, trying to calm her.

At least he agreed with her that someone was doing this on purpose. Flies might have gotten into her apartment through some action on her part, but not toads. And she was convinced the devil's head cake order was a ruse to get her out of the house.

She'd told him all about how, after fleeing from that crazy fellow who'd thrown her devil cake at her, she'd driven straight back to her apartment. But there, when she turned on the light, she noticed something that resembled a little brown log on her coffee table. Then it moved.

Another hung from the drapes. Two scurried toward the kitchen. As she'd realized what the strange tickle she'd felt on her foot had been, she screamed and ran out of there.

"I want to meet that new helper you hired," Paavo said, holding her close. "She's got to be behind this. Maybe the flies, too."

"But why? I'm her source of income."

"None of this was happening before she came to work for you," he pointed out.

"It can't be her." Angie didn't think she could cope if she had to go back to handling her business all by herself. "It just can't be."

"Did you see any signs of a break-in?" he asked.

"Who would know, with toads jumping all over the place? I'll call some company to come get them in the morning, and I'll make sure they look under the pillows on the sofa and under the bedcovers and all. I really don't want any more surprises like that."

He gently stroked her arm. "I'm sure they will."

"Toads! What's my apartment turning into? The plagues of Egypt or something?"

"Stay here a few days," he said, tilting her chin up with his finger, forcing her to look at him, and brushing her lips with his. "I'd like that. You can stay even longer if you want."

Her face lit up at his offer, but quickly turned sad again. "I can't. I've got to get back to my business." He dropped his hand. She sat up straight and clasped her hands together tightly. "I've got cakes to bake and deliver. Customers who are counting on me." She shook her head. "I just hope the toads and flies haven't crawled into the cake flour—or in the oven. I don't think the smell of burning toad would do wonders for my mood, or my food!"

He had to smile at that. At least she hadn't completely lost a sense of humor. "I'll help you check the place out tomorrow," he offered with affection.

Whoever was doing this was trying to squash her and her business. No way would she let them. She raised her chin. "I appreciate that. And I'm not going to let whoever is behind this stop me! I'll handle it."

He flung his arms across the back of the sofa. "Just be careful, okay? Whatever's going on, I don't like it."

"Me, neither. It's not as if anyone I know is mad at me, or..." Just then, a light bulb went on in her head. There was someone. Connie. But would Connie...?

"What is it?"

"Nothing." She needed proof before she would smear her friend, or, her former friend. "I need to think about this a bit," she said and unsuccessfully tried to stifle a yawn.

"You can go in and lie down on the bed." He leaned forward on the sofa, not touching her, elbows on thighs. "I'll sit out here a while, give you time to relax, maybe get to sleep."

She looked at him. Then, for the first time in days, she really saw him. Her man. Her wonderful man. He was the one she had turned to in a frightful state after discovering ugly crawling creatures in her apartment. Sure, they were only dumb little toads, but after everything else, she couldn't cope with them.

He'd been in bed after working hard all day, but he immediately took her in and did all he could to comfort her and help her calm down.

Throughout all this, he'd been loving, supportive and helpful, and instead of thanking him, she'd railed against reptiles and carried on about cakes. What kind of awful, self-centered,

Type A workaholic was she turning into? That made her feel even worse than finding toads in her apartment.

She placed her hand on his back and languorously rubbed it. "Paavo, I want you to know I'm sorry about the way I've been acting. Today. Yesterday. The day before. I don't know what's wrong with me or even where all my time goes anymore."

"It's okay. You're doing something you want to do." He remained leaning forward, not looking at her but staring at the unlit fireplace.

"Am I? Sometimes, I wonder. Because I want to be with you, too." Her voice dropped to a whisper. "More than anything else. Believe me. "

Wordlessly, he glanced over his shoulder at her. Sky-blue eyes, eyes that made her heart spin, caught hers and held. His voice turned soft, scarcely more than a whisper. "I'm glad to hear you say that."

"I don't know what I should do—not even what I want to do," she said, as her own voice took on a sudden huskiness. "I'm not happy with what this cake business is doing to us."

"Angie, it's all right." He turned toward her. "Your business is growing. You'll find a way to work it out. And I'm not going anywhere."

She threw her arms tightly around him and squeezed her eyes shut as she pressed her cheek to his hair. "It's not all right," she whispered intensely. "Not at all. I've ignored you; I don't mean to, and I don't want to. I love you, Paavo. So much. You know that, I hope."

"I know," he whispered. "And I love you."

"Still?"

"Always."

She lifted her head. Their gazes met, and then their lips.

Mason Markowitz bolted upright, a cold sweat on his forehead. Wide-eyed, he surveyed his surroundings under the Folsom Street freeway. The candles had long since gone out and the dawn was beginning to light the sky.

She had come to him once again in a dream. Alone, she walked beside an ocean, smiling and happy. The sun shone down on her, so bright it wrapped her in a hazy glow, her features indistinct.

The other women, the ones he had failed, suddenly stood in front of him. One of them opened her mouth, and blood gushed from it, pooling around his feet; then alive, it crawled onto his ankles, up his legs.

He scooted off the old newspapers with a shout, and crouched, looking all around him. The air stirred; he could almost hear the flapping of Baalberith's cape of wings, almost see the horned and taloned beast hovering over him, laughing, laughing, laughing.

He pinched himself hard. Please let me still be asleep, he prayed. But he wasn't. He fell to his knees, his hands clasped over his head. The lord of the flies and his minions must not prevail. He must stop the ascension of the Dark Queen.

He prayed for the strength to do that which he must.

CHAPTER TWENTY-ONE

he pest exterminators were waiting outside Angie's apartment when she arrived the next morning. She began phoning from Paavo's house as soon as businesses opened and found a service available to help immediately.

Now, she explained that she didn't want the toads killed, just gathered up and moved somewhere else. Some toad-loving place, not a big city apartment building.

They eyed her as if she were crazy. Maybe they were right. As she waited in the hall, the lead serviceman made a quick run through the apartment, then came out to assure her the toads were harmless and that there weren't hundreds of them, but twenty at most.

She didn't care what the number was, as long as no squishy reptile greeted her when she entered the apartment.

Where would anyone have found a bunch of toads anyway? Did pet shops carry them? She had no idea. If not, did that mean someone knew about a toad hangout, and they went there and set traps or something? Toads were little boy things, not the sort of creatures she or her sisters had had anything to do with as children.

It was all too weird.

She called Scout and told her not to show up until one o'clock, and then put in a call to Rysk, where she left a message. She needed all the help she could get.

Next, she phoned her sister Caterina. Cat was a woman who always wore elegant clothes and loved spas, massages, week-long visits to health farms, personal trainers, tennis coaches, and beauty makeovers. She lived in a bay front home in Tiburon, a pricey town just across the Golden Gate.

Angie reached her on her cell phone. To her surprise, Cat was in the city, heading for the Furniture Mart, a wholesale outlet on Market Street. She invited Angie to join her.

Cat aspired to be an interior decorator. She'd been aspiring for about ten years now. As far as Angie knew the only house she'd ever decorated was her own, over and over, and still hadn't gotten it right. Tubular chairs and plastic sofas didn't look good no matter how expensive they were.

Angie hurried to the Mart, eager to see it as it wasn't open to the public. Cat met her at the door.

"Well, little sis, what brings you here?" Cat asked as they entered a room with rows of sofas. They were staged by style, with none of the accents of a furniture store. Cat forged ahead, as if cataloguing the sofas in her head, then headed for a sea of armchairs.

It wasn't my good judgment, Angie was tempted to say when her sister didn't even look back at her. She had to rush to keep up. "I wanted to ask your advice," she called.

"Advice?" Cat skidded to a halt, as if no one ever asked for her advice before. They certainly hadn't done so on home decoration. "Don't tell me you're finally going to move those dreadful old antiques out of your apartment! I've prayed for this day, Angie. I truly have. Let's go to the lamps. I know a darling wrought iron that would look wonderful in your place. I've got so many ideas to share with you."

Angie bit her tongue. Cat and her friends were big on sharing. She dashed after her sister. "Wait. That isn't it. It has to do with... friendship."

"Friendship? What do you mean? Maybe a nice loveseat? Something in a leopard print—wouldn't that make a statement to your friends!"

As Cat zigzagged through floor lamps, Angie tried again. "You seem to have a number of friends."

"Oh! Why yes, I do. I'm glad you noticed. I have a zillion friends. Why, we send out over five-hundred Christmas cards every year." She fluffed her platinum hair. Angie hated the color. "To keep friends, every time you get a chance, immediately make sure you do lunch. It works like a dream!"

"Lunch?"

"I try to go out at least twice a week, and with a different friend each time. Never go with the same person twice, Angie, it's a waste of—Ah! Here we are. I wonder if we want two of them for an even more dramatic statement?"

While Cat pondered some truly ugly loveseats, Angie said, "That's not what I meant."

"No? I know—sectionals. You can put a big sectional in the corner."

"No, no! I was wondering if you've ever had a friend turn on you? Start to, almost literally, dish you dirt?"

Cat's mouth dropped, appalled. "One of your friends is doing that to you?"

"I think she's trying to destroy my business!"

"What?" Cat grasped Angie's hand and dragged her to a turquoise and purple chaise lounge near the door where they sat. Cat's brown eyes opened wide and her hands clenched in little fists as she demanded, "Who is this backstabber?"

"I... I suspect it's Connie. God, it makes me so upset!"

"She's jealous." Cat stated.

Jealous? "I can't believe that," Angie countered.

Cat stiffened; an eyebrow arched. "I've met Connie. We've spoken, *mano-a-mano*, so to speak. I know what I'm talking about."

"Oh, my." Angie stared at her. Could Cat be right?

Cat nodded knowingly. "You came to me because I know how to handle people. Trust me in this. She's envious."

It made no sense. But Cat seemed so sure. "Do you think?"

"Why else would she be trying to destroy you and all you've worked so hard for?"

"I don't know." Angie's voice was tiny. Everything in her cried out that wasn't Connie's nature.

"She's hateful!" Cat announced with a shout.

Angie was taken aback, but the more Cat spoke, the more it seemed possible. "Maybe you're right."

"Of course I am! Are you an Amalfi or not?" Cat demanded crossly.

Angie swallowed hard. "I am."

"Then stop being such a wimp!" Cat pointed at her. "You need to get even! This very minute. Make her rue the day she ever messed with you. Don't let this harridan screw you one second longer!"

Angie stared hard at her big sister, then pounded her fist into her palm. "Who needs her anyway?"

"Damned sure you don't! Let her know you're tough. Nobody messes with an Amalfi!"

"I'll do it!" Angie leaped to her feet, ready to dash out the door to do battle.

"I'll come with you to the parking lot," Cat said. "I've got something you need in my glove compartment. I don't know why someone gave it to me, but it'll do you good."

"Oh?" As they rushed through the Mart, Angie wondered what it could be.

Cat reached into her car, rummaged around, and then pulled out a little paperback. *How to Manage Your Anger in Ten Easy Lessons.*

The cake ordered by a small lingerie company looked like a giant blue lace garter. Angie, as master decorator, and Scout, as her apprentice, regarded the frothy monstrosity with mixed awe and morbid fascination. Angie nearly dropped the pastry bag she was using to make rosettes in the frosting when the doorbell chimed. No one ever used her bell. It was tiny and low and seemed to be nothing more than a knot in the wood of the doorframe.

Rysk stood in the doorway smiling at her. "You called?"

"Yes, but you didn't have to come by today. We don't have any deliveries ready, and—"

"We?" His eyes lit up as he asked a bit too eagerly, "Is Scout here?"

She smiled and stepped aside. She'd been right about those two. "She's helping me. Come on in."

"Er, sure. Why not?" The mask of insouciance and bland disinterest was back on his slim face. He sauntered slowly through the living room, taking in every detail as she pointed him toward the kitchen.

"Hey, Scout," he greeted her when he reached the kitchen.

Scout glanced at him, with surprise, but soon her mouth wrinkled as she went back to cleaning up from the last cake. "Look at what the cat dragged in." Sponge in hand, she gazed at Angie. "Flies, toads, and now snakes. What's your apartment turning into, a zoo?"

"I've asked Rysk to work for me. Now that I've leased a minivan, he can use it to deliver cakes."

She snorted. "He's lucky to find his way to the john. It's your money, girl, if you want to throw it away on that loser, don't say I didn't warn you."

Angie had basically put aside Scout's warnings about Rysk since she was in need of his help, but now she realized Scout had been right. "I do need references," she said, facing him, "before I can actually hire you, of course."

"Yes, well..." he hesitated.

She didn't like the hesitation. "I need to know your real name, where you live, and that you have a driver's license. You will be driving a leased minivan for me."

"I understand," he murmured as he opened his wallet and gave her his driver's license.

"You'd better check his references well, Angie," Scout cautioned. "Fifty bucks on the street could get him a driver's license that says he's Leonardo DiCaprio." Tossing the sponge in the sink, she stood with her arm pressed to Angie's shoulder and peered down at Rysk's identification.

"I wonder how well she checked out yours, Vannix," he sneered.

"Edward Bowie," Angie read aloud as she wrote down his license number and address.

"Edward?" Scout snickered. "Somehow I don't see you as an Edward."

He eased back, arms folded, so that most of his weight rested on one leg. "Guess that's why I got the nickname."

"You live in the Mission district," Angie read. "By yourself?"

"It's cheap. And I don't have a roommate." He looked at Scout as he said that.

"Any moving violations?"

"Just parking tickets... for the last three years, anyway."

"I do want some references to call before you leave here," Angie began, when she heard a knock on the door. Paavo's knock.

She should have realized he'd come over today to check out

Scout. Last night, he'd been convinced Scout was the cause of all her problems.

Scout was close-mouthed and private. Even though they'd worked together for five days now, she was still as much a mystery to Angie as when they'd first met.

One thing that wasn't a mystery, though, was why Scout couldn't find a job as a pastry chef. After five minutes in the kitchen with her, Angie realized Scout knew nothing more about pastry than what was written on the back of a Betty Crocker piecrust box. In other words, nothing. She realized Scout must have seen her deliver a cake into the restaurant and put two and two together with a hope and a prayer Angie might need a helper.

Although Scout's lies were disappointing, Angie had to admit that if she'd been in Scout's predicament, going hungry, she'd have lied too. That was the one reason she didn't fire her on the spot. But the real reason was that the woman worked hard, learned fast, and had a great eye and a steady hand for whimsical decorating.

Angie liked Scout and refused to believe she had been behind any of the strange goings on.

"Scout, Rysk," Angie said as she led Paavo into the kitchen. "I'd like you to meet my boyfriend, Paavo Smith." One glance at Scout and Rysk's expressions reminded her of how intimidating Paavo could appear when he put on his "cop face and stance." And he wore it now in spades.

A glance back at Paavo told her what *he* was seeing as he inspected her helpers—pale, emaciated, sooty dyed hair, weird make-up, and strange clothes on both. He didn't look happy.

She gulped then forced a big smile. "Paavo, I'd like you to meet Scout Vannix, and Edward Bowie, who goes by the name Rysk, with a 'y'."

Paavo was shaking their hands when Angie added, "Paavo is a homicide inspector."

Rysk's eyes darted a moment toward Scout. "Ah, interesting work," he said.

"Yes, it is," Paavo responded, giving each a long, piercing look.

"Nice to meet you," Scout said quickly, then to Angie. "I can handle everything here if you'd like to visit with your guy. It's no sweat, girl."

Paavo didn't give Angie a chance to reply. "Are you new to the city?" he asked Scout.

"Chicago," she answered with all the friendliness of someone hooked to a lie detector.

"What brought you here?"

She concentrated on washing a cake pan. "Earthquakes, fires, floods, power brown-outs, gangs, homelessness, looting…. All the things that make city life worth living." She glanced at him. "What'd you expect? Oh, yeah. It's a pretty city."

"An expensive city," he added.

"Chicago's no walk in the park either." Scout's tone had turned snarky, with a glint of fire in her eye at all these questions.

Angie quickly jumped in before things got any worse. "Rysk is here to talk about a job delivering cakes for me."

Paavo faced her, one eyebrow lifted. "Your business is even better than you'd indicated."

"Well…" Angie murmured.

The full force of Paavo's cold gaze turned to Rysk. "Interesting nickname," he said.

"I think so." Rysk was wearing one of his more outrageous outfits—a black turtleneck, red vinyl vest and purple velvet trousers. Green coloring showed on the spikes above his forehead, and all three earring studs sparkled. At least he'd gone easy on the eyeliner.

Paavo's eyes narrowed. "Have you been in the city long?"

"All my life." Rysk raised his chin.

"Me, too," Paavo said. "Mission High. You?"

"Washington."

That, in itself, told Angie a lot. Washington High was in a middle-class, family oriented section of the city. Paavo's own high school was in a much tougher neighborhood.

"What were you doing before you started working for Angie?" he asked.

Rysk put his hands on his hips. "Hey, Angie, your boyfriend sure is a cop. I haven't been grilled like this since I worked at a hamburger joint and put my hand on a burner by mistake."

"You're not used to it?" Paavo asked, pointedly eying the hair and clothes.

Rysk stiffened. "This is a live-and-let-live kind of town."

"Doing what?"

Rysk shook his head. "You don't give up, do you? Okay. I worked at a dot-com company for gamers. Lots of guys like me did. Unfortunately, after our initial start-up flurry, the whole thing bellied up." He shrugged. "Easy come, easy go. Something else will show up eventually. I'm working on my own game in my spare time."

"About what?" Paavo asked.

"I call it Destination. It's not a fantasy setting—too many of those around. Instead, it'll be set in different periods of American history." He rocked back and forth enthusiastically and Angie saw the glance of interest Scout gave him.

"It sounds fascinating," Angie said honestly.

Rysk regarded her with growing kinship. "Yeah, I hope. There'll be levels. The ultimate, god level, will be for hard-core gamers."

"You did time somewhere, didn't you?" Paavo asked Rysk unexpectedly, bringing the conversation back to a jarring reality. Angie had once heard that, if a person was an ex-con, he was supposed to admit it to a police officer when asked.

Rysk stared back at him, his expression blank. "No."

This was going too far, Angie decided. "I think I should talk to Rysk and then let him go on his way," she said, trying to hustle Paavo out of there.

"How about you both write down your social security numbers and I'd like to see your driver's licenses," Paavo said to Scout and Rysk as he tore a sheet from his notebook and put it on the table with a pen. "I'll check them for you, Angie. It'll save you time."

Angie just stared at him, her cheeks burning at the way he had taken over, questioning her ability to hire her own employees... although she really had no idea how to check their credentials.

Still, he would have needed a bag over his head to have missed her outrage. "I *know* you always check out people you hire," he said, trying to appease her. "You're busy. I'm being helpful."

Angie was trying to remember when she'd ever hired anyone except a cleaning lady—oh, and a couple of security fellows at one time. But in both cases she'd used agencies.

"It's all right, Angie," Scout said, jotting her SSN down and handing Paavo her driver's license. "I, at least, have nothing to hide. And, Angie, I trust that your boyfriend is who he says he is." She handed the pen and paper to Rysk, eying his reaction.

Angie's eyebrows rose as she realized the trust issues ran both ways. Again, Scout was right.

Risk weighed the pen a moment, looking from Angie to Paavo. "I'm okay letting Law and Order here do his thing." He scrawled some numbers on the paper; Angie already had written down his license information.

Angie took the papers and brusquely stuffed them into Paavo's hand.

"I'll leave you to your business, Angie," Paavo said, tucking the sheets into his breast pocket. He glanced at Rysk and Scout. "Nice to have met you both."

No one smiled.

"I'll be back in just a moment," Angie said as she followed Paavo out of her apartment to the elevator. He pressed the call button. "Why did you treat them that way? I want them to work for me. To help me."

Paavo faced her, his jaw firm. "Get rid of them."

"Why?"

"They're both hiding something."

"They're such a cute couple, how can you say that? They seemed truthful to me," Angie stated as the elevator arrived at her floor.

His mouth wrinkled. "So I noticed."

Without another word or even a goodbye kiss, he got on the elevator, leaving Angie speechless as the doors shut.

CHAPTER TWENTY-TWO

The results of Paavo's identity checks on Scout and Rysk slowly dribbled in. An Illinois driver's license showed Scout Vannix, age twenty-five, living in Chicago.

Paavo contacted the Chicago P.D. to see if she had any kind of record. She came up clean in both city and state. As Paavo stared at the photo, he wondered at the sadness on her face.

While it was hard to tell if she was lying, according to Angie she was beyond private, keeping everything bottled up inside, which meant it might burst out into... what? She troubled Paavo. Every instinct told him she was there for a reason that had nothing to do with baking cakes.

Rysk worried him even more. Searching DMV, local, state and Federal records had turned up nothing at all on Edward Bowie. His social security number and driver's license were fakes.

Paavo usually read people pretty quickly, but there was something impenetrable about that guy, and it troubled him.

He was clearly older than he seemed, and older than many of the mostly college-age kids who ran around dressed like

Goths and vampires. Paavo would place his age at twenty-seven or eight. He'd seen guys like that before, the baby-faced ones who kept a youthful appearance as long as they didn't become dissipated. Put teenage-style clothes on them, cut their hair a certain way, and they could fool most people.

Edward Bowie—Rysk—was one of that type.

Along with age came wisdom. And there, too, Rysk wasn't the cool, mellow, relaxed dude he pretended to be. But whether that wisdom caused him to be dangerous was another question.

Rysk and Scout were both into the Goth look, as Taylor Walters had been. Paavo needed to find out more about that sub-culture, and just how dangerous it might be.

Walters' autopsy came in as he was searching for something, anything, on Edward Bowie. Walters had such a mixture of drugs in his system, if he hadn't jumped from the bridge, his brain might have burst anyway. But one drug in particular stood out. Thiopental sodium, the same drug as had been found in the autopsies of Julie Kim and Lucy Whitefeather. It was a drug that, in non-lethal doses, could be used to induce a type of hypnosis that would allow a person to fall under the control of another. The autopsy told Paavo and Yosh two things: it explained how Taylor was induced to climb out on a bridge between two buildings and jump, and that Taylor's murder was either the same person, or involved with the same person, that had killed those women.

Whatever had happened, the death and demon-worshipping Vampyre world was riddled with drugs. The autopsy report further convinced Paavo that Angie should have nothing to do with people in that subculture.

The problem was to convince her of it.

"Edward Bowie doesn't exist," Paavo announced as soon as Angie picked up the phone.

"That's hard to believe considering I hired him yesterday and he'll start delivering cakes for me today," she said with more than a little sarcasm.

"His driver's license was a phony, and his social security number a lie."

"Or the DMV records just might be wrong. Everyone knows they're a mess. And he might not have wanted to give you his social security number when he did nothing wrong! He's a nice guy, Paavo. A little mixed up in the way he dresses and does his hair, but that's not a crime. I like him. I want him here, and he's given me no reason not to hire him."

"You're not being reasonable--"

"Give me proof I shouldn't employ him and I won't, but right now, I've got work to do. Scout is in the kitchen waiting for me."

"Watch them both."

"I will. Don't worry."

"I do worry about you."

She paused, finally, and took a deep breath. "I know, and I really don't mean to trouble you. But I'm going with my intuition on this one." They agreed to meet soon, and the call ended.

As Angie headed from the living room to the kitchen, she was startled to see Scout in the hallway between the bedroom and den.

"What are you doing here?" she asked, approaching her.

"Just looking for the john," Scout said.

"It's off the bedroom. You used it yesterday."

"That's right. I forgot."

After Scout disappeared into the bedroom, Angie walked to the door of the den. Why was Scout back here?

She studied her desk and even opened a couple of drawers.

Paavo's worry was causing this suspicion, but what if he was right? Her eye went to an old address book, now open on her desk.

Angie hadn't used it in ages.

Scout had to have been looking at it, but what could she possibly have been looking for?

Scout was already back in the kitchen when Angie returned. "Did you go to the den?" she asked.

"The den? No. Well, I looked in and saw the bathroom wasn't connected to it, if that counts. Look, if something's in your craw about the den, just speak out. I don't want any bad feelings here. If I did wrong, say so."

"No. Just curious. It's nothing."

Scout gave her a sidelong glance, and then, her voice loud and bitter, added, "If you're going to be suspicious of anyone, it should be Rysk. He's the one who's a mystery."

Why the sudden outburst? "He strikes me as a nice person," Angie said.

"That's easy to pretend... for a little while. Just watch your back."

"Why don't you like Rysk?" Angie asked.

Scout shrugged. "It's not that I don't like him. He's a puzzle." She had an odd expression on her face, then turned back to the cake mix.

They were putting the finishing touches on a cake that looked like a computer when Rysk showed up. They'd made the monitor into a face sticking out its tongue. The cake had been requested by a computer repair group.

He entered the kitchen. "Hey, cool. I've had computers do that to me."

"Haven't we all?" Angie said with a chuckle.

Scout glanced at him, then at Angie. "While you're boxing these, I'll run down to the market and get another pound of butter. We're almost out."

"Get two. We'll use it." Angie handed Scout some money. The Hyde Street Market was just a couple of blocks away.

"I don't think she likes me," Rysk said at the sound of the front door shutting.

"What's with you two?" Angie asked.

"I guess I got off on the wrong foot when we first met."

"Where did you meet?"

He grinned. "At a dance. She's a good-looking woman."

Ah! How interesting! Before she had a chance to pursue it, Rysk picked up two of the cakes and carried them to the new minivan. Angie had finished packing the third and had begun the fourth when he returned.

"This box isn't sturdy enough for the computer cake," she said. "I'm going to look for something to strengthen it in the den."

She walked into the den and immediately realized that if she doubled the boxes, one inside the other, that would do it. She whirled around and returned to the kitchen to find Rysk on the floor and scrambling to his feet. He bumped his head on the underside of the kitchen table as he did so. Scout's backpack lay open. She'd left it under the table.

"What are you doing?" Angie asked.

"I thought I saw a big glob of frosting on the floor," he said, rubbing his head. "I wanted to clean it up before someone slipped on it."

"Really?" She pulled the chair aside, but didn't see anything.

"It was just a shadow, I guess," Rysk said.

She looked at him quizzically.

"You got what you need for the last box?" he asked.

"Yes. Why is Scout's backpack open?" She was sure it hadn't been open earlier.

"Is it?" He reached down and zipped it shut. "Guess she left it that way. Say, you don't think..." His gaze shifted between her and the backpack. "Look, Angie, if you're going to be suspicious of anybody, it should be Scout. She's the one who's a mystery."

Hadn't she just had this conversation?

"I think Scout's a nice person," she said.

"It's easy to pretend... for a little while. Just watch your back."

Deja-vous all over again.

"Why don't you like Scout?" she asked.

Rysk shrugged. "It's not that I don't like her. I do. She's a puzzle, though. An intriguing puzzle."

Angie studied the almost wistful expression on Rysk's face. Could he have been looking in the backpack for information about Scout? Her address or phone number?

It was all becoming, as Alice said in Wonderland, curiouser and curiouser.

Before she had a chance to ask him more, Scout returned with the butter, Rysk left with the computer cake deliveries, and the cake-baking marathon began again.

Mason Markowitz stood in the nighttime shadows and gazed at the luxury apartment building. He'd walked the streets since the infernal armies of Baalberith had invaded his sanctuary and swarmed over his possessions, corrupting them with their paws and hooves and tails.

He needed the woman. He would wait here for her, for all eternity if necessary.

His head pounded. That must be why the vision was so unclear this time. He rubbed his temples, trying to see, trying to understand.

No matter. With patience, the answer would soon be his.

CHAPTER TWENTY-THREE

The white angel food cake appeared perfect as Angie took it out of the oven and placed it on her kitchen table. There, in less than an hour, it would be transformed into an angelically smiling bunny. A newly pregnant woman's husband had called to order a cake of a dead rabbit. He wasn't pleased when Angie told him that rabbits hadn't been used in pregnancy tests for more than fifty or sixty years, and no longer had to die to prove that a woman was knocked up.

Eventually, Angie talked him into substituting a cheerful, cottontail rabbit holding a test tube. He didn't think that was very comical, but she refused to make a cake that looked like a sweet little bunny wearing a toe-tag. No one else, she was sure, would do such a thing either. Besides, who would want to eat it?

He relented. Angie almost gave in to the urge to slip in a note giving his wife condolences for being married to such a jerk. The longer she worked with the public, the more she wondered about these people and their sick senses of humor.

Anyway, the cake she envisioned would be cute and highly edible.

"I can handle this if you want to get out awhile to see your cop or a girlfriend," Scout offered.

"Thanks. I don't think so. Visiting my sisters is quite enough for now."

"You have sisters?" Scout asked.

"Four. No brothers."

"That must have been fun when you were growing up," Scout said, her voice suddenly wistful. "Do they all look like you?"

"Kind of, except for one who dyed her hair platinum."

"A blond?" Scout looked interested. "Do you gals get together often?"

"Once in a blue moon, I'm afraid, except for holidays. They're all older and married. Do you have any brothers or sisters?"

To her surprise, Scout's eyes reddened, and she hastily lowered her head. "A sister. She's only eighteen," Scout said.

"Is she back in Chicago?" Angie asked, wondering if the cause of Scout's tears was homesickness.

"No." Firmly, Scout shook her head, squaring her shoulders. "She's out on her own. Our mom died, and our father remarried, and his new wife—well, we both left home at an early age."

"I see," Angie said, not sure that she did, but feeling bad that she'd upset Scout and not wanting to cause her any more heartache.

"You're lucky to have family around you," Scout said. "And I imagine you have a lot of girlfriends to have fun with as well. You're a lucky person."

"I don't know about that," Angie said ruefully, her mind going to Connie. She couldn't discuss her. The subject was too hurtful.

"Really?" Scout said. "Do you—"

She was interrupted by Stan's shave-and-a-haircut knock on the door.

"Hi. The luscious smell of freshly baked cake wafted across the hall from your place to mine," Stan said. "I took it as an invitation."

"Come in. We'll have some cake left over when we cut out the rabbit ears."

"Rabbit ears? Are you making a TV cake? I thought everyone used streaming these days."

Scout glanced up as they entered the kitchen and laughed. "Now, that's funny," she said.

Stan glanced at Angie. "Why?"

Angie didn't bother to explain, but made introductions.

As she peered at the two of them, a new idea popped into her head. If Rysk was as shady as Paavo had indicated... "Stan used to help me with these cakes," Angie suddenly announced to Scout. "He's quite good at it, but his job at the bank takes up too much of his time." *That'll be the day.* "He's an assistant vice president, almost, so he isn't able to be here much."

Stan gawked at her. "But you threw me ou—"

Angie kicked him.

"A vice president," Scout said, measuring water into the mixing bowl. "That's impressive."

"Almost," Angie replied. "He lives alone, and comes over here to help me get rid of leftovers."

"Does he?" Scout glanced up at him as she stirred the white icing.

"I like being helpful." Stan puffed out his narrow chest.

"Are you saying you're a man who likes to bake?" Scout asked playfully, adding a little more water. "I didn't know there was such a thing."

"I like to eat," he answered.

She laughed.

Scout's ability to laugh at Stan's awful jokes was a definite plus, Angie thought.

"Stan can help us decorate the cake," Angie said. "He's quite artistic."

"I am?" Stan looked stunned.

Angie nudged him closer to Scout. "You help Scout with the icing while I cut the cake into shape. We need lots of pink and blue icing."

"I'll get rid of the pieces you don't need," he offered. "This is great, Angie. I'm glad you've finally found someone who actually wants to be helpful."

"What's that supposed to mean?" Angie asked.

"Connie hated helping you. I thought you two were friends," Stan said. "Was I ever wrong!"

The room began to swirl as blood rushed to Angie's head. Even Stan knew Connie didn't really like her! How gullible had she been? She'd honestly thought they were best friends. This was too much. She didn't know whether to laugh or cry.

"Who's Connie?" Scout asked.

"No one I wish to talk about," Angie announced curtly. "Let's finish this cake."

"I love helping," Stan said to Scout. "And I love cake with thick frosting."

Angie's doorbell caused her to leave them. Rysk was right on time to pick up cakes for delivery. She had asked him to leave off his earrings, eye makeup and colored hairspray, and wear clothes a little less off-putting to her customers. He showed up in blue jeans, a Nike tee-shirt, and a brown leather bomber jacket, with his hair combed to the side instead of sticking straight up. To Angie's amazement, he was quite good looking.

"Hi!" she said once she got over her shock. "Come on in. The cakes and addresses are in the kitchen. You have four deliveries today. By the way, Scout's here, and so is my wonderful neighbor, Stan."

"Oh?" Rysk walked into the kitchen to see Scout smearing some icing onto a bite of cake.

"Hey, Scout," Rysk said.

She frowned at him and plopped the cake into Stan's mouth. Stan's gaze was lustful, but Angie suspected it was more for the dessert than the woman. Rysk's smile vanished.

"This is my neighbor, Stan Bonnette," Angie said. "Stan, meet Rysk."

The two men shook hands while eying each other like two stallions each guarding their position.

"So, you're Angie's driver," Stan said after swallowing.

"That's me." Rysk hooked his thumbs in the belt loops of his jeans. "And I'll help doing other things if she wants."

"Not if she's got half a brain," Scout murmured, returning to the bunny cake and smoothing a circle of pink frosting.

Stan lifted an eyebrow at that. "Angie's a great gal," he said. "We've worked together on all kinds of projects. I'm sure Scout is a great asset, too." He flashed her a big smile.

"But for how long?" Rysk asked, his glare never leaving Scout's face.

"I enjoy working here," she responded, avoiding eye contact with Rysk. "Making these cakes is fun, not work. And who can complain about working in cool digs like this, with good food for lunch each day, coffee, whatever."

"That's for sure," Stan said. "Have you filled up your cookie jar, yet, Angie?"

"It's still empty," Angie replied as she tagged the cake boxes for Rysk's deliveries.

"Angie!" Stan wailed.

"Help is coming your way, my good man," Scout said. "I promised Angie I'd bake up some of my specialty, coconut-and-bittersweet-chocolate cookies. I've eaten so much of her food, I owe her a real treat, and believe me, that they'll be."

"They sound exquisite," Stan was all but orgasmic. "I'll help. Do you want to start now?"

"Exquisite?" Rysk mouthed to Angie. She shrugged.

"I've got to finish putting this cake together," Scout said.

"I'll help," Stan replied. "Two hands are better than one, and the sooner we get done with this rabbit the sooner we can get to real baking. Angie, this is a woman after my heart."

Angie laughed, but she noticed that Rysk didn't seem to find Stan's carrying on in the least bit amusing. She looked over her little crew.

Scout was concentrating on blending the coloring into the icing. Stan was drooling over the cake, and Rysk was watching Scout.

Pure desire was in his eyes. Yes! Angie knew it. Any two people who argued as much as they did, had to be in love or they'd have killed each other by now.

Now, what to do about it? To start with, somehow, she had to show Paavo how wrong he was about Rysk.

That night, Scout visited the Crypt Macabre. It was filled with the usual night crowd, but she'd noticed extra security by the doors. She wore a black dress cut quite short and black high-heeled ankle boots.

"Miss Vannix," the deep voice called from behind her.

Scout's bones chilled. Slowly turning, she faced the Baron. His eyes held hers firmly as he glided closer. "Baron," she whispered.

"I regret we haven't had a chance to get to know each other better." He gave her a leering once over, then held out his hand.

She gave him hers, even as everything inside her clamored to turn and run. But it seemed her turn had finally come to receive the Baron's attention. She had to be sure not to mess it up.

"It's been a drag on me, too," she said, working to maintain a jaunty, hip demeanor. "But you always have chicks lined up around you ten deep. I can't even get close."

He chuckled. "You can get as close as you'd like, anytime, Miss Vannix."

She smiled. "The name's Scout."

"Scout." The name curled around his tongue and his gaze darkened. "I've watched you for some time. I could feel your eyes on me. You have powerful eyes... Scout."

"Not me." She was unable to stop herself from taking a step backward. "I'm just old reliable Scout. Nothing special."

"You sell yourself short." He tucked her arm in his and, holding it close, led her to a small bar. "I like your dress, and this necklace." As he lifted the amethyst stone, his fingers brushed her neck. He moved his head closer as if to study it. Her breath held. The room seemed to sway and visions of him kissing her throat filled her head. Or... her heart pounded... was he biting into it like a vampire?

"Your order, miss?"

Startled, she saw the bartender looking at her expectantly. He was pouring a scotch and soda for the Baron.

She ran sweaty palms over the short, tight, black satin shift. He was regarding her with a knowing smile that unsettled her even more than her strange vision had. "Gin and tonic, please," she said.

Drinks in hand, he led her to a small, round table.

"I understand you work on cakes, Comical Cakes," he said, his voice smooth and his dark eyes penetrating.

"How do you know that?" she asked.

He laughed aloud. "Do you really think there's anything I don't know?"

"I'm fairly new in town." She placed her drink down and self-consciously tugged at her hem. The Baron's eyes narrowed ever so slightly and she let it go. "I'm still learning who the Daddy Fish is in this pond."

"You're from Chicago," he said, continuing to make her feel as if she were under a microscope.

She grew more uneasy and cupped her drink. "I thought it was where all the real people hung out, but it's deader than sea scrolls compared to this place."

The Baron cocked his head and gave her a lazy smile, one that brightened his eyes. "You're an interesting woman, Scout Vannix. I will admit you puzzle me, but I like puzzles. I'm going to enjoy our time together."

Her mouth was dry. This version of the Baron, the one who clearly expected women, her included, to fall at his feet, seemed far more dangerous than the cold leader making general pronouncements.

"There's nothing special about me," she said, trying to come off as mysterious. If he liked mysterious, that's what he'd get. She needed to get close to him, to learn about him and others who were near.

"What do you say I order a Comical Cake?" He chuckled and gave her a crooked grin. "Do you think you and your friend would make one for me?"

She was surprised, but forced a smile and then made herself lean closer. "I'm sure we'd be honored."

Suddenly, his attention was caught by something over Scout's shoulder. His face tightened. "Excuse me a moment. There's someone I must speak to. But I'll be back."

Her gaze followed his. A young, pretty Asian woman stood in the doorway, looking immensely self-assured and poised as she gazed out over the crowd, far different from most of the young people here.

The Baron hurried to her. Taking her hands, he pulled her

close. The top of her head barely reached his shoulder. He wrapped his arm around her and they disappeared into the shadows.

With all her concentration on the Baron, Scout realized with a start that his assistant, Fieldren, was standing beside her.

"She's a new member," he murmured. "Her name is Julie Sung."

It was all Scout could do not to react. She knew that was the name of a young woman in the city who had been found murdered.

This place was not only creepy, it was sick.

Scout hurried from the club.

CHAPTER TWENTY-FOUR

Angie was beside herself. She'd had an appointment that afternoon at a home in Marin County to discuss baking cakes for a party of twenty, but no one was there when she arrived. This was the second time in three days that had happened to her. Was someone playing tricks or were people really so careless as to make appointments and then not keep them?

She really didn't have time for this. At least she was getting smarter about scheduling, however. She'd brought a cake with her that needed to be delivered to a horse's birthday party not far from her appointment. She never thought she'd be baking cakes for a horse, but 'Heidi' was being boarded some twenty-five miles outside the city, and the owner visited her on weekends only. That was why the owner wanted a cake that looked like the mare with a big smile on her face.

Angie couldn't imagine eating something that looked like a beloved pet or animal. She was meeting real ding-a-lings in this line of work.

Still muttering to herself about the thoughtlessness of the public, she got into her Ferrari. A vaguely familiar, yet disquieting smell hit her. A stain smeared the bottom of the cake box. As she peered closer, the smell grew stronger. The bottom of the box was wet.

She slid close to the driver's side door, ready to jump out of the car, as her hand slowly reached to open the cake box. Thoughts of flies and toads pounded her. What now?

She flipped back the lid and shrank away from it.

Nothing moved. Nothing jumped out.

But poor Heidi was now a bright red color, and it wasn't frosting. The familiar smell was blood, and it had been poured onto her cake. Shifting the box, she saw that it had seeped through onto the leather seat and was dripping down to the floor mat.

OhGodohGodohGod! Disgusted and horrified by the sight, Angie didn't want to touch it, but the blood was ruining her car seat.

She managed to whisk the cake box onto the floor mat without the cake falling through the bottom of the box. She would have loved to report this to the police, but quickly dismissed the thought. They scarcely investigated small crimes. She couldn't see them getting involved over a ruined cake.

After scrubbing the blood from her hands, she phoned the horse's owner to tell her someone had vandalized her cake. Instead of sympathy, the woman threatened to sue. At this point, Angie was too frustrated to care. She'd love to hear what a judge would say about taking up a court's time because of a cake delivery.

Immediately, she drove back to the city and to the auto detailer she'd used in the past. After dropping off her car, she called Rysk to pick her up. He was using the minivan to deliver four cakes in the city.

Rysk arrived fifteen minutes later to find her standing at the door to the detailer's shop watching the owner trying every trick he could think of to get the blood off the car seat and floor mat. The soft, light beige leather car seat, so far, remained stubbornly pinkish.

"You were delivering a cake?" Rysk asked as he walked up to her. He wasn't looking too Gothic today. She was glad. Her mood was black enough for both of them. "That's my job," he added. "You don't need to do that."

"It was on my way to see a potential customer, who didn't bother to show up for the appointment," she explained. "I thought I'd save us both time."

"Why would anyone put blood on your cake? And how did whoever did it know you'd be there?"

"You're right! This had to be planned." She faced him. "I've had flies and toads in my house, now blood on a cake. And lately, people either aren't home when I show up, or swore they hadn't made the appointment. Is it me? Or is it the cake business?"

"Let's walk," he suggested.

Just being on a sunny street filled with people looking carefree and not plagued by slimy creatures or blood made Angie feel a little better. "Thanks for coming to help me out," she said.

"My pleasure. Anyway, you sounded pretty low, boss lady."

"I was... I am." They were on Pine Street, and it was a step hike up to California. They began the climb.

"Is someone mad at you about something?" he asked. "A customer maybe?"

"The only one I can think of is Connie." She quickly told him a little about Connie and their argument.

"Blond and pretty, hmm?" Rysk asked with a grin. "Think she'd be interested in going out with me?"

Angie knew he was kidding. At one time she would have automatically said no, but she had to admit that he cleaned up very nicely. She also decided he must be a good five years older than she thought when she first saw him in his Goth get up. Someday she might discuss with him the benefits of giving up that punk look altogether. "I don't think so," she said finally.

"The story of my life," he lamented.

At the top of the hill a strong wind made the air crisp and clean, and the bright blue of San Francisco Bay painted a calming picture. "Connie used to be my best friend," Angie said softly. "It's hard to imagine her doing something like this to me."

"I've gotten a few women mad at me in my day," he said. "They turn from sweet little things to... to looking just like the cake that the guy threw at you a while back."

She laughed. It felt good to stand in the sunshine and laugh. She hadn't realized how much she'd missed it.

"Tell me," Rysk said, his expression suddenly serious, "did Scout know where you were going today?"

"Scout?" She glanced with surprise at him. "I mentioned it to her, but so what?"

He nodded, but didn't reply.

Angie didn't get it. He was interested in Scout, yet acted suspicious of her—just as Scout was of him. It didn't make sense. "Scout has done nothing but help and support me. You can't believe she did this."

"You hardly know her," he pointed out.

"I hardly know you, either," she countered. "And I don't believe you could be so mean."

"I'm glad to hear it," he said.

They walked through the small Nob Hill park between the Fairmont Hotel and Grace Cathedral. A couple of elderly men were there with tiny dogs and a young woman in Spandex jogged by.

"How did you and Scout meet?" Rysk asked.

"It was an accident, I suppose," Angie said. "We talked, and I found out she used to work in a pastry shop."

"She did?"

"Well, no, not really. But she needed a job. I suspect she saw me enter the restaurant delivering a cake, needed a job, and stretched the truth to get it. It's water under the bridge. She's a friend, now."

"How much do you really know about her?" His gaze was serious, much too serious to suit her.

"Well," she lifted an eyebrow and grinned. "She's single..."

He grimaced.

Enough for now, she decided. "Let's go see what the bad news is on my car."

"We got him!" Calderon shouted as he strutted into the homicide bureau. "Son of a bitch!"

Paavo, Yosh and Rebecca all looked up from their desks to hear the story.

"He squealed worse than a pig," Benson said, a big smile on his face. "Yelling he was innocent. Can you believe it? He tried to say he was the one who was going after the killer."

"Are you talking about Mason Markowitz?" Rebecca asked.

"Paavo and Yosh found his apartment, or whatever you'd call it," Calderon said.

"If it was in a basement, it'd be called a dungeon," Benson added.

"Where did you find him?" Paavo asked, relieved that the suspect was in custody.

"It was easy." The two arresting officers poured themselves celebratory hours-old coffee and grabbed a couple of the morning's doughnuts. "We figured he'd be living on the streets after we found his room, so we put out word to patrol cops to be on the lookout for him. We got a call from one in Russian Hill who'd picked up a vagrant who was acting crazy. Bingo! It was Markowitz."

"Russian Hill?" Paavo asked, a sinking feeling in the pit of his stomach.

"Jones and Green. A nice neighborhood."

Yes, it is, Paavo thought. Angie lived on that corner. His gaze met Yosh's. Yosh knew where Angie's apartment was.

"He told you that *he* was looking for the killer?" Paavo asked after the two settled into their desks.

"That's right. He's sticking with the story about being a demon hunter, but swears he had nothing to do with any of those women's deaths. He admits to going to the area where Whitefeather and Sung were murdered, as well as to Sausalito, but he claims he was there only to 'feel' the demon who did it, whatever that means," Benson said before filling his mouth with jelly doughnut.

Paavo glanced up at this statement. "He admits to having been at the crime scenes?"

"You got it," Calderon said. "We didn't say a word, just let him talk. We've got his prints, plus, he wears sneakers that match the ones the Sausalito PD had prints of at their scene. We've got the guy nailed."

"Along with his admissions," Benson added.

"His attorney must have had fits about that," Paavo said.

"He doesn't have one yet, but I'm sure he'll find one soon enough," Benson said. "This is such a high-profile case, I'll bet those guys will be crawling out of the woodwork to defend him."

"You've got that right," Yosh said with a frown. "He might be a vampire killer, but they're the blood-suckers."

CHAPTER TWENTY-FIVE

Since Angie and Scout had finished up early and Rysk had completed his deliveries, Angie took the minivan to the Jazz Workshop. It was too early for it to be open to the public yet. The detailers were still working on her Ferrari's stained seat and it would need at least another day's work. The floor mat cleaned up, but the blood had seeped through the leather into the cushion itself.

As Angie walked into the nightclub, Dominic Klee and his jazz band cut the song they were practicing and launched into "Sophisticated Lady." She smiled and waved at him, then continued through the club to the back room.

Her sister Maria, Dominic's wife, was busy creating a computer image mock-up of a newspaper advertisement. She didn't even look up when Angie entered the back room. "Good to see you, Angie. Want to help?"

"Sure," Angie said, looking over the mockup. She selected the image of a trumpet, Dominic's instrument, and angled it. "I'm sorry to bother you, but I just don't know what to do."

"You're no bother, little sis." Maria was the middle sister—older than Francesca and Angie, and younger than Caterina and Bianca. She was the sister Angie least understood. She moved the trumpet back the way it had been before Angie touched it.

Maria was highly religious and always have been, even as a child. Everyone assumed she would become a nun. Instead, she ran off and eloped with a jazz musician who was leading a fairly wild life—at least, until he got married. At times, Angie wondered if Maria didn't regard her marriage to Dominic Klee as some sort of penance, maybe for lust. She was happy, though, and Angie couldn't imagine a more disparate couple—except maybe her and Paavo.

Maria was also a blithe spirit. She didn't seem to see the world around her, but looked beyond it to a different plane. Few things bothered her. She wore no makeup and rarely cut her long, black hair, wearing it loose or in a single braid down her back. Even her home held the simplest of furniture.

Although Angie didn't understand Maria, she hoped this sister might give her the advice she was seeking.

"So what's up, Angie?" Maria asked, pouring her a cup of peach-flavored tea, caffeine free, as she stepped back and studied the newspaper ad layout.

It was one of Angie's least favorite drinks, but she took it out of politeness.

"I'm trying to learn what it takes to be a really good friend. How do you go about it?" Angie grabbed the computer mouse and switched some lettering from the bottom to the top of the ad. Much better, she decided.

Maria cocked her head and then moved the lettering back to the bottom. "Me? I don't know if I am one, frankly. I have too many faults. I'm not a good enough person." That was typical Maria-speak. Angie knew her sister didn't believe a word of it. "Why are you asking about this?"

"I'm just feeling... a little down, I guess," Angie admitted. It wasn't fun not being able to call Connie whenever the idea for something fun or interesting popped into her head. Other people she got together with from time to time, like Nona Farraday, were more of acquaintances than all-around friends. "Maybe there's something wrong with me as a person," she said dejectedly.

"Who has you questioning yourself this way?" Maria asked, horrified by what she was hearing.

"Well, Paavo said—"

"Men! You can't listen to them. They just don't get it."

"I know," Angie agreed. "Still, it might be my fault that I don't have lots of friends like you do."

"Me? Don't look to me as an example." She sighed soulfully. "I'm afraid my friends aren't of this world, Angie."

That was a bizarre statement. "They're not?"

"No. They're from..." She cast her gaze Heavenward.

"They are?" Angie said, forgetting her dislike of peach tea and swallowing a mouthful.

"The saints listen to me, listen to my troubles and woes, and my happy times as well. They give me love and guidance. I couldn't do without them."

"I've heard people say they talk to saints, but you sound like they answer you back." Surely Maria was joking, Angie thought, as she stared dubiously at the tea. What did they put in it that gave it such a disgusting flavor?

"Of course they do. Otherwise, what would be the use of talking to them? I tell them all my secrets, and they never tell anyone else. They're very good that way."

"I would guess so," Angie murmured.

"Other people come and go in my life. Some are a pleasant surprise, others disappoint. But the saints are forever. They're my friends, Angie. My true friends. If you made them your friends, you wouldn't have to worry about them ever shitting on you."

"No," she gulped, shocked at hearing her saintly sister use

such a word. On Maria's lips, it sounded all but sacrilegious. This conversation wasn't helpful. "I guess not. I'd better get going."

"Wait." Maria reached onto a shelf on the back wall. "Take this. It'll help."

With a sinking heart, Angie read the title of the little paperback, *Living A Saintly Life*. As she left the jazz club, she heard Maria call out, "Oh, Angie, thanks for your help with the ad. It looks great now."

Angie could have used a little one-to-one with Maria's martyrs when she came out of the nightclub and found all four tires of her minivan slashed. AAA had to load the van onto a flatbed and give her a lift to a tire shop, where she borrowed an avocado-green 2010 Impala from one of the mechanics.

She had an errand to run.

"I've had all I can take!" Angie marched into Everyone's Fancy and straight up to Connie at the sales counter.

The heads of two customers browsing the gift items jerked up.

"Angie." Connie shushed her and glanced over at the women with a wan smile. "What's the matter with you?"

"It's become clear to me that you're jealous of my success and doing all you can to foil my attempts at creating a great and growing company," Angie declared as she leaned over the counter between them. She clenched her fists to keep from grabbing her treacherous friend. Her reflection in the big mirror behind Connie only added to her fury. Her hair was a mess, her green Marc Jacobs dress smudged with grease from kneeling on the street to look at her tires, and sticking out of her Prada tote was the book Maria had given her. *Saintly life my eye*, she thought. "I demand you stop it right now."

Connie stared at her a moment, then said in a high voice. "Are you nuts? Or have you been sipping the cooking sherry?"

"I've had it." Angie's voice grew louder. "No more phony calls, no more bugs, no more slimy creatures--"

"Stop!" Connie fairly shrieked in outrage. "What are you talking about?"

The two women gaped from Angie to Connie, and backed up toward the door.

"You know very well! You can't hide any longer!"

"I'm not!"

"You're jealous!" Angie shouted.

The bing-bong that sounded when the shop's door opened, rang now as the potential customers dashed out.

"Jealous?" Connie was beside herself and shouted back. "You think I'm jealous of your stupid comedy cakes? I just lost two customers!"

"They aren't comedy! They're comical."

"I said comedy, and I meant comedy. Your business is a joke!"

Angie gasped at the attack. "I didn't come here to be insulted!"

"Then go back to your cheesy business."

Steam could have come from Angie's ears and nose she was so irate. She teetered on her pumps to reach further over the counter. "I still have a business, despite your best efforts!"

"I did try to help you, for all the thanks it got me. Stan told me all the nasty things you said about me and my shop. And that you've dumped him, too, as a partner. I suspect the two new people who are helping you are the ones causing you trouble. They probably don't like you as a boss any more than I did!"

"What nerve!" Angie cried, unable to overlook the fact that Connie sounded just like Paavo with this distrust of her employees. "Why does everyone think I'm incapable of hiring good help?"

"You can leave now, Angie. I don't want to see you anymore."

"I'll gladly leave and never come back. But first, I'm warning you—stop meddling in my business!"

"What are you talking about?" Connie screeched, looking completely frustrated at this point. "I never meddle in anything. That's your forte. If meddling were an Olympic sport, you'd take the gold every time."

Angie was beyond furious. "Keep away from me and my tires! And my cakes."

Connie folded her arms. "I wouldn't be caught dead anywhere near you or your precious car or your ugly, unfunny, hard-as-bricks cakes."

"Our friendship is over," Angie declared.

"Friendship? You don't know the meaning of the word."

Angie paled. "Is that so?"

"Yes, that's so."

"Well!"

"Well to you, too! Now get out of my store!"

"I just--"

"I never--"

"Fine, then!"

Angie marched out in a huff. It was all she could do to keep back the tears. What went wrong?

CHAPTER TWENTY-SIX

"Boy, is that guy Looney-tunes," Bo Benson said as he stepped onto the elevator at the Hall of Justice with Paavo and punched the button for the fourth floor. Paavo had just returned from Angie's. He was sure he'd find her home baking, but she wasn't there. Her cell phone went straight to messaging. Her movements were beyond understanding at this point.

"Who's that?" Paavo asked.

"Markowitz. The stories he tells about witches and demons are right out of *Beetlejuice*."

"Building his insanity plea, is he?" Paavo asked. Instead of heading toward room 450, he turned in the opposite direction.

"You got it." Benson stayed with him. "He keeps talking about spiders and blood and vampires and evil creatures walking the streets posing as humans. I thought my view of humanity was bad, but he thinks there are even worse monsters in the world."

"What's that about spiders?" Paavo asked. "He doesn't also mention flies or toads, does he?"

"It wouldn't surprise me. He was raving about vampires and

demons, mostly. I think he even mentioned some Count. Or was that Dracula? I'm not sure. All I know is we aren't going to get a confession out of him. I don't think he's capable of it, and even if we got one, it won't be easy to find a judge who'd let it stand. The guy's in the twilight zone."

Paavo turned into the men's room, holding the door open for Benson. "Would you have a problem if I talked to him?" he asked. "There are a couple of things I'd like to ask him about."

"There *is* no talking to the guy," Benson said. "He's beyond conversation."

"Do you mind if I try?"

"You shouldn't get involved anymore in this case. You've got other things on your mind."

"Not really. I'm wrapping up the Walters case. Everything points to suicide, probably brought on by drugs," Paavo said thoughtfully. "Actually, Markowitz just might know--"

"That's not what I meant," Benson interrupted. "I'm talking about Angie."

Paavo said nothing. As much as he wondered what Benson knew about him and Angie, he didn't want to discuss her. He walked up to a urinal.

Benson also positioned himself at one. Both zippers simultaneously descended. "You want to propose, and she's not giving you the time of day," Benson said.

"Where did you hear that?" Paavo's jaw was tight.

"Doesn't matter. Everybody knows it." Benson cast his gaze upward. "If I were you, I'd take all this as a sign from God."

"You would?"

"Right. A sign that there are a hell of a lot of women out there, and you got no business limiting yourself to just one of them." Benson grinned as he and Paavo headed for a sink. "Especially one who would rather be baking cakes." His grin turned into laughter. "That's not the type of woman I'd ever be interested in. No way!"

Paavo knew Benson was just giving him a bad time. Nevertheless, his comments grated.

He snapped a paper towel from the rack. "I'm going to see Markowitz."

"So much for my good advice," Benson said with a chuckle as a stiff-necked Paavo strode quickly out of the bathroom. "Man, it's your funeral."

Scout paced the dingy room she was renting, impatiently glancing at the telephone. They'd always arranged to check in every four days unless something urgent came up. Where was he?

It all seemed so hopeless. Her kid sister, Greta, had last contacted her many weeks ago. She had sounded ridiculously happy. "The man of her dreams," she'd called the Baron. Mysterious, kind, guardian, and lover, everything Greta could have wanted, he was.

References to evil, witches and vampires hadn't frightened Scout at first. They were commonplace enough among the Goth-Vampyre subculture in which Greta traveled. After a while, though, Greta's texts and emails grew less coherent, her thoughts and actions much darker. Worried, Scout had managed to track her cellphone to San Francisco's Haight-Ashbury district.

Once there, Scout found some Goth hangouts and quickly learned about the Baron. She found people who had talked to Greta, but they hadn't seen her for some time. All assumed she was still with the Baron.

But Greta had vanished.

Scout could have just walked up to the Baron and asked him, but one look at his club and at the people going into it, and her gut reaction told her he'd clam up, have her escorted out, and her chance at finding out anything at all would be gone. It was best to get inside and look and listen for any clue as to her sister's whereabouts.

Hours were spent hiding outside the Baron's club watching people, hoping against hope that one of them would be Greta. After a week of doing that, she saw she wasn't alone—someone else was curious about the Baron, a strange old man named Mason Markowitz.

They had talked for hours, and she learned that he had insights to the Baron, the happenings in the club and the dangers surrounding it, that she hadn't dreamed of.

The more she learned about the Baron, the more he scared her. He knew too much, and his followers were loyal and close mouthed.

Seeing a woman who called herself "Julie Sung" at the Baron's club had rattled her badly. She had read everything she could find about Julie Sung's murder as well as Lucy White-feather's. Even the woefully dense young woman who called herself Mina Harker was eerily weird. People in these death cults sometimes took on the name of a murderer or someone who'd been horrifically murdered just to see what kind of reaction they'd get out of people. Vampire fans knew Mina Harker was Dracula's victim in the Bram Stoker classic.

The ironic part was that most people didn't recognize the names of victims. The killers got the fame; the victims, a grave.

But Julie Sung's murder had been recent. To have the name used by a woman in the Baron's club could mean the Baron liked to play some very sick games, turning living women into some necrophiliac's wet dream. Or it might mean something even worse; it might be something the police should know about. She hadn't met anyone calling herself Lucy White-feather, but she'd stopped asking. As despair over Greta's whereabouts filled her, she went less and less often to the club. She too afraid of what she would learn.

Angie's boyfriend was a homicide detective. Maybe she should tell Angie about her suspicions and have her relay them to her boyfriend? She could tell Angie what she'd been doing, and all that was going on.

But what if the cop boyfriend confronted the Baron? There was no proof of anything, just a drugged-out woman calling herself Julie, playing a death game. The Baron already knew Scout worked for Angie. If her boyfriend suddenly showed up asking questions, he might tie it all back to Scout. He might bar her from going to his club. As much as she hated everything about it, there was no denying it was her sole remaining link to Greta.

The fear that the real Julie's fate had also been Greta's plagued her. She sat, her hands shaking and her stomach churning.

She shouldn't think such a thing. Greta had to be alive and well. She'd show up again at the Baron's, or one of her friends, just like she used to. The Baron couldn't have had anything to do with the death of Julie Sung or anyone else. He had no need to. He had all the women he could handle around him, hanging on him, wanting him.

To say anything to Angie or Paavo could get in the way of her goal: to find Greta and get even with the Baron for what he'd done to her. God, she hated him!

Once Greta was safe, she would happily kill him with her bare hands.

She paced. What if the Baron had someone spying on her? It would have to be Rysk. His turning up at an event where she and Angie worked was far too coincidental. Delivering ice? How stupid did he think she was?

What was she going to do?

She sat with her phone in her hands. Why didn't it ring? Markowitz was her best chance to find Greta, and now, had he also abandoned her?

He must have thought she'd failed him. For some reason, he kept asking her to find out all she could about Angie and her friends. He was the one who told her about Angie's cake baking business, and that she could meet Angie by fearlessly chasing him away.

Markowitz had scared her at first with all his talks about demons, but the more she was learning, the more she was wondering if he wasn't much closer to the truth than she'd ever dreamed.

But now, where was he?

Angie slammed down the phone. It was midnight. Who did that Baron Severus think he was calling this late at night to ask her to bake a cake for his club? That was the third time he'd called and asked her for a cake. Her body ached so much from baking and decorating five cakes that day she'd had a hard time falling asleep, only to be awakened by that man!

She thought she'd made it clear to his assistant when she went to his home that she wasn't interested in working for him.

Even if she had considered working for him, she wouldn't now.

She shut her eyes and rolled onto her side. Connie's voice screaming at her that she'd be a gold medal winner in meddling came back to her.

I should have said that she'd get the gold in backstabbing! That would have shut her up.

If only she'd said that, instead of standing there on the verge of tears. She rolled over to her other side.

Then, when Connie said she didn't know the meaning of friendship, she should have reminded her of all the times she'd lent a sympathetic shoulder when Connie came over crying about some new boyfriend who'd dumped her or who turned out to be a jerk or had a wife he'd forgotten to mention.

She should have said that!

Connie would have felt badly, and maybe she would have been the one ready to burst into tears.

Angie rolled onto her back and stared at the ceiling.

She wished she could talk to Paavo about this. Was she really that bad of a friend? A bad person? How come she didn't have a zillion friends? Why only one close friend whose hair-color was out of a Clairol bottle, and who wouldn't help with a cake business, and who not only fought dirty, but wouldn't admit it when confronted?

She flipped onto her stomach, punched the pillow, and then dropped her head on it. She finally knew Connie as she truly was.

Why then, did she feel so bad about losing Connie's friendship?

Angie glanced at the clock on her bedside. One-thirty a.m. *Thank you, Baron.*

CHAPTER TWENTY-SEVEN

Paavo walked into the small interrogation room outside the cellblock of the County Jail temporary annex on the seventh floor of the Hall of Justice. Whenever the regular jails grew too crowded, the annex would be reopened.

Markowitz would be a resident of the cellblock at least until his arraignment, and possibly longer since his attorney was arguing that he needed a psychiatric evaluation and to be placed in a mental hospital rather than a high security prison.

Markowitz was perched on a metal chair, at a plain metal table, his hands folded. He didn't look at all like the crazy killer Benson and Calderon said he was. His hair was white, and his blue eyes were more world-weary than Paavo had ever seen on a man, making him look far older than his sixty-eight years. A serial killer his age was almost unheard of.

"I'm Inspector Paavo Smith, Homicide."

He lifted his gaze to Paavo's and held a moment. Suddenly, the room felt smaller and oddly bright.

"Ah, you've come," Markowitz said.

Paavo took his time sitting down opposite him. "You were expecting me?"

"For centuries he's waited. You know he's out there," Markowitz replied.

"Who's out there?"

"*Ars Diabolus* warns against allowing the Dark Lord to take a Queen and gain power. In here"—he tapped his temple—"I know. We have little time."

"What do you mean by Dark Lord?"

Markowitz leaned forward and whispered. "Baalberith, high in the hierarchy of hell." He straightened, his voice louder as he said, "I must stop him!"

"Who is this Baalberith?"

"Behold Baalberith, beloved of the Ammonites. He has had many names. His bones are bronze, his limbs like iron. The wild beasts are his food, and he sleeps in the reeds and the marshes."

"Wait, I don't--"

"Behold!" Markowitz's voice grew louder, his gaze so intent over Paavo's shoulder that Paavo was forced to glance at the blank wall behind him, just to make sure nothing was there. "He rides closer on his pale horse, eighty-five legions behind him, trumpets harkening all to his command. All his dominions are in darkness, and his purpose is wickedness and evil. He is destruction. He is nightmare."

"Mr. Markowitz," Paavo called, but still the man stared. "Mr. Markowitz."

Finally, Markowitz cast his eyes on him, the look cold and dark.

"I saw you with a dark-haired woman," Paavo said. "What is it you want with her?"

"Baalberith searches for his Dark Queen. The time is at hand."

Paavo's gut twisted at the words. "What Dark Queen? What do you mean?"

"Yes, yes!" His eyes sparkled. "There is such danger! I must find her, stop her. He brings their souls back, you know."

"Whose souls?"

"Only from the Dark Ladies. They and his Queen form a pentagram. Through it, comes the power that is his." Markowitz suddenly clapped his hands.

"What about the dark-haired woman?" Paavo insisted, growing more irritated by these rantings. "What did you want with her? Why were you watching her apartment?"

"I know her soul. I must get out of here! We aren't safe. No one is safe! Just like that boy. He thought he could fly like a bat."

"What boy?" Paavo asked. The hair on the back of his neck stood as a vision sprung to mind of Taylor Walters with his black cape spread wide, standing on the top of that bridge and then letting himself go, hoping to soar, but instead falling.

Markowitz's slightly bent forefinger pointed upward. "He was possessed. His demons were told by one more powerful to destroy him, and they did. *You* know! *You* were aware of the demon's presence. *You* felt his presence. *You* knew he was watching you." Markowitz began to rock, faster and faster.

Paavo remembered the chill he'd felt at the site of Taylor Walter's death. And at Mina Harker's. And Lucy Whitefeather's. He pushed the memories aside. "Flies and toads were in Angie's apartment. Did you put them there?"

Markowitz's eyes widened and his body began to quake. "Alien eyes and evil presence. Rituals all around." He grasped the table, but his arms and shoulders shook with tension. "Hurry! You understand the danger."

Paavo decided to go along and hope that some of Markowitz's ravings made sense. "Tell me about it."

Markowitz began to wring his hands. "The evil one is creeping ever closer. He knows that we know. We must take care."

"Where can I find this evil one? Does he have a name?" Paavo decided to bring the conversation down to the mundane.

Markowitz gripped the table, leaned toward him, and shrieked. "Baalberith, I told you! Fool! You are as much a fool as the others! I must get out of here. The time is short. Don't you understand? I alone can stop him. *I must be free.*"

Paavo stared at the man's angry, tear-filled eyes and was jarred by what he saw. The man truly believed in this evil force. Whoever or whatever it was, it scared him badly.

"Do you understand that you're being held here for murder?" Paavo asked calmly.

"He's very clever! The cleverest of all, they say. He trapped me."

"You're accused of the murder of three women," Paavo continued.

"There will be more, unless I can get out of here and stop him."

"More? How do you know?"

"Let me out!" His body rocked from side to side, his voice almost keening. "I must act before he grows stronger. If he gains his ultimate power, all will be lost!"

"The only one who can set you free is a judge if you're found to be innocent."

"But that will be too late!"

"Your lawyer needs to explain the process to you."

Markowitz lunged at him. Paavo slid his chair back and the manacles on the prisoner's legs stopped him from reaching the detective. "You don't know what you're doing! You must free me."

"If you know something about the murders, tell us," Paavo said. "Give us something to go on to prove you're innocent."

Markowitz lifted his gaze to Paavo's, his face contorted in rage. "You could see the evil around you if you would just open your eyes. If you don't, I can't help you. No one can. You will be lost. You! And all that you hold dear."

Angie was walking out of the studios of KYME radio, a sales contract in hand for the station's ten-year anniversary cake— one that would look like an oversized old-time radio. She once worked for KYME... very briefly. Station *Why me?* she used to call it.

She approached the elevator when a heavy-set, wild-eyed woman ran up to her, calling out, "I want to thank you!"

The woman, with thick, curly red hair cascading over her shoulders, jiggled all over as she vigorously pumped Angie's hand.

"Thank me?" Angie asked as soon as she could extricate herself.

"I'm in accounting so you don't know me, but I had to tell you we're all so glad you're in the cake business. We were afraid they'd order another of Lolly Firenghetti's cakes."

"You were?" Angie didn't follow.

"They're simply awful. Unless you add detergent to the batter, your cake will taste much better. We're all so glad—we do love good cake!"

"Do you know Lolly?"

"Unfortunately, yes. She's made cakes for us for the last few years. But they've just been flat sheet cakes with drawings of a radio in frosting. Yours will be ever so much more clever. And we've heard they taste great! We aren't the only company that's dumped Lolly, you know."

No, I don't know, Angie thought, but didn't say it. Instead, she simply said, "Thank you."

"It's not your case, Smith!" Lieutenant Hollins shouted. It was his job to keep the detectives in line and out of each other's cases.

"I had questions," Paavo explained, "and Calderon and Benson didn't seem to have any answers. Listen, I'm sure this Markowitz knows about Taylor Walters. He said the boy thought he could fly."

"So what? It's still suicide." Hollins reached for the roll of Tums he kept on his desk.

"There's a connection between the two. I want to know what it is, and what's going on here."

"Calderon told me Markowitz doesn't even know Taylor Walters' name, let alone anything else about him."

"Markowitz is either lying to Calderon or is too addled to remember. He gave Taylor a flask of holy water. We have his fingerprints to prove it," Paavo said. "And now, Markowitz claims that more women are in danger." The words, "Dark Queen," kept echoing in his head, along with Markowitz's interest in Angie... a brunette.

"You believe this nutcase?"

"To a degree, yes," Paavo insisted. "I want to talk to him again when he's calm."

"They upped his medication. He'll be beyond calm and into comatose for a while. Anyway, how do you know he doesn't have an accomplice? Why would you assume he's innocent?"

"I'm not assuming any such thing. I simply want to question him again about my case—Taylor Walter."

"Calderon and Benson are perfectly capable of asking whatever you need to know." Hollins glowered at his subordinate.

"They can ask, but will they get answers?"

"They're working on it. Better than you, I might add. It was all the shrink and his jailers could do to quiet him down again after you left. His attorney had a shit-fit that some cop not even involved in the case was up there questioning him. He's asking that Markowitz be put on a suicide watch because of this 'trauma.' Do you want the case thrown out before we even have a chance at it?"

"Of course not, but—"

"Look," Hollins visibly tried to tamp down his impatience. "I know you're upset because you're thinking about proposing to Angie--"

Paavo paled. "You know—"

"And I know she hasn't exactly been cooperating with your plans—"

"Who told—"

"I hear she's got a business—baking cakes. Tell her about the Investigation Bureau Deputy Chief's retirement party. It's next week. They'll need lots of cakes. Tell her the Deputy Chief likes mocha cakes. With buttercream frosting."

"I'll tell her," Paavo said, and did a mental eye-rolling. "But as for Marko—"

"Look, this is a tough time for you. Big decision time. Hell, I remember when I was thinking about getting married the first time." Finally, Chief Hollins seemed to relax enough to crack a smile. "I was a basket case. I couldn't sleep. Couldn't even drive. All I could think about was whether she'd like the ring, and if her parents were gonna throw a fit."

"My wanting to propose or not has nothing to do with Markowitz. And I don't want to talk about Angie," Paavo said through gritted teeth. The fact that he'd also been anxious about the ring and Angie's parents galled him.

"Good," Hollins said, with a paternal pat on the shoulder. "In that case, I'll repeat myself one more time. I don't want you to see Markowitz again. Knock it off, right now. As your soon-to-be in-laws would say, *capisce?*"

The combination of exhaustion, wine, and watching the city far below her was enough to make Angie's head swim. She sat across from Paavo in the Fairmont Hotel's Crown Room, at the very top of the famous hotel. The tables of the restaurant were situated against the windows, allowing diners to a great view of the city.

Paavo wasn't helping her much. He had seemed distracted yet glad to see her when he picked her up.

"How's your business coming along?" he asked after they were served a salad of spinach, endive and Gorgonzola.

"Busy," she said, and poked wearily at her salad. "I don't know how Lolly Firenghetti handled so much business alone."

"Who?"

"My competition. Never mind. Tell me more about the Deputy Chief's retirement party," she said with a smile.

Paavo had already explained that the deputy's secretary, Carla, hadn't yet ordered a cake, and had planned on a traditional sheet cake. As a result, Angie had plenty of time to convince her to order something personal and special. "Just keep in mind one thing," he cautioned. "The Deputy Chief has absolutely no sense of humor."

By the time the entrees arrived, veal scaloppini for Angie and oregano crusted salmon for Paavo, he asked her about Connie.

"I haven't spoken to her since our last argument," Angie said. "The more I think of it, the more I wonder if Connie really is the one behind my cake problems. I mean, she seemed not to understand what had happened and why I was upset. None of this makes sense. Is my business targeted? I don't get it."

"Maybe you need to try talking to Connie again. Don't accuse her, but say you might have been mistaken about her. It can't hurt."

"I guess I can do that." She stifled a yawn. "You seem a bit distracted tonight, Paavo."

"Do I? I'm sorry."

"One of your cases?" she asked.

"One that's mine, one that's Calderon's." He gazed at her and thought of Markowitz's words. "Remember that panhandler who approached you outside Fugazzi Hall?"

She was surprised by the question. "Vaguely. Why?"

"His name is Mason Markowitz. Can you remember what he said?"

"Not really. Something about danger, that he had to talk to me." She also remembered that he'd approached her a second time and that Scout had chased him away. She could just see Paavo's reaction if she told him that. He already spent too much time worrying about her.

"Anything specific? Think hard, Angie. Did he use the words Dark Queen?"

"No. I'm sure of that." She tried to remember more, but couldn't. "His appearance, more than anything, startled me. I hardly listened." Maybe she did need to tell him about Markowitz's second approach. "What's going on?"

"He's behind bars. But be careful, anyway."

"I always am." The man being locked up was a big relief. Normally, she would have wanted to know more, much more. Who was Markowitz? Why was he arrested? What was his connection to her? To Scout? What in the world was a Dark Queen? But the man was behind bars, she had too much on her plate as is, and she was *not* going to get involved.

"Good," he said as if in answer to her unspoken thoughts.

As he finished his dinner, he looked quite nervous. Was he that worried about Markowitz? That wasn't like him.

"Would you like dessert?" he asked.

After his disappointment when she turned dessert down last time, she quickly said yes.

"Okay, great." He looked around as if ready to order, but their waiter wasn't nearby at the moment.

She'd never seen him so anxious for dessert before. He usually didn't have much of a sweet tooth.

"Excuse me a minute," he said, standing.

She understood. The little boy's room called. She nodded, and he dashed off.

Just then the waiter came by to clean the table. She scooted close to the window and rested her head against it a moment as the man worked. Her eyes shut.

"Angie?" A voice called from far away, the voice she loved beyond all others. She smiled, but her eyes were so very tired, she couldn't seem to open them.

"Angie, you're so sleepy, let's get you home."

She forced herself awake to see Paavo standing at her side. The restaurant's bill had already been paid. How long has she's slept there? "But dessert..." she mumbled.

"It can wait," he said, then took her hand to help her stand. "We'll have dessert another day."

CHAPTER TWENTY-EIGHT

After Paavo drove a very sleepy Angie back to her apartment, he headed for Lobos Alley, where Lucy Whitefeather's body had been found.

No lights shone in the alley, and the only doors led to the backs of buildings.

He got out of his car. The sound of the car door shutting echoed, as did his footsteps on a sidewalk glistening with mist. The alley was icy cold, so cold it was difficult to draw a deep breath.

The sense of evil, of something terrible here, was like a physical assault.

Next, he went to the alley where Julie Sung's body had been found. There was the same sense of a presence. Not as if he was being watched, but that something had been in this area that was so evil the area still reeked of it.

He'd felt this before—at the site of Taylor Walters' suicide and even in Sausalito where 'Mina Harker' had been murdered. Markowitz's words played in his head. *You could see the evil around you if you would open your eyes.*

He wasn't a man who believed in spirits. He practiced no religion, although over the years he'd come to believe God exists. Perhaps it was because of what he saw every day with his job—not the bad, not the killers—but the other people, the ones who knew and loved the victims, and those miraculous times when good people survived or performed feats beyond heroic to save another person. Most of what he saw as a cop was bad, but some good happenings went beyond luck. If he were a religious man, he'd say they were miracles; but he wasn't, and so the word didn't occur in his vocabulary.

Still, if he could believe in God, why was he so quick to dismiss the possibility of an evil presence? And why was he trying so hard to convince himself that Taylor Walters' death had been a suicide?

***

The creature walked the shadows of the Fillmore's decrepit flats in the heart of the city staring at the gutters, the cracks in the sidewalk, the ants and spiders crawling everywhere, all around him, wherever he stepped.

He needed a with roots in the southern hemisphere, *Ars Diabolus* had told him. He'd find her here, tonight. He had no choice. Time was running out. At one time, most of the residents in this neighborhood were African-American. These days, newcomers from Asia and other parts of the world diluted his pool. Still, he was certain he could find the right woman for his purpose.

A car weaved toward him, then sailed past. A man and woman were inside, and the woman's arms flailed. As the car crossed the intersection it slowed, and the passenger door opened. The car jerked to a stop, and the woman got out, slamming the door shut behind her.

The driver, a young African-American man, also leaped from the car. He yelled something, but the woman didn't stop. She waved a backhanded middle-finger salute at the fellow and stomped toward the intersection.

Toward him.

The driver cursed and pounded the car roof with his fist, then climbed back inside and sped away.

The woman's step slowed a moment. She pulled her jacket tighter and tucked her head down, her heels clicking ever faster.

Two blocks away a major street bustled with taxis and buses. That was her destination. He couldn't let her reach it.

She noticed him then, in the darkness. Her eyes flitted from side to side. Big, lustrous eyes. Her cheekbones were high, her skin creamy-smooth with a honey-warm tone. Long legs tottered on high heels, and her body was enough to make him weep with joy.

He, with power over life and death, had chosen her to live forever at his side. To be his Queen's fourth consort. His mistress.

After this final deed, all that remained was for him to await his Queen.

He had to stop her here, long before she reached Geary Boulevard. Too many people were on the lookout for him. He'd had to abort a couple of attempts because of busybodies. It was just as well. This woman was the best one yet.

Her shoes were the answer to his prayers. Once trapped, she wouldn't be able to outrun him.

"Lady, don't be scared," he said, stepping out of the dark shadows toward her. "Are you all right? This isn't the kind of neighborhood to be walking around in this time of night."

"I'm fine." She hurried past him.

"Do you want a ride somewhere?" He followed her. "Maybe

just up to Geary Street where you can catch a cab? My car is at the corner. I hate to get in and drive away, leaving you on this street. It isn't safe."

She shook her head and kept going.

He jumped in front of her, blocking her path. Her eyes widened and her step slowed for just a moment as if she couldn't quite believe he was still bothering her. She started around him. He knew she hoped to pass by without incident; that she was hoping he would give up.

He sidestepped in front of her again.

"Get the hell away from me," she said.

He smiled, reaching his hand toward her. She jumped back. "I feel bad about leaving you alone," he said softly. "I know you're scared, but believe me, I'm here to help you."

She took another step backwards. He slipped his hand into his pocket, fingering the syringe. He just had to grab her and hold her long enough to jab it in her.

Her gaze dropped to his hand. "Go to hell." She glanced over her shoulder, then again at him. When he took a step toward her, she whirled around and ran.

He chased her.

She turned at the corner, and he followed.

He grabbed her arm, and she fought him, slapping him, socking, and kicking like a hellcat. He shoved her hard against the wall of a building, slamming her head against it.

The blow stunned her as her boyfriend's car slowly passed by the street she'd just left, as if he'd felt bad about the argument and was looking for her.

She squirmed as if hoping to run to him for help. But, too soon, he was gone.

The Dark Lord pressed his body against hers, his hand over her mouth. She tried to bite him, but his hand pressed so hard, she couldn't move her jaw.

Tears filled her eyes, a look of horror coming over her at her first look at the syringe. Her fierce attempts to free herself began again, but he was too strong for her.

He jabbed the needle into her neck, and in a moment, her struggles ended.

CHAPTER TWENTY-NINE

"How have you kept your friends over so many years?" Angie asked her mother as the shoe salesman disappeared into the storeroom.

"I don't know," Serafina said dismissively. "Now, has Paavo hinted about proposing to you yet?"

"Not at all. But tell me about your friends."

Serafina shrugged. "We keep each other. That's all I can say. They find me if they want to see me. Or, I'll give one of them a call and see if we can get together. That's all there is to it. You can't make anybody like you, Angelina. Ah, my shoes."

The salesman sat at a stool and raised Serafina's foot to his shin. He took off her beige pump and put on a black one with a square heel.

"I'm not sure. What do you think, Angelina?" Serafina asked.

"I like it," Angie said.

Serafina reached for the shoe box, then glared at the salesman. "What's this? Size nine? Why would you bring me such a big size? Are you crazy? It looks like a boat! I'm a six and a half. I used to be a five and a half, before I had my children."

The salesman was dumbfounded. "But I measured--"

"Take this *gondola* away and bring my correct size. Oh, *aspetti*, I like my shoes loose, now that I'm getting older. A seven and a half, double A, will be fine."

He shuffled off, scratching his head.

She faced Angie. "What's all this friend stuff about? Connie's your good friend. It's a husband you should be worrying over."

"I don't see Connie anymore," Angie confessed. "Once your friends move out of your life, do you just forget about them?"

"Of course not. I've got girlfriends that I don't see or talk to for years. When we do get together, it's as if all the time in between has gone in a poof. We feel like we saw each other only yesterday, and we talk and laugh like young girls again."

"Well, it's easy to keep friends like that."

Serafina's eyebrows popped up, then her eyes bored into Angie. "What's going on with you and Connie?"

"We had a complete falling out."

"Those things happen between friends. You'll both get over it, I'm sure. Ah, here are

my shoes."

The salesman sat before Serafina and lifted her nylon-covered foot to the shoe. Her big toe went in, so did three others, but the little toe didn't. She turned the shoe, aimed all toes at the side, then tried to slide them into the vamp. It didn't work.

She put the shoe on the floor. Angie helped her to balance on one foot as she squeezed her foot into the new shoe. Once she got it in, nearly crippled with pain, the salesman had to practically stand on top of her to pull it off again.

"There's something wrong with that shoe," she complained, rubbing her toes and casting him a steely, black-eyed glare. "It must be mis-marked. My husband used to own several shoe stores. We never had mis-marked shoes in his stores. Are you sure you know what you're doing?"

The salesman was pale now. "Let me see what I can do," he murmured, and rushed away.

"Maybe, at times, I took Connie for granted," Angie said as her mother cast daggers at the salesman retreating back. "It's this cake thing."

"Are you sure it's what you want to be doing?"

"I'm good at it."

"That's not the same thing," Serafina said. "What's more important to you?"

The salesman came back, with four other styles in size seven and a half. He showed them, one by one, to Serafina, who shook her head more emphatically with each. "I can't believe this," she bellowed. "I want to talk to your manager!"

Sweat poured from the salesman's brow. "I'm sorry, but--"

"Oh, wait," Angie said. "Look. Here's a size six in the shoe my mother wants." She picked up the very first shoebox the salesman had brought out and held it upside down. "You must have overlooked it," she said to him.

Mouth agape, his eyes jumped from her to her mother. "But that's--"

"Size six?" Serafina cooed. "Let me try it."

She put the shoe on. "*Bellissimo!* And it fits perfectly." She gave the salesman an arch stare. "It's good I have my daughter with me. At least she knows what she's doing."

As they walked up to the counter to pay for the shoes, Serafina said, "Now, I want to know why Paavo hasn't proposed yet. You talk about your business and your girlfriend, but not about Paavo. Angelina, *figlia mia*, a girl must have priorities."

Paavo wasn't about to let Markowitz's strange comments go by without trying to determine what he meant by them, no matter how upset Calderon and Benson might be once they found out what he'd done. The talk about demons sounded nonsensical, but he had to learn what was behind it. Clearly, Markowitz believed what he was saying, which meant he might well have acted on those beliefs. To understand the actions, Paavo had to understand their cause.

He went down to the Property Control Section in the basement of the Hall of Justice, where Markowitz's papers had been stored as evidence.

Notebooks, scraps of paper and newspaper clippings had been gathered into oversized manila envelopes. Paavo checked them out and sat in one of the cubbyholes. His interest lay in the notebooks. Simply getting past the handwriting was a challenge.

Once he could read most of the words, he realized it wasn't the handwriting per se that was so confusing, it was their meaning. They didn't fit together in a normal way; but after a while, he began to understand, and soon found himself caught up in Markowitz's world.

It was a world of evil, a world where children could be born with no souls, feral, and people could bargain with the devil for worldly success and other-worldly damnation. It was a world of complete darkness and amorality, in which humans were chattel and food.

Markowitz wrote of the alienation of youth and the lure of those who tempted the deepest, darkest parts of human nature with promises of power, wealth, and immortality. For those who were lost, Markowitz saw little hope of redemption, and his cold calculations and logic left even a cynical cop shaking his head.

Paavo read on. Much of the writings were ravings and rantings, illustrations or doodles. Mason didn't want to save souls, he just wanted to stop the demons. His notes told of those he'd hunted. He was clearly insane.

Then something caught his eye. Scribbled along a margin were strange words: Crypt Macabre.

"Well, now that we're all here, I can announce my big news," Angie said as Stan, Scout and Rysk stood in the kitchen. She and Scout had just finished a camisole—the lingerie company had liked the garter and ordered another cake—plus they had made two teddy bears for kids' parties and one pair of breasts for a plastic surgeon's conference on silicone implants. The thought of eating them made Angie squeamish. Stan was munching his way through a plate of cake that had been cut from the decorated portions, and then covered with leftover frosting. Rysk was ready to go on his deliveries, and Scout was loading the dishwasher.

They all stopped and turned her way.

"We've been given our biggest job yet," she said proudly. "Paavo told me a deputy chief in the Hall of Justice is going to retire. I contacted the woman in charge of the retirement reception, and guess what? She wants us to bake a cake for his party!" The other three applauded and Angie took bows.

"We'll need to do one big sheet cake that's in the shape of a police badge," she said.

"That's supposed to be funny?" Stan asked and reached for another slab of cake.

"It isn't, but neither is the Deputy Chief. The secretary, whose name is Carla, and I tried to think of something humorous that wouldn't offend him, but she was too nervous about that. The more we talked, the more she decided Comical Cakes wasn't such a good idea. So, I suggested the badge. She loved it, and even gave me his old patrolman badge number.

She said he'd love it as well, and there's no place else she could get a detailed, custom cake that way at such a reasonable price. I'm giving them a good deal because of Paavo, and because the police deserve it. I don't want to make a profit off them."

"You aren't getting paid?" Scout asked. Stan gawked, so appalled he even stopped stuffing his face.

"They'll pay for our costs, but that's it. Don't worry— it'll be great publicity. Other than the badge, we need to make six plain sheet cakes, all with dark blue icing. It'll be quite wonderful."

"Shit," Rysk said under his breath.

"You have a problem helping the police?" Angie asked.

"Oh no. Not at all. It's just what I always dreamed of doing," he mumbled.

"Look, if this makes you uncomfortable, I'm sure Stan could help me and Scout deliver the cakes. You'll help me serve, won't you, Scout?"

"The police?" she asked, looking thoughtful. "Where is this party going to be given?"

"It'll be held in the Hall of Justice," Angie replied. "They have a cafeteria, and they'll be putting up banners and balloons and flowers, trying to make it festive."

"Got it," Scout said with a nod.

"Come on, you won't back out on me, will you?" What was it with these two? This job should be the proverbial piece of cake, given the other cakes they'd had to do.

"Cops will be at this party?" Scout unexpectedly asked.

"Not patrol, or maybe a few. This is mostly for the Bureau of Inspection's staff housed in the Hall of Justice."

"I see," Scout said, brightening up. "It sounds like a big project."

"I'll help," Rysk said as if coming to a decision. "You'll need me and Scout both."

"Great," Angie said. "Stan, that leaves you off the hook."

He paused, fork in mid-air, long enough to mutter, "Can't say I'm sorry."

"When is it?" Scout asked.

"It'll be Friday, starting around five. Most of the people will be coming by right after work."

"Friday the thirteenth? Great planning, there," Stan said, putting down his fork and contentedly rubbing his stomach. "Do you really think you should be having a party that day?"

Angie laughed, but no one joined her. "Who cares?"

"Maybe someone should care," Rysk said, giving Scout a strange look.

Angie looked from them to Stan. He shrugged.

"It's a piss-poor copycat!" Calderon slammed his fist against his desk and glared at Bill Never-Take-A-Chance Sutter, who'd earned his nickname because of the way he approached his work now that he was close to retirement. Sutter got up from his desk and walked to the water cooler without a word.

"You don't know that at this point!" Rebecca Mayfield shouted. She and Sutter had been sent out on the latest homicide call and found a crime scene exactly like those of the ritual murder killer. "You haven't looked at any of the evidence."

"You don't know enough about my case to know that this murder is nothing like the other two. Nothing at all!"

"Whoa, you two," Yosh said, entering Homicide with Paavo right behind him. They had just returned from testifying in court, a homicide inspector's most frustrating activity. "What's going on here?"

"We've had another ritual murder," Rebecca said. "And Calderon's prime suspect was locked up in jail when it happened."

"You don't know it was a ritual murder!" Calderon countered immediately.

"No, but I'm also not blind." Rebecca walked over to him. "A young woman. African-American, this time. Her name was Tashanda Reed, twenty-two years old. She was killed last night. Apparently she and her boyfriend got into a fight, and she got out of his car heading north on Steiner. He figured she'd go to Geary Street for a taxi, but he couldn't find her. That was the last time she was seen alive."

"Was her body found like the others?" Paavo asked, finally finding enough of a pause to ask his question.

"In an alley, surrounded by candles, nude. No heart," Rebecca said.

"The boyfriend did it, I tell you," Calderon nagged. "They fought, he killed her, then set it up to look like the stories in the paper."

Paavo glanced at Rebecca, who scowled and shook her head.

"We've got Markowitz cold," Calderon continued. "You couldn't ask for better evidence, including the statement of eyewitness Taylor Walters, now deceased, who placed him at the scene. We've got enough evidence, in fact, to go for the death penalty. It looks like the DA is going that route."

"But those weird, smelly candles were used," Benson said. "We didn't let anyone know about them."

"Smelly?" Yosh asked.

"Like the kind of stuff your grandmother might have rubbed on you when you had a sprain. It also keeps away bugs. What did they call it? Liniment? No, wait, camphor. That's what it was. Anyway, we kept that fact from the press."

Paavo mulled it over. The camphor-scented candles did make it even less likely to be a copycat.

"But people might have talked about them anyway," Calderon interjected. "The case is too sensational to keep everyone's lips sealed. One person blabs to two, they each tell two more, pretty soon, it's all over town." He faced Rebecca. "Lean on the boyfriend, I tell you. He'll confess. I know it."

Paavo couldn't help but wonder what Mason Markowitz would say about this. Markowitz had predicted the murders would continue. Looked like he was right.

<hr>

Paavo waited until late that night, long after the other homicide inspectors had left for home or hit the streets to talk to snitches and others who only came out after the sun went down.

He went to City Jail and asked to speak to Markowitz, showing his credentials. The guard remembered him from the last visit and gave him a dirty look as he led Markowitz to an interview room.

Markowitz's hair was tangled, and he appeared even more haggard than previously. The orange jail suit hung from his bony frame. His eyes bulged, and he was too excited to sit. "I can't wait here any longer! It's happening soon!"

Here we go again, Paavo thought. "What is?"

"All the signs were there, and now with the alignment of Pluto and Aquarius, we must act."

An astrology lesson wasn't the reason Paavo had come here tonight. "Why did you say the murders would continue?" he asked.

"Why? Why not?" Markowitz raised his hands out at his sides, palms up. "Of course they would. What would stop them?"

"You're here."

"So?"

"Your fingerprints were found at critical scenes, and so was your shoe print."

"We must stop Baalberith before he kills again."

"He has," Paavo said, and then wondered where *that* had come from. "Or, I should say, someone has."

Markowitz's eyes were bright and watery. "Who did he kill?"

Paavo shook his head.

"A woman? Was it a woman?"

"Yes."

"The fourth! The Dark Ladies are his. I must get out. I must stop him. Stop him before he takes his Queen." Manacled, he stood and shouted. "Let me out. Only I can handle him. Only I have the power!"

As much as Paavo tried to calm him, he couldn't. Finally, he gave up and called the guard.

CHAPTER THIRTY

Angie had a bunch of magazines spread in front of her. She received a cake order from the mother of a man who just won a mechanical engineering award for coming up with an improvement to some kind of sophisticated diode. She couldn't begin to understand what a naïve diode was, let alone a sophisticated one.

Or, what could possibly be comical about it.

Head in hand, she scrolled the internet, hoping something might jump out at her.

Angie's phone began to ring—a welcome diversion from tools and building plans. Between cakes, her mother, and agonizing over Connie, her head was splitting.

It was Paavo. He told her he was hung up on a case, and hoped they could go to dinner tomorrow night, or the night after that.

"Sure. No problem," she said, even as she realized her voice was flatter than the bottom of a springform cake pan.

"Is anything wrong?" he asked.

Everything, she wanted to say. Aloud, she replied, "No, not really."

"You haven't seen any strange characters hanging around your apartment, have you?"

"No one stranger than Scout and Rysk," she answered.

"Any more flies or toads?"

"No."

"Have you talked to Connie?" he asked.

"Me?" Her bottom lip trembled as everything that was upsetting her, starting with her fight with Connie, came rushing back.

"Angie, you've got to call her. The two of you need to have a calm, adult talk."

"I know," she murmured. -

"Listen, we arrested the guy we thought killed those women, what the press called the ritual murders, but there was another murder last night. We're all trying to piece this mess together."

"My God! Paavo. You mean the killer's still out there? Be careful, please!"

"Me? You're the one I'm worried about. Since Markowitz was interested in you, be doubly careful. Don't go anywhere alone and keep your doors locked all the time."

This so-called interest of Markowitz's just didn't make sense to her. "It's got to be a mistake. There's nothing special about me. All I do anymore is bake cakes." *And fight with friends, and blow off my boyfriend.* Sometimes, she really didn't like herself.

"He was caught lurking around your building. He might have been looking for you, or maybe Scout. There's some tie in with him and the Goths or Vampyre culture. It's not clear yet."

The thought of a potential killer having been nearby was unnerving. "Isn't he still in jail? Or was he released?" she asked.

"Still in jail." Paavo didn't even try to hide his worry. "Why don't you go stay with your parents for a while until we can tell what's going on here?"

She rubbed her forehead. "I don't get it. Why would anyone care about me? I'm not *doing* anything."

"Neither were the other women he's killed!" Paavo shut his eyes. "I'm sorry. I didn't mean to shout. It's just that Markowitz has me seriously worried about you."

"Okay. I'll just finish up the last couple of jobs and then stopped until this is over. The deputy chief's cake is the only big one I've still got to do."

"Angie--"

"I'll be careful, Paavo. And I won't go out alone. I promise. Now, don't worry so much, and go find the killer."

She hung up, depressed and frustrated. Knowing Paavo was probably feeling the same way didn't help.

She went back to internet searching for engineering humor. A little later, her phone rang again. Hope that Paavo was calling back welled up in her. She didn't know what had gotten into her, why she was so touchy and always in such a foul mood all the time. This perpetual PMS was getting old.

Or, just maybe, it was Connie.

She picked up her phone. The caller was Scout.

"Hello," she said brightly.

"Did I leave my backpack in the kitchen?" Scout asked. She sounded upset. "I can't find it."

Angie went into the kitchen. "You did. Do you want to come by and pick it up?"

"Glad it's safe. I don't need it today. I'll get it tomorrow."

"Okay," Angie said, thinking Scout seemed more distracted than usual. "Take it easy, and I'll see you tomorrow."

"Thanks, Angie."

Another vaguely dissatisfying phone call, Angie thought, as she ended the call. She looked at the backpack under the kitchen table. Hmm. She really shouldn't...

On the other hand, what if Paavo and Rysk were right?

What if she was being shortsighted, naïve, dumb—all their unspoken insults?

She sat on the floor and slid the backpack toward her. Unzipping it, she folded back the front flap to peer inside.

An unopened bottle of water. A sealed tube of Ritz crackers. Something told her she was looking at what might have been Scout's dinner that night.

An old sweater. A large manila envelope. Nothing else.

Being careful not to tear the envelope, she opened it and slid out the contents. Newspaper clippings about the ritual murders were the first things that caught her eye. They alarmed her. Why would Scout be interested in them?

A small white envelope was included. Inside were photographs. One was a young woman, blond with pink and purple streaks. Except for the hair, she looked like a young version of Scout. This must be the sister she'd lost contact with. The combination of the sister's photo and the newspaper clippings made Angie's spine tingle.

The sister's eyes were painted black, and she wore lots of cheap silver, or possibly tin, jewelry. A knit top of white and black zebra stripes was worn under a black jacket. Beside her stood a couple of geeky looking young men, scrawny and pimply, and behind them, others danced near small tables—a club scene of some kind.

The other photos were of Goths. A street scene of people entering a basement room stopped her. With alarm, Angie recognized the street and house. *The Baron's!* Was that the club for which he wanted to purchase a Comical Cake?

More pictures of people entering the club spread around her. She didn't recognize any of them, and many were a bit blurred.

The photos made it look as if the crowd was hanging around one side of the Baron's house. Angie had heard that a lot of these strange Goth gatherings were held in private clubs and homes. The Baron's house was big enough and the side the people were at faced the old St. Michael the Archangel graveyard, so it wasn't as if anyone would be disturbed by a raucous dance club.

Angie thought about the way Scout dressed when she first met her. She dressed like the people milling around the Baron's club in the photos.

Angie could use the excuse of returning Scout's backpack to go to the club and maybe find her or at least learn what the girl was up to. Besides, the Baron had claimed he wanted to become one of her customers.

She had just promised Paavo wouldn't go out alone at night. But they'd been talking about cake deliveries to strangers' homes. That was certainly different from taking an Uber door-to-door, and going to a dance club filled with people so she could meet Scout.

Surely, that wouldn't be a problem.

CHAPTER THIRTY-ONE

Connie smiled at Paavo as he walked into the coffee shop that same evening after her store's closing time. "Thank you for coming," she said when he joined her.

"I'm glad you called," he said. "How are you doing?"

"I'm okay." They made small talk until the waitress took his order, then Connie said, "If I saw some guy lurking on the street across from my house, should I call the police? Can they do anything?"

"There are laws against loitering and vagrancy. You can call the local station. Is the guy watching you?"

She picked up an empty sugar packet and smoothed the paper. "Probably not." Suddenly, she crumpled the packet and pushed it aside. "Hell, that isn't why I called. How's Angie?"

"She misses you and your friendship," he said bluntly.

Connie's face fell. "I was so furious at her, it amazed even me. I wanted to stay mad at her, I really did. Life is much easier when I don't see her since that means I don't get involved in any of her goofy plans." She stirred her coffee. "I just go along my quiet way, running my shop, seeing nearby shop owners and neighbors, watching TV, cleaning up the apartment, trying to find a good man..." She glanced up at him bleakly. "And it's boring. I miss her."

"What happened? Was it her cake business?" he asked.

"In part. You know how one-track her mind is. When she starts something, a team of rampaging bull elephants can't divert her attention. That made me mad, but if I hadn't been so upset about her—and you—I wouldn't have been so touchy. I'd have kept helping her out."

"Me?" he asked.

She nodded. "I can tell you want to ask her to marry you and she'll say yes. But then"—Connie yanked a napkin from the holder and dabbed the corner of her eye—"then she wouldn't have time to be my friend anymore."

He was stunned. "You thought that?"

Her tears flowed harder. "I was feeling sorry for myself, thinking about my divorce, and the guys I tried to get together with and how nothing ever seems to work out, and how you and Angie are so perfect together, and how she wouldn't need me anymore. And then Stan said--"

"Stan?" he blurted.

She nodded. "He said she was taking advantage of my good nature. That she only pretended to be my friend because I worked for her."

Paavo shook his head, disgusted. "I should have known that little worm was behind this. Angie's got to keep him out of her life."

Connie's sniffles grew louder. "What if he's right?"

"Listen to me, Connie," he put his hand on her arm, "Angie would never give up your friendship. She's talked my ear off, mopey and weepy, because she thinks you don't like her anymore. She's been asking all her sisters how to be a good friend—not that she's gotten very good advice, mind you. I know how important you are to her. Nothing can get in the way of that."

"Really? You wouldn't know it from the way she talked to me at my shop. She has quite the mouth when angry."

He grinned. "Don't I know it. Although, to hear Angie tell it, you more than held your own. She was licking her wounds for quite a while."

She chuckled. "It did get pretty ugly."

Paavo was glad she could laugh about it. "Do you think you'll be able to forgive her?"

Her eyes widened. "I'm afraid I already have!"

"I'm glad to hear it," he said warmly. "One more question. Do you think Angie also suspects I'm thinking about proposing?"

"Well, normally, she'd be picking up the queues just like I have. Probably well before I noticed, to tell the truth. But she's so consumed with this cake business I don't think she knows which end is up. Is that why you haven't asked her yet?"

He nodded. "I've been waiting for the right time. You know Angie. I might not be the one-knee-on-the-floor type, but I'd like the setting to be memorable for her."

"But you will ask her?" Connie said.

"If she ever stops working with those damned cakes long enough for me to get a word in."

Connie ran around the table to hug him. "That's good. I'm glad for you both."

"You're pretty sure she'll say yes, then?"

Connie laughed. "Try to stop her!"

Scout was walking out the door of the Crypt Macabre when

Rysk caught up to her. "Leaving already?" he asked, joining her on the sidewalk.

"Yes." Scout shook her head. "Sometimes this girl finds that whole scene hard to take."

"Me, too," Rysk said, falling into step on the sidewalk beside her. "Why do you go there?"

She stopped walking. She shouldn't want his company, and she should say something to cause him to turn in a huff the way she usually did. But when she met his gaze, harsh words melted on her tongue. "I wonder that myself," she admitted. "Have you been going long?"

"A little over a month."

They began to slowly stroll toward the three-hundred-dollar Dodge Omni she'd picked up when she first arrived in the city. Amazingly, it still ran. "I guess you've met a lot of women at the club," she said, trying to sound casual.

"I'd like to hope the thought makes you jealous," Rysk said cockily, "but I don't think that's why you're asking. Looking for someone?"

Dismay struck her. He was too clever by half, but she already knew that. "I was told a friend used to hang out here. Did you ever meet a young woman named Greta? Eighteen. Pink and blond hair, blue eyes, slim, pretty."

"Greta? No. The name's not familiar. I've seen girls who look like that—several, in fact."

"I know. It's a type, isn't it? I was told she and the Baron were an item, but I haven't seen her with him."

"The Baron goes through his women pretty fast. He's got a new one every week, minimum. I saw him make a move on you. What happened? Did the lady killer strike out for once?"

They reached her car. "He's not the type that makes this girl's heart beat faster," she said with a grimace.

"Oh? Who is your type?"

She couldn't keep her gaze from drifting over him and liking, despite herself, what she saw. It was the last thing she'd ever admit. "Expensive suits. MBA. Ryan Gosling hair and looks."

"Ouch."

She unlocked the car door, trying to stifle her smile. "I'll see you at Angie's tomorrow."

He regarded her quizzically. "Okay, see you."

With a quick tug at her black miniskirt as Angie got out of the Uber, she stood on the sidewalk and faced the Baron's house, Scout's backpack slung over her shoulder.

She had waited until ten at night, when she guessed Scout might be there. She could have texted her, but most likely Scout would have told her not to go, and she was quite curious about the place after seeing Scout's photos.

But, she wasn't going there to snoop around. She was going as a friend, with no need for disguises or trying to fool anyone, although she wondered if she shouldn't have dressed up more Goth. With the mini, she wore a black turtleneck, black tights and black ankle boots. Although she didn't normally dress, she wondered if it wasn't more New York City black than Goth.

She watched as two women, one in a floor-length hooded black velvet cape, the other in a man's black suit, shirt, tie and Florsheim wingtips, both looking more dead than alive, walked past the front door of the decrepit Victorian. The home's walls and eaves were dark with soot. Two gray gargoyles leered down from above the doorway. At the side of the house, the two women walked down some stairs. A door opened, then quickly shut.

Despite being completely curious about the Baron and the whole Goth scene, Angie was suddenly far less sure of herself than a moment ago. As she followed the women's steps, she couldn't help but think of how much nicer it would be if Connie were with her. They could have dressed up in wild Goth clothes and make-up, laughing at themselves and each other. A heaviness descended on her heart as memories of the crazy times they'd spent together came back to her.

She knocked softly on the door. A puffy, baldheaded man with a pasty, bluish-gray skin tone, and wearing a black jacket buttoned snuggly against his oversized neck, opened it. "Yes?"

"I'm a friend of Baron Severus," Angie said.

His eyes lighted as he took in everything about her. "You are?"

"Yes. I bake cakes. He wants me to make him one."

He looked ready to laugh at her. She squared her shoulders, ready to argue. "I see," he said quietly. "Do you have any, uh, identification?" He held out his hand.

She ignored it. "I didn't drive, so I left my license at home." She'd learned that going to strange places like this, she was better off not bringing much with her. The thin handbag held only lipstick, compact, comb, money, cell phone, and apartment key. "You don't think I'm under age twenty-one do you?"

He frowned.

"Look, all I want to do is check out the scene," she said, trying to sound like Scout. "I was told this is a neat place, and the Baron is a friend. You can ask him."

Blue head raised an eyebrow.

"Do I need someone to vouch for me?" she asked. "The Baron's assistant knows me, too. I just wanted to go inside for a simple little visit. I won't bother anyone, I promise. If I do, you can throw me right out of here, okay?"

He continued to glare and to hold out his hand, moving it a little closer to her.

"I won't hurt anybody." Angie widened her eyes. *What's with this guy?*

He dropped his hand to his side with a loud smack. "Are you a cop or undercover agent?"

"A cop? Me?" What would Paavo think of that? She couldn't wait to tell him! "I don't know what you're talking about," Angie said, shaking her head in bewilderment.

He suddenly broke into a chuckle. "Go on inside. This should be interesting."

She walked around, canvassing the room and smiling while searching for Scout. Music wasn't live, but played on some kind of old-fashioned boombox. The people were mostly young, but a few older men were there, all looking way too lustfully at what appeared to be under-the-drinking-age girls. Their clothes made Scout's and Rysk's weird outfits seem like the height of fashion. Angie decided to find Scout and leave, fast. She could understand why Scout never talked about the place.

"Hi," she said to a young grungy fellow who'd propped himself against a wall.

"What's happening?" he mumbled. He looked stoned.

"I'm looking for Scout. You know her?"

"If she's a friend of yours, she's one of mine, too. I'll help you find her. I'm Fred Limore, and you're...?"

"Thanks, Fred, but I'll just have to find her on my own." Angie backed away from him.

"Wait."

She waved a hand in a way he couldn't mistake for anything but a brush-off and went to a woman this time. "Hi," she said. "I'm Angie. Are you a friend of Scout's?"

"Scout? No, my name's Mina Harker."

In a pig's eye, Angie thought. The woman was ten miles high, but then, so was just about everyone else here. Where was the Vice squad? "Do you know Scout Vannix?"

"You're not very friendly." The woman wandered away, leaving Angie gaping after her.

So I've been told.

"Miss Amalfi?"

Angie turned to see a tall man with a kind of soft, squishy look about him. After a moment, despite the red lipstick and black eye shadow, she recognized Wilbur Fieldren, the Baron's assistant. She'd know those particular black parrot-seed looking fingernails anywhere.

"What a pleasant surprise," he said. "I'd had the distinct impression you weren't into this kind of thing."

"Live and learn," she replied.

"My sentiments exactly."

Angie thought a moment. Scout, apparently, wasn't here. No sense wasting the trip. "I'd like to meet the Baron," she announced.

"Wonderful!" Fieldren said. "He's been anxious to meet you for some time. Come with me."

Angie was surprised that the Baron wasn't a bigger man than he was. He was fairly tall, although everyone seemed tall to her. His hair, like almost everyone else's here, was black. If she hung out with this crowd, it would save her a fortune in highlighting costs. And if she wanted color, she could buy a bottle of black shoe polish and do it herself, which was how the hair of many of the people here looked.

The Baron stood as she approached and shooed away the three young women who had surrounded him. He then stared with interest at Angie. His hair, pulled back into a rubber band, emphasized a deep widow's peak, and his eyes were a strange purplish color. She suspected tinted contact lens.

"My favorite city's favorite baker," he said, holding out both his hands.

"You're very kind, especially since you haven't tried my cakes yet," she said, placing her hands in his. He pulled her closer and kissed her cheek, then smiled down at her. She could feel him taking in her black onyx and gold earrings, the matching ring on soft manicured hands, the cut of her clothes, her Fratelli Rosetti shoes, her tiny Gucci handbag.

"I'll try anything you'd like to offer." His voice was a deep rumble. "You are very special. Very special, indeed. I am honored that you finally chose to come to me. I've hoped to lure you here."

"And here I am."

"I'd like you to create a cake for me." His eyes were surprisingly soft, and something about the way he looked at her made her feel warm and wanting to please him. It was weird. "Perhaps not a comical one, but a serious, Goth cake."

"Black on black, in other words?" she asked.

"Ah... a joke. Yes, I can understand why you do comical cakes."

He had a nice laugh. She was getting some insight to his club's popularity. "Actually," she said, "I came here looking for a friend of mine, Scout Vannix. Do you know her?"

"Of course I know Scout. A very nice young woman. I also know she works for you. Why are you looking for her? Is she missing?"

"She suggested I come. You've got a great spot here."

"I'm most grateful to her, but I'm afraid I haven't seen her tonight."

"So, she must come a lot?"

"Fairly. Has she said anything to you about us?"

"Only that this is a pretty neat spot."

He smiled suggestively. "Feel free to try me in any way you'd like."

He had charm, but not *that* much. "What do people do at your club besides dance?"

"We enjoy each other's company."

"In other words, nothing special."

An eyebrow cocked. "If you're looking for a more unique experience, at times we take part in a ritual. Do you like ritual?"

"Maybe. What kind of ritual?"

"We don't do it here, but in the abandoned church next door. It's got a great atmosphere. We pretend we're something we're not. You can pretend to be anything you want. Most of the people here dress up as vampires. Vampires are in these days, as you might have heard."

"Yes. I did hear that, not that I understand it, though."

"No? Actually, that's perceptive of you. Vampires simply regard humans as food. Others have much more interesting ideas about humans."

"What kind of others?"

His face, his whole demeanor, grew more intense. "Demons, for instance. They see humans as a challenge."

"Oh?"

"A challenge to win over to the side of evil. A challenge to tempt and see how much, or more often how *little*, you need to offer a human to get them to submit."

Her breathing quickened. "You sound as if you aren't human yourself."

The Baron laughed, a strong, loud laugh that caused heads to turn. "I suppose I do. I've role-played a demon so many times in our rituals that it comes natural to me."

"I hope you haven't sold your soul, Baron," Angie said, forcing a smile.

He glanced at her, eyebrows lifted. "Now, why would you say that?"

"Isn't it obvious? If you have, you would be doomed to hell for all eternity."

The Baron's eyes sharpened. "Some of us who live in the night would say that the real hell would be to spend all eternity with the good people in Heaven."

"Oh, dear," Angie said. "I think on that note, it's time for me to leave."

He took her hand, stopping her. "I do hope I haven't frightened you with this talk."

"You haven't frightened me." She pulled her hand away, lifting her chin and meeting his gaze.

"Give us...me...a chance." He lightly placed his hand on her arm. "You'll enjoy it here. We have many ways to help with your enjoyment. Something that will bring great *ecstasy*, shall we say?"

She tried to move away. "I think it's time for me to leave now."

His hand tightened, and he drew her toward him. "Why don't you come with me? We should talk more privately."

Angie blanched. "No, really."

"Well, look who's here!"

She turned at the familiar-sounding voice and saw Rysk. Relief and astonishment swept through her. What was he doing here?

"I didn't know you were into this scene," he said. That night he wore tight leather slacks and a flowing white shirt.

She yanked her hand free from the Baron's grasp. "Scout told me about it," she replied. "I thought I'd check it out. I didn't know you came here, too."

"You know both Angie and Scout?" the Baron asked Rysk, his eyes hard.

"Sure," Rysk folded his arms and smiled at Angie. "I know all the beautiful women in the city. Angie's an old friend."

Angie saw that for some reason, Rysk didn't want the Baron to know he also worked for her. Maybe it was a macho thing. Driving around Comical Cakes wasn't, she guessed, a job to be proud of.

"I was just trying to convince your friend to visit us often," the Baron said, giving Rysk a penetrating gaze before he turned once again to Angie. "She has much to offer, and I know we have much to offer her in return."

Rysk glanced from one to the other. "You're quite right, Baron."

Angie didn't think she heard much conviction in his voice.

"I'll keep it in mind," Angie said to the Baron, then looked her arm onto Rysk's. "I was just about to leave. I'm going to call an Uber. Want to wait with me?"

"Oh..." Rysk glanced at the Baron who stared back with a frown. "Sure," Rysk said.

"Nice to have met you, Baron," she said, taking Rysk's arm.

The Baron cocked an eyebrow. "And I will not feel alive until you return. Come back soon."

"I will." As she turned away, from the corner of her eyes she saw the Baron give a nod to Fieldren.

"Why do you come here?" Angie asked Rysk as they reached the door.

"It's a way for me to spend my nights. I like the music, the conversation, the women. What can I say? What brought you? I don't see this as your scene."

"I was hoping to find Scout. I talked to her on the phone this afternoon and she sounded so down, I was worried about her."

"She told you she comes here?" he asked.

"Not exactly." A reason for being here popped into her head. "The Baron wants me to do a cake for him. He mentioned it to Scout."

"Really?" Rysk eyed her as if he found it hard to imagine she'd bake a vampire cake.

"You've seen Scout here, right?" she asked as she stepped to the street looking for her Uber. It wasn't in sight yet.

"This is where we met," Rysk said, avoiding her eyes.

"Do you like it here? The Baron?" she asked.

"He's not anybody I'd mess around with."

She peered at him curiously. If he didn't care for the Baron, and there were plenty of other places to go for music and dancing, why come here? It had to be because of Scout, she guessed.

The Uber she'd called soon pulled up to the curb, and Rysk opened the door for her.

He obviously was more interested in Scout than he pretended to be. She knew it! God, but she was good.

CHAPTER THIRTY-TWO

Paavo felt a distinct affinity for the terror Markowitz spoke of in facing demons as he approached the front door of Angie's parents' home. He knew he'd been taking the coward's way out, wanting to talk to Angie first rather than her Old World parents. Maybe that was why his plans just weren't working. He decided to make amends.

The housekeeper let him in, and in a moment, he was wrapped in a warm greeting from Serafina. *"Buon giorno, Paaverino. Come stai?"*

How Angie's mother, who was all of about five-foot-two, could call him "little Paavo" was beyond him. Angie swore it was an endearment that didn't translate well.

"I'm not so good, Serafina." He followed her into the living room, but stopped and faced her.

She studied his expression, then took his hand. He could feel the calluses and lines that had permanently formed in her bent fingers from years of hard work before the family wealth grew. "It's about you and Angelina, I take it. What's wrong?"

"I want to propose to her," he said after a while.

"Brava! I knew it! I'm so happy, Paavo," she gushed with

sheer happiness, giving him another rib-breaking hug and kissing him soundly on both cheeks. Tears glistened in her eyes. "You're a good man. *Buonissimo.* When will you ask her?"

"That's the problem. She's so busy with her business, I can't seem to find the right time."

"When you ask her, it'll be the right time, no matter what. I know my Angelina."

"I'd like to do it the right way, in a nice setting," he said. "Also, I'd like to talk to Sal. I know he objects to me marrying Angie."

"Come, sit down." She led him to a sofa and sat beside him. "Salvatore is no problem. Don't worry. He pretends he doesn't like all his daughters' husbands, except for Caterina's husband, and that was only because Caterina is so pushy, he was glad to get her off his hands."

Paavo knew Serafina was trying to help, but it didn't do anything for the knots in his stomach. Angie was Salvatore Amalfi's baby girl, his princess. "Thanks," he said. "Is Sal here? May I see him?"

When Angie's father entered the room, his hangdog expression told Paavo he had a good idea why Serafina had called him. Despite that, he had, as always, a distinguished air about him. He was almost as tall as Paavo, although frail from a heart condition. His nose was Romanesque in an olive-complected face, his hair almost completely gray, and his eyes as piercing as a hawk's.

"Paavo has come to us like a good man should do," Serafina said as she rejoined Paavo on the sofa, patting his hand. "He came to tell us he wants to marry our Angelina."

"Hmph," was Salvatore's only response.

"Sit down! *Madonna mia!* Didn't you hear what I said? Be civil."

He sat on an armchair on the far side of the room. "I knew this was coming," he grumbled to Serafina as if Paavo wasn't in the room. "What do you think I am, stupid? I knew him and Angelina were thinking of something like this. I can't say I like it, but nobody cares any more what I think. In the old country, girls listened to their fathers. We'd say who they should marry. Not anymore. Not here."

"I know you have particularly high hopes for Angie in many areas," Paavo said, his heart thumping.

Salvatore nodded. "*É vero.* We sent her to good schools, even the Sorbonne for a year. That cost so much I couldn't believe it. I thought she'd accomplish many things. I keep waiting."

"She tries, Sal," Paavo said, and added with frankness, "She tries very hard to please you. Sometimes, I'm afraid, too hard."

"I wouldn't know it! Anyway, nothing works. Maybe I put too much pressure, I don't know. Or she puts too much on herself."

Paavo drew in his breath. He could do this, he told himself, despite feeling like he was tussling with a porcupine. "You've made it clear you think she can do a lot better for herself than to marry a cop. I don't want my job to be a problem for Angie, not another area for her to feel pressured or that she's failed in her father's eyes. That's why I'm here to talk to you."

Sal went to an antique sideboard and poured himself a straight shot of Jack Daniels. He gestured toward the Baccarat glass decanter and Paavo shook his head.

Sal sipped the whiskey and then sat again. "Why don't you get out of her life? It'd be so much easier."

Serafina clucked her tongue in annoyance, but kept quiet.

"I've tried," Paavo admitted, thinking back just a couple of months earlier when he tried to ease himself out of her life while she had a crazy Fantasy Dinner business going. It had backfired big time. "It hasn't worked. I love her. She... she makes my life worth living." He stared at the floor a moment, then raised his eyes to Sal. "She loves me, too. If I had any doubt of her feelings, I wouldn't be here. I might not have the world's greatest job, but I'll spend my life doing all I can to make Angie happy."

"Ah, *amore!*" Serafina's eyes were shining. She clasped her hands together and smiled mistily. "You must give your consent, Salvatore."

Sal tossed his drink back and returned to the bar.

"Enough! Your heart!" Serafina ordered.

"My heart. Who cares? I'm old. All my girls are going to be married. They won't need me, anymore. Who the hell cares anymore about an old man." He nevertheless left the decanter alone.

"*Madonna sanctissima!*" Serafina cried. "Why do I have to listen to you feeling sorry for yourself when Paavo is telling us he loves our *bambina*? Our youngest little girl? Oh, such a pretty baby she was. It seems like only yesterday." Serafina heaved a deep sigh and dabbed her eyes with a small handkerchief she pulled from her pocket.

"Hmph. Love is easy to talk about before marriage, but it takes much more than that to make a marriage work," Sal said, sitting down again without the drink he wanted.

"Nothing is more important than love." Serafina's hands fluttered to her heart. She sighed, and with her eyes gleaming and her face rosy, Paavo could see the young woman who had caught the eye and heart of a proud man. "You were crazy about me when we got married."

"Yeah, I was, but I was crazy about a lot of women. That doesn't mean I wanted to marry all of them."

"*Che dici?*" Serafina sounded angry, although Paavo had no idea what she'd just said.

"It's not what you're thinking, Serafina. You were always special to me." Salvatore threw his hands up in exasperation.

"Hmph!" She turned back to Paavo. "We didn't have a big wedding. No, we had no money. No nothing. Not even my father and mother attended. We took a train to Reggio—that's in Calabria. It was such a mess of a city. But we were young. In love, despite what Salvatore says now."

"I didn't say we weren't!" Sal shouted.

Paavo cringed. This wasn't going at all the way he'd hoped.

"No, just that you could have had your pick of women, and somehow I was the lucky one," Serafina yelled right back at him. "Where is *l'amore?* At least, it is with you, Paaverino." She then stood up and gave him another hug. With a new tear in her eye, she said, "I'll leave the two of you to work things out."

Paavo and Salvatore faced each other in the ensuing silence, their expressions showing that both felt they'd been caught up by a tornado.

"Angelina is a lot like her mother," Sal said. "It's quite a bit to put up with, you know."

"I know. I love them both."

"Serafina will mother you. You know that, too, right?"

"I'll enjoy it," he admitted.

"I suppose there's nothing I can say to change your mind."

"I'm afraid not," Paavo said.

"Have you asked Angelina yet?"

Paavo drew in his breath, then shook his head dejectedly. "To tell the truth, I tried to, even before talking to you. I had hoped we would face you together. But when my plans didn't work out, I realized I should talk to you first."

"I appreciate your honesty." Sal looked Paavo over even more carefully. "So, what's keeping you from asking Angelina?"

"She's been too busy with her new business."

"She's that involved in her work?" Salvatore's eyebrows lifted. "Does that mean I might get a son-in-law and a business woman for a daughter at the same time?"

"Could be," Paavo said, not with a little wonder.

Sal sighed. "I know better than to attempt to stand in the

way of Angelina and Serafina both. All right. For this marriage, you and Angelina have my blessing."

"I'm glad you called," Angie said, clasping Paavo's arm as they walked along Fisherman's Wharf. He'd asked her if she had time to join him for a late lunch and was pleasantly surprised when he'd suggested the wharf. The two of them had had some of their nicest times together strolling along the water's edge.

"I'd hoped you could get away from a hot oven for a while," he said. "And I needed something bright and pretty in my day."

"The Wharf?" she asked with a smile.

"Exactly," he said teasingly.

They stopped and bought shrimp cocktails from a sidewalk vendor then walked along a pier. As they ate, she told him how she was progressing with her cake design for the deputy chief's retirement party. "The thought of serving cake to a bunch of cops must have really gotten to Scout. She couldn't make it to work today," Angie said with a laugh.

"I still worry about her and Rysk," Paavo admitted. "They're both mysteries."

"You were a mystery for a long time." Angie smiled. "But I stuck with you, didn't I?"

"That's different. Anyway, I'm not a mystery, although my family is."

"I'm afraid that in many ways you're still a mystery to me, Inspector Smith. That's one of your many attractions."

Cocktails finished, they stood against an old wooden railing and peered down on the water and a couple of fishermen making their boat ready to head out to the Pacific. Paavo reached over and took Angie's hand, running his thumb over her knuckles. "If I'm such a puzzle, why do you stick with me?"

"Because of your nature." She squeezed his hand and turned toward him. "You aren't a man to lie or cheat."

"Never with you, Angie. That's how we should always be with each other."

"Absolutely," she said as she remembered something she needed to tell him about. "Actually, even though I joked about Scout earlier, I found out something that might help you understand her better."

"Oh?" He looked interested.

"She's looking for her sister. Apparently, the girl is one of the many runaways who found their way to this city. Scout sounded so upset and troubled on the phone, that last night I went looking for her."

Something in her tone must have conveyed to him that he wasn't going to like what she had to say because his hand tightened on hers. "You went looking for her at night? Alone?"

A seagull cawed and swooped right by their heads. They ducked, then began walking once again. "But just one place. And I took an Uber there and back to be safe. Anyway, she goes to a Goth hang-out. It's called the Crypt Macabre. It's at the house of this weird guy who calls himself Baron Severus. He's like, I don't know, maybe the Hugh Hefner of the Goth set."

He froze. "The Crypt Macabre?"

"You've heard of it?" His reaction puzzled her.

He again began their stroll again. "Just the name. Where is it?"

She gave him the location and then continued to describe it. "It's weird, kind of spooky, and some of the people there seem to be living a Dracula fantasy." She chuckled.

He stopped again. "It's nothing to laugh about. I've seen it in connection with... with things that are dangerous. If they knew you were there snooping around—"

"I was not snooping!" She hooked his arm and tugged at him. He fell into step at her side. "I've given all that up. I was minding my own business, just looking for my friend. And anyway, Rysk was there. He even walked outside with me and waited until my Uber showed up."

"Rysk! That's even worse! I already told you, Angie, Edward Bowie doesn't exist. He's a fake. And if he and Scout both go to that club..."

Angie stopped walking. His reaction to her little adventure had been making their stroll less than enjoyable, and the turn it had just taken killed her enthusiasm for it completely. "Look, I don't know why Rysk and Scout go to a place like the Baron's. From everything I've seen working with them both, they aren't really into the whole Goth culture, despite their outfits."

He leaned toward her. "What are they then, *really*?"

Her hands clenched. "I don't know!"

"That's what I'm saying. I don't know. Neither do I, and for that reason I don't like them around you. You need to fire them right now!"

She gaped at him, scarcely believing what he'd just said. "You're telling me how to run my business?"

"I'm telling you how to be safe," he all but shouted.

She shook her head, hurt and stunned by his words, then hurried away, not even looking back when he called.

When Angie got out of the Uber she'd taken back to her apartment after getting so upset with Paavo, she was shocked to see Rysk across the street studying the building next door. Upset about Paavo, she didn't feel like talking to Rysk, but before she could run into her building, he saw her.

"Angie," he called.

"What are you doing here?" she asked as he approached her.

"Just looking around. I thought I'd check to see if you and

Scout needed help with baking, but you weren't home." He slid his hands into his pocket. "You haven't mentioned any more pranks. Is everything okay?"

"Nothing new, thank goodness." Her head swiveled from side to side. She didn't like the thought of some malevolent prankster in her neighborhood. "Have you seen anything or anyone suspicious?"

He laughed. "Don't worry. No bogeymen are out here."

"That's good. Well, I'm sure I'll need to help with a couple of deliveries tomorrow afternoon," she said.

"See you then." His voice held more resignation than enthusiasm.

CHAPTER THIRTY-THREE

Paavo was in one of the foulest moods he'd ever been in when his feet hit the concrete stairs leading into the Hall of Justice after his aborted date with Angie. His head was muddled with the heartburn-inducing walk and he wondered whether he was in his right mind to consider a lifetime with someone so stubborn.

So lost in thought was he, he almost missed spotting Scout as she walked out the main door. Seeing him, she stopped in her tracks and turned to reenter the building. He sprinted up the steps and grabbed her arm.

"Hey!" she yelled. "Watch it!"

"What are you doing here?" he demanded.

"I, uh, came to try to get out of jury duty. What's it to you?"

"Do you know Angie went looking for you last night at the Crypt Macabre?"

She paled. "I don't know what you're talking about."

He kept his hand on her arm and pulled her out of the doorway to the side of the building. "Start talking. Who's Baron Severus? What's the Crypt Macabre? And why do you go there?"

"Not that it's any business of yours, but since I like Angie, I'll tell you." She jerked her arm free and defiantly stared at him. "My sister is a runaway. I knew Greta went there when she was in the city, so I've gone to try to find her or someone who knows her. I've had no luck so far."

"That's it?"

"That's it."

"What about this man?" He pulled a couple of photos from his inside breast pocket and showed her one of Markowitz.

She shook her head. "Never saw him before."

"This one?" He held up Taylor Walters' photo.

There was a long pause. "I've seen him at the club," she said softly. "He was complaining, um, I don't know why. I don't remember."

"Was it about an old man following him?"

"No. Maybe. I'm not sure."

"Did anyone there tell him the old man's name?"

Her eyes were wide, searching everywhere except at him. "I don't know. He talked to the Baron. I don't know anything more. I'm sorry."

She ran down the steps in her hurry to get away.

"What do you want?" A bleary-eyed, heavy-set man with short brown hair, smudged eye make-up, and a sickly gray-tinged face opened the door of the big Victorian on Vallejo Street. He was wearing a bathrobe and slippers.

"Paavo Smith, police," Paavo said as he flashed his badge. "Are you the owner of this house?"

"No. He's still sleeping."

Obviously, the owner wasn't the only one who'd been asleep. It was three in the afternoon. "When will he be up?" Paavo asked.

"Around six. Maybe seven. Or eight."

"I'd like to speak to him now." Although Paavo had left messages for both Calderon and Benson to check out Markowitz's connection to the Crypt Macabre, he had a few questions of his own for Severus.

"What's this about?" the man asked arrogantly.

"Who are you?" Paavo retorted.

The fellow straightened his spine. Had he been wearing shoes instead of slippers, Paavo wouldn't have been surprised to see him click his heels. "I'm Wilbur Fieldren, the Baron's assistant."

"I'm here on a homicide investigation. I want to see Severus now."

"One moment." He shut the door. Nearly ten minutes went by before the door opened again, and Fieldren waved Paavo inside.

Stepping into the house was like entering a meat locker. The sense of evil he'd had at the crime scenes struck him tenfold. He followed the assistant through a gaudy hallway to a small, dark parlor. The room had a strong, almost medicinal smell. He couldn't quite place it, but it was disagreeable.

The Baron was seated by the fire. He wore a heavy brocade robe and his head was flopped forward, chin to chest. He slowly lifted it as Paavo entered the room. At first, Paavo thought he was an old man, but then he realized the Baron was simply dissipated and in need of sleep.

Paavo explained who he was and then said bluntly, "I'd like to ask you about Mason Markowitz."

"Never heard of him," the Baron grumbled. Obviously, being pulled from his bed didn't agree with him. Frankly, Paavo wasn't in the world's best mood either, and if this guy wanted trouble, he was ready.

"He's heard of you," Paavo said coldly. "And your club."

"So have a lot of people. What's this about?"

"It's about murder, Baron Severus. What's your real name?"

"I don't see that as any concern to anyone but me. Why am I being questioned?"

"I'd like to know why Mason Markowitz is interested in you and your club, and why you deny knowledge of him."

"I'm not denying anything. The man is a stranger to me."

"Have you ever seen this man?" He withdrew a glossy lineup photo of Markowitz and handed it to the Baron.

"Never." The Baron handed it back. "Is he Markowitz?"

"What about Taylor Walters?" Paavo asked as he placed the photo back in the envelope.

"Taylor... oh yes, the boy who killed himself. I was sorry to hear it, but not surprised. He was a junkie."

Paavo was finding the Baron an interesting liar. He seemed to deal in half-truths and had a shell that was difficult to penetrate. The Baron, he was sure, had a lot of practice in deception. "What else?" he asked.

"I didn't know him well. He was troubled, unhappy, with few friends. That's all I can tell you."

"Did he tell you about an old man leaving holy water at his house?"

"I heard about it. He was extremely upset by it—unnaturally upset, if you ask me."

"Someone told him the name of the old man who was after him. Who could that have been?"

The Baron yawned. "Your guess is as good as mine. Probably better, Inspector, because I don't give a damn. Ask Fred Limore. The two were thick as thieves."

"What do you know of Scout Vannix?"

The Baron's eyes widened at the woman's name. "She's also troubled—and trouble. I have no idea why she hangs around. She's too uptight for our group. I'd be just as glad if she stopped coming. In fact, she won't be admitted anymore. This *is* a private club, after all. Happy now?"

"What about her sister?"

The Baron looked at him curiously. "Who *is* her sister?"

"Greta. Greta Vannix."

His frown didn't come quick enough, and Paavo saw a twinge of something flicker across his eyes before his nonchalant mask descended once more. "Months ago, a girl named Greta came here. I don't remember if I ever heard her last name. I scarcely remember her, and I have no idea where she is now."

"And Rysk?"

"I'm tired of these twenty questions. He's a jerk. I pay no attention to him."

"I'll need to know your whereabouts around midnight over recent days."

"I can answer right now. I'm here every night. I never go out. I have no need to. Everything I want is here."

"You have parties here nightly?"

"What's your problem, Inspector? It seems to me you're just fishing, and I don't have time to waste."

"Thank you, Baron." Paavo stood. "Our talk has been most enlightening."

"No, it has been most disagreeable." The Baron stood. "I don't want to hear anymore from you, now or ever, unless you bring a warrant."

"A warrant for what reason?"

"That's just it. There is no reason."

When Paavo went out into the sunshine, he breathed deeply, trying to fill his lungs with clean, pure air.

CHAPTER THIRTY-FOUR

An awful night's sleep reliving his argument with Angie didn't help Paavo's mood one bit the next day.

Another bout of rants and raves was the last thing he wanted to deal with as he strode into the interview room and scowled at Markowitz and Markowitz's attorney, Cecil Keller.

In fact, he'd never felt less like doing his job than he did now.

"Well, well, well! The good inspector," Markowitz said with a friendly smile.

Paavo scowled at Keller. What had he done to his client? Drugged him? Keller, however, was gaping at Markowitz in surprise.

"I want you to tell me about Baron Severus," Paavo said.

"Ah, yes. A terrible man. He deals with drugs, you know," Markowitz said brightly.

"He does?"

"Demonic masters use surrogates to do their bidding." His voice dropped to a whisper. "You have to beware of people. All of them. They're all evil."

Paavo glanced again at Keller, who shrugged.

"What about this Dark Queen you talk about? Is Baron Severus connected to her?" Paavo asked, hoping to find some common ground with Markowitz in order to get some answers.

"I know she is being watched," Markowitz said calmly after a long while. "I felt the evil around her. Poof!" He laughed and kept his smile as he added, "Poof! It's all around us. All around."

Paavo wasn't sure that he didn't prefer the ranting Markowitz to Little Miss Sunshine. "You mentioned surrogates?" he prodded, his thoughts on Scout and Rysk. Were they surrogates? Or were they something more? "Tell me about them."

"You shouldn't worry, my boy," he said with an eerily peaceful smile. "Help is on the way."

"It is?"

Markowitz's gaze was fixated somewhere on the far wall, and he seemed to not even hear Paavo's question.

"Mr. Markowitz," Paavo decided to try again. "Can you tell me about the Crypt Macabre or Baron Severus?"

"Never go there, young man. Evil lurks. It will steal your soul. Our time of trial is at hand."

Markowitz bowed his head, eyes shut, and began to speak in what sounded like Latin.

Why wasn't the man screaming about leaving as he had done before? What was going on?

After a couple more attempts to get Markowitz to respond failed, a completely baffled and frustrated Paavo left.

The librarian gave Paavo a strange look as she handed him several references on the demon Baalberith.

He sat at a table and read them. All told a similar tale of a demon who wove a net of fornication and wealth to trap his victims. Scorned by a beautiful young woman who threw herself into a fiery pit rather than endure Baalberith's love, her selfless act caused him to be demoted to a second level demon. As a result, Baalberith went on a rampage of killing and the possession of souls while searching through the centuries for the one woman who would love him, the one who would become his Queen and raise him from the second order of demon, a Dark Lord, to the first—to become Baalberith once more.

Paavo was unsure of what to think of all this. Demons were supposedly capable of taking over a human body, overwhelming its original soul, and making it act in uncharacteristic ways.

Demonic possession was, all in all, an easy excuse for a lot of evil. He was just about to leave the library when his eye caught the fiction section. Curious about Angie's comments about the Crypt Macabre, he found Stoker's *Dracula*.

Mina Harker's journal entries were prominent in the book, as were tales of her friend, Lucy Westenra. Flipping through the pages, he came across the name Renfield, the crazy minion of the Count. Renfield... Fieldren...

Markowitz had talked about demons having surrogates.

Paavo placed the book back on the shelf with a shake of his head. He was becoming a little too comfortable with all this. He felt like he was caught in a cross between *The Conjuring* and *The Exorcist*.

Angie was surprised but relieved to see Paavo at her door at nine o'clock that night. She had just indulged in another long soak in the tub, aching and weary from baking cakes all day for the Chief's reception. At this rate, she was going to become waterlogged.

"I thought you were busy working on those awful murders," she said, leading him to the living room. She was upset by the way they'd parted at the Wharf, and when he hadn't called all day, her unhappiness grew. His showing up was a good sign, but when she sat and he didn't, the good sign took a turn south.

"I came here for two reasons. The first is to apologize. I was wrong about Scout and Rysk being behind your troubles. I still don't trust them, but nonetheless, I'm sorry."

"Apology accepted, although unnecessary. I know you're looking out for me, and I appreciate it. I'm also glad to hear you believe you're wrong about Scout and Rysk," Angie said, thrilled, yet unable to hide her confusion. "But how do you know that?"

"That's the second reason. We caught the woman who had been trying to harm your business."

She stared at him, shocked. "What did you say? The woman? What woman?"

"Lolly Firenghetti. She'd taken to following you, doing damage to your cakes, pretending to be customers with phony orders."

Angie's head reeled. "She did that?"

"Someone called in an anonymous tip. We caught her on the roof next door with a cage filled with live mice. She knew someone in the building, and once when she was visiting, managed to swipe the key to the main door. With it, she could get into the apartment building, and go up to the roof. She'd climb up to your roof deck and then go down the steps to your backdoor. You don't have a double lock on it, and she was able to get pass the single lock and let herself in, do whatever mischief she planned, and then leave."

"Mice! Oh, my God!" She shivered. "I've never even seen Lolly! How could she hate me that much?"

"You were cutting into her business, and she hated that fact."

"I've heard she's a somewhat overweight, middle-aged woman. How did she manage to climb around on rooftops?"

"The roof next door is just a couple feet below yours, and the buildings are side-by-side. Plus, she was plenty motivated and angry. The cop who went up there to arrest her has the bruises and bite marks to prove it."

Angie shook her head in amazement. "I can hardly believe it's over. And to think, she's Italian!"

He grinned. "So much for Cosa Nostra." He was actually quite relieved to learn the mishaps were caused by human mischief. For a while, he'd even considered an unnatural source. He definitely was spending too much time around Markowitz and kooks like the Baron.

"I'm a little bothered," he said, "that someone is watching you enough to call in the tip, but at least it had a good outcome."

"Don't worry. It was probably a cake lover. All I have to say is you're my hero."

All weariness and unhappiness forgotten, she held her arms out to him. He walked up to her, drew her to her feet and took her in his arms. They had a lot of celebrating to do.

***

Angie awoke in the middle of the night. Paavo was no longer at her side, but had quietly left while she slept. She wrapped her arms tight around the pillow he'd used, holding it close.

But soon, an attack of paranoia had caused her to get up and check for flies, toads, or mice, despite Lolly Firenghetti's arrest. In the kitchen, blue-frosted cakes covered every counter, even the top of her range. Imagining what mice would have done to those cakes—and to her apartment—was heart-attack time.

No strange creatures were there, just a sea of blue.

Tomorrow, Friday the thirteenth, was the Deputy Chief's reception, and she prayed everything would go well, for Paavo's sake as well as her own. She wanted him to be proud of her.

It would be nice if someone were proud of her.

Maybe after tomorrow, things would be better.

Rysk left the Crypt Macabre at two a.m. and stared up at the stars a moment. Not many were visible above the lights of the city, but he knew they were there, just as he knew of the many levels of activity going on around him.

Scout hadn't been allowed inside the club that night, but to his amazement, she'd asked for him to come out to talk to her. She had a request. An outrageous idea he should have run from as soon as she started talking. But he couldn't.

He gave her a promise, and tomorrow, no matter what, he was going to keep it.

Mason Markowitz paced his cell, unable to sleep. Tomorrow was the day. He had to get out of here. The safety of humanity depended on him.

Would his plan work? Dare he depend on others? He had no choice. He could only wait for tomorrow and pray.

Paavo drove home through the quiet streets. Tomorrow, when the big reception was over, somehow he'd get Angie to have a dinner with him that was free of arguments or interruptions, even if he had to take her to his house and cook for her himself.

He was tired of waiting, tired of not being sure if she'd say yes, despite what everyone else had to say. He wanted to hear the words from her lips.

Tomorrow, whatever it took to get her attention, he'd ask her to become his wife.

⁂

"Where are you, Greta?" Scout whispered even though, in her heart, she had no more hope. Her mind swirled in too many directions to sleep, and she paced around her small rented room.

Tomorrow, she would put Markowitz's plan into action. It would be dangerous, but she didn't care anymore... or did she?

She'd met someone who made her *want* to care, who made her feel there might be something enjoyable about this crazy life. At a time like this, though, how could she even acknowledge such stirrings, let alone consider acting on them?

She had no business acting on anything until she found Greta. To the outer limits of her ability and beyond if needed, that's how far she told Markowitz she would go. Tomorrow would be the test.

She must not fail.

⁂

One more infernal day until night fell and everything the *Ars Diabolus* predicted would come true. The Dark Queen would be his, and with her ascension, he would gain the ultimate power. He would become the Supreme Dark Lord—Baalberith.

Behold Baalberith! All the angels and saints would bow down before his power.

Tomorrow, all would become his.

He looked at the not-quite-full moon and raised his arms high to it. In twenty-four hours all the world would know the truth of his prophecy:

I am Destroyer. I am Beast. I am Nightmare.

CHAPTER THIRTY-FIVE

Finally, the big day had arrived.

"The cake and the set-up look great," Angie said, smiling at Scout and Rysk as she looked over the Hall of Justice cafeteria. "You two have been simply terrific."

The administrative assistance and clerks from the Bureau of Inspectors' various offices had joined Angie, Rysk and Scout to transform the cafeteria into a party room. Helium-filled balloons along with streamers festooned the ceiling. More were used as centerpieces on each table, and a colorful banner across the entire back wall read, "Happy Retirement Deputy Chief O'Malley. You're the Greatest."

The pièce de résistance, however, was Angie's cake. It was four feet across by five feet long, and was a perfect replica of the San Francisco police department badge, complete with the Chief's number.

It might not have been comical, but the oohs and aahs it received did her heart good. She was glad she went with serious, rather than funny.

Not only did she know the Chief of Police had no sense of humor, but hers vanished as well when she eyed Rysk. He was dressed more garishly than usual. His glow-in-the-dark green spikes were gelled to hard peaks, eye shadow smudged all the way around his eyes. His nails were painted the same dark crimson as his lips, and tonight he wore earrings in every one of his three ear holes, not to mention a nose ring. Dressed head-to-toe in black, he was an incongruous sight amidst all the blue uniforms and suits.

Angie could have spit when he showed up at her apartment that way. The urge to act like a school principal and send him home to scrub his face and wash his hair tempted her, but there wasn't time. If she didn't know any better, she'd have thought he was in disguise.

Scout, thank God, was at least normally dressed in a navy slacks and a white blouse. So far, no one paid any particular attention to Rysk, all being in a party mood. Besides, this *was* San Francisco.

"I never thought I'd be waiting on a bunch of cops," Rysk admitted as he studied the room that was just beginning to fill up.

"Everyone I've met here has been a great guy or woman," Angie said. "Give them half a chance and you'll like them."

Rysk tightened his lips. "I'd like to think they'd do the same for me."

"What? That spiked green hair won't warm them to you?" Scout asked with laughter in her voice. It was the first time that evening she showed any sparkle. She seemed preoccupied, as she'd been the day before while they baked. Angie had hoped to talk to her about what was bothering her, but time, and Scout's mood, hadn't yet allowed for it.

"What's more important is how you feel about it," Rysk said to her.

"You can shave it all off for all I care." Scout went about her business putting out plates and paper cups.

Rysk looked so crestfallen, Angie couldn't help but grin—and did her best not let him see it.

Paavo wanted to check his incoming emails before going down to the Deputy Chief's party. The others, except for Rebecca Mayfield, had already left. She gazed glumly in his direction as he sat at his computer.

An email from the FBI had his name on it.

Before visiting Baron Severus, he had wiped the glossy photo of Markowitz free of prints. When he gave it to the Baron to look at he only touched its edges. He didn't think the Baron would be as careful, and he wasn't. A perfect thumbprint resulted.

The FBI produced a match. George Arthur Hyde, age forty-three, born in Ithaca, New York, arrested three times for possession of narcotics and twice for dealing. Each time, he'd gotten off for tainted or lack of evidence. Markowitz had been right when he'd called the Baron a dealer. What else had he been right about?

As he carried the report to his desk, he noticed Rebecca Mayfield staring sadly at her computer.

"Rebecca," he said. "What's wrong?"

"Nothing," she said, a slight wobble in her voice.

He sat down at the chair beside her desk. "Are you sure?"

He watched her stiffen her spine, as if preparing herself to speak what was on her mind. "I just hope you've thought everything through and know what you're doing. That's all."

"About Markowitz?"

"No. About Angie."

"Angie?" He didn't understand.

Her large blue eyes studied him a long moment. "Look, I've learned that it's easy to put up with a cop when you're just dating. During that time, we're exciting—our jobs are danger-ous. We're tough, clever, in-the-know with lots of the wild stuff going on in the city. If we stand up our date, well, it's obviously because a life-or-death matter came up. They understand. Then you get married, or even engaged, and your partner suddenly isn't half so understanding."

"Don't you think I know all that?" Paavo asked.

"You know it, but only intellectually." She dropped her gaze. "I speak from experience. Been there, done that."

"You're divorced?"

"No. Never got that far." She lifted watery eyes and sniffed. "I was almost engaged—we'd talk about the possibility of marriage. It was when I was a patrol officer. I didn't listen to all the cops who said I'd be best off if I stuck to others like me when I dated. I found a civilian, and damn it all, I fell in love with him. I was sure he was The One. All was fine until I got shot. It was small, no lasting effects. But he freaked out completely.

"He gave me a choice. Him or my career. It was awful. I tried, but in the end, I guess neither one of us loved the other enough to be willing to work things out. It was also clear that he couldn't deal with my job—not the hours, not the danger. It destroyed us."

"I'm sorry," he said.

"Me, too," she whispered. "But that was then. I've gone out with cops ever since. Of course, now that I'm in Homicide, where most of them want to be, they kind of see me as way up the ladder from them, and that brings its own set of problems." Then, she smiled wryly and shook her head. "Good God, why am I telling you all this?"

"Because you care, and we're friends," he said.

She met his eyes. "Yes, that's what we are."

He nodded.

Elbows on the desk, she folded her hands and smiled

wanly. "I'm just feeling melancholy. I guess if anyone can make a cop and civilian marriage work, it's you and Angie." She smiled at him. "You're both too darn stubborn to let it fail."

He nodded. "Thanks. And I know you'll find the right guy, Rebecca. Probably another by-the-book cop. Want to walk down to the Deputy Chief's reception with me?"

She shook her head and gazed around the bureau—the ratty steel desks, the ancient computers, the stacks of papers and books and file folders. "I think I'll sit here awhile. I worked hard and gave up a lot to get here. Might as well enjoy it."

Scout snuck out of the reception. The room was slowly filling with people, but the deputy hadn't yet arrived.

She hurried through the hallways to the opposite side of the floor and went in search of a pay phone. She didn't want her cellphone number traced.

Making sure no one saw her, she stepped inside the booth, pulled the door shut, and dialed.

"Richards, Adams and Blaustein," the receptionist answered.

"I'd like to speak with Mr. Keller," she said, asking for the firm's junior attorney.

"May I tell him who's calling?"

"My name is Dolores Rice. Mrs. Dolores Rice. I'm calling about his client, Mason Markowitz. I believe I have some information that will be very useful to him."

Keller came on the line quickly.

"I can't keep my mouth shut any longer," she said, trying to make her voice high and nasal. "Mason Markowitz is innocent. He was with me the night Lucy Whitefeather was killed. We were together all night, and I can prove it."

There was a long pause. "How can you prove it?"

"I've got a receipt from the motel we stayed at. Mr. and Mrs., it says." She spoke hurriedly. "He signed it, and I took his copy. I was supposed to throw it away. My husband was out of town that night, you see."

"Why didn't you give me this information sooner?"

"I didn't think it would go this far. Mason and me, we agreed this was our secret. It's because of my husband—we're retired, and I get a wife's pension. I can't afford a divorce, but I can't let Mason stay in jail for something he didn't do. It's hard to do this, Mr. Keller. Very hard."

"You're now willing, however, to come open with this information?" he confirmed, excited.

"I wouldn't be calling if I wasn't. Mason is a good man. He believes that there's evil in the world, but he's no killer. He wants to rid the world of evil, to rid it of demons. Okay, I'll admit that's a bit strange, but don't we all have some quirks now and then?"

"It's more than a quirk to some people."

"I don't care. He's innocent, and I can prove it. Now, do you want my information or not?"

"Of course I do, but let me talk to my client."

"I'm leaving town, Mr. Keller. I can't take this. It's got my nerves all jangling. I'll call you in a couple of hours. You tell me what I can do, now, right now, 'cause I won't be here later."

"Wait. Try to relax. We'll keep this as quiet as possible, I promise."

"I know what lawyer's promises are worth."

"How can I reach you?"

"You aren't listening to what I'm saying. This will end my marriage, the life I know. I'll call you at eight o'clock." With that, she hung up.

Scout knew that Keller was a hungry young lawyer who had been working to become a partner. He was tired of being stuck with the kind of pro bono work that the firm meted out to its junior associates. Having been given a possible way to win a case that everyone suspected was a slam dunk for the prosecution, he'd find a way to meet with Markowitz immediately. Of that, she had no doubt.

Smiling, she went back to the reception. Time to find Rysk.

Angie was ecstatic. The reception was a resounding success. She stood beside Paavo as the various dignitaries made speeches about the years of able service Deputy Chief O'Malley had given the city and the department.

Last of all, they waited through an interminable speech as O'Malley recounted said years of service... one by one.

Finally the time came when Deputy O'Malley had to cut the cake. Paavo smiled proudly at Angie as the Chief praised her cleverness and had a number of photos taken standing beside it. Angie hoped that one of the photographers was from the *Chronicle*, and that a photo with her cake would be chosen for the city's major daily. That should bring lots more business her way.

She had to admit she almost cried when the Chief made the first cut after all the hours she'd put into making the badge perfect. And now, it was going to be eaten. *Sic transit gloria.*

She and Scout soon took over cutting and serving. She'd learned quite a bit about who was whom in the police force from Paavo, and she gave out pieces to the bigwigs first. That seemed to please them.

After the dignitaries wandered away with their cake and coffee or punch, Angie and Scout put a number of pieces of cake on plates, and cut up the remainder to make it easy for latecomers to serve themselves.

"You know, Angie," Scout said, pouring more punch, "I've heard that there are a number of police up on the seventh floor in the County Jail Annex who aren't able to leave their posts to come over here for a piece of cake. I was wondering if it would be all right with you if Rysk and I brought them some."

"How very thoughtful," Angie said, surprised that they'd come up with such a suggestion—and that she hadn't—considering how alienated from the police they had both initially acted. "I've heard there's a corridor between this building and the jail so you won't have to go outside."

"Yes... I've heard that, too," Scout said.

Carla, the Deputy Chief's administrative assistant and the one in charge of the party, agreed to the proposal. Scout and Rysk sliced up a large piece of cake, and placed it on a cart along with paper plates, forks and napkins. Then they wheeled it out of the room.

Angie slowly surveyed the crowd. People seemed to be enjoying themselves, and her cake was a big hit. Scout and Rysk should return soon, the party would end before much longer, and the cleanup would be relatively fast. Almost all the cake had already been eaten.

Paavo, too, looked pleased by what he saw. "This party is a winner," he said proudly, as he stepped to Angie's side. "You've done a great job. Everyone is impressed. The cake not only looked good, it was delicious." She smiled, her heart warmed by his words.

"Thank you," she murmured.

"When it's over, shall we go celebrate?"

Her smile deepened. "Wonderful idea. I'll be ready to relax. I'll admit to having been quite nervous about this. I particularly wanted everything to be perfect for your sake."

"You're always perfect to me."

"You know what I mean. I wanted you to be proud of me. Also, there's something else I've been thinking about."

"What's that?"

"This cake business. With a lot of hard work, I know it can

be profitable, but I don't think it's what I'm looking for." She took his hand. "Scout has a natural gift for it. Lots of the designs were hers. I'm thinking about asking her if she'd like to take it over. What's your opinion? Maybe, if she had Rysk's help..." She winked at him.

He wrapped his arm around her shoulders. "That sounds like a perfect plan." She couldn't help but smile at the look—was it relief?—in his eyes, and eased herself even closer to him.

As they spoke, the buzz of voices in the room grew progressively louder. Lieutenant Hollins stepped in hurriedly, caught Paavo's eye, and gestured for him to approach.

"What's going on?" he asked after excusing himself from Angie.

"Mason Markowitz escaped!" Hollins took his arm and led him over to Calderon. Angie followed at a discreet distance, her curiosity piqued. "Markowitz had been taken out of his jail cell and placed in a much lower security interview room where he was talking to his attorney," Hollins told his two detectives. "Apparently, some woman gave the cop guarding the room a piece of cake at the same time as a plumber arrived saying his company had received a call about some problems in the cells. Between the two of them, the guard was distracted enough that, as the plumber was looking for his identification, he took a bite of cake and went out like a light. It was laced with knock-out drops.

"Next thing, the couple opened the door to the interview room, bound and gagged the lawyer. Keller said it was clear the woman and Markowitz knew each other. The guy removed his coveralls, Markowitz put them on over his prison clothes, and the three of them walked out of there with the cake cart, easy as you please."

"What the hell?" Calderon bellowed. "A spiked cake? And cake cart?" He turned and glared at Angie who was standing near enough to overhear everything and now stood mute and frozen.

Her eyes widened as she looked from Calderon to Lt. Hollins to Paavo.

She started to step closer to defend herself, when Paavo bolted toward her, and whisked her into a corner.

"This isn't really happening, right?" she whispered, no coherent thought in her head beyond Paavo's boss and coworker glaring at her.

"It's happening, Angie. Sounds like Scout and Rysk helped a madman escape."

Lt. Hollins and Calderon approached. Noticing the activity, Yosh also joined them.

Angie felt faint and weak as Calderon stuck his angry red face in hers. "Who the hell are those people you hired?" he barked. "Are you part of this, too? I know Paavo didn't agree with my arresting Markowitz. Is this your way of helping him get even with me?"

She couldn't believe his words. Confusion over her supposed involvement and anger at what he implied about Paavo filled her. But before she found the ability to speak, Paavo's arm circled her waist.

"Leave her alone." He glared at Calderon.

"Why should I?" Calderon clearly wanted to bellow the words, but he also needed to keep what just happened quiet. "Look at what she's done!"

"I didn't do a thing, and neither did my people." Angie's cheeks burned, and she was sick to her stomach. "I can't believe they were willingly involved. Someone made them do it!"

"Who? You?" Calderon sneered.

"She's got a business to run," Yosh said. "She doesn't have time to get involved in a jailbreak and you know it."

Nothing like damning with faint praise, Angie thought.

"There's no reason for Scout and Rysk to help Markowitz escape," Angie insisted.

"Did those two ever mention him?" Calderon demanded.

"Never!"

"Enough," Paavo said. "Angie, I want you to go to my house and stay there."

"What? Now, I can't even go home? What's going on?" She could see he was hiding something from her.

"If Scout and Rysk are behind this, they might go to your place to hide out, and might even bring Markowitz with them. I don't want you facing the three of them. It's best if you aren't alone. Stay at my house. You'll be safe there."

"But Scout and Rysk are my..." She swallowed the word. She'd been saying all along that they were friends, and now look at what they'd done. She could have cried. "Maybe Markowitz isn't the killer everyone thinks he is," she said weakly.

"That isn't for them to decide. It's for the law." Paavo wore his cop face now. The Great Stoneface, she had called it—firm, forceful, and unreadable. "They're obstructing it and will be arrested when caught. I want you far away from them."

She nodded.

"I'll get one of the uniforms to escort you."

"You really think they could be a danger to me?"

"I want to be sure you're safe so I can concentrate on finding Markowitz."

"Wait," she said. "You told me I shouldn't be alone. What if I go to Connie's place instead of your house? It'll give us a chance to talk, and give me something to do rather than worry about you and all that's going on."

He thought a moment, then nodded. "Okay. I'll ask that an officer stays with both of you until this gets resolved."

Angie sighed with relief. "That sounds good."

Officer Crossen, who knew Angie from past cases, had just

stopped in to give his best wishes to the Chief and to eat some cake when Paavo approached him.

Before long, Paavo was gone, and Angie and Crossen went to the parking lot where the second nasty surprise of the night awaited her. "It's not here," she said as she stared at the empty parking spot where her van had been.

"What kind of car is it?" Crossen asked.

"It's a minivan, a white Ford something-or-other." Panic set in. Any minute now she was going to start hyperventilating. What unlucky star was she born under? "There are no white vans out here of any make."

"Are you sure this is where you parked it?"

"Of course! I parked near the door so we wouldn't have to carry the cakes too far."

He just nodded and scanned the parking lot as she spoke. "Did the two people who worked for you have keys to the van?" he asked.

"No. I let Rysk drive it to make deliveries, but he didn't have his own set of keys."

She held up a bundle of keys for him to see.

"What would have stopped him from having a duplicate made while he was on a delivery?" Crossen asked.

Her face fell. "Nothing."

He put his hands on his hips. "I guess we know what they used as the getaway car. I'll let Inspector Smith know. What's the license number?"

CHAPTER THIRTY-SIX

Angie rode in silence beside Officer Crossen, too upset to say a word.

Not only had the Chief's retirement party been ruined, but her employees had released a possible serial killer or killer assistant back into the community. Once word of this got out, her business would be in shambles. Forget giving her business to Scout. She wouldn't have a business to give. And the damage to her good name would be even worse! She'd have to move, somewhere far, far away, where no one knew her. Somewhere like Idaho, maybe.

Going to see Connie was the only good thing about this. She never should have fought with her. More than anything, she wanted to see Connie and beg forgiveness even if she had to get on her knees to do it.

She and Crossen stopped at Connie's gift shop to find her part-time employee in charge. The older woman told Angie that Connie had gone to the bank, and then planned to head for home.

Crossen then drove her to Connie's nearby apartment. She knocked on the door. No answer.

"If she isn't home," Crossen said, "where do you want to go next?"

"Her assistant said she'd be home after the bank. Let's go inside and I'll call her. Don't worry. I've seen Connie do this many times." She then walked to the decorative round knob at the top of the banister right across from Connie's door. Wiggling the ball slightly, she worked it off. Underneath was a key. "Voila!" she said.

Taking the key, she unlocked the door and she and Crossen walked inside. She was trying to find the light switch when she saw a movement in the dark, felt a rapid whoosh of air toward her head, and all went dark.

Lt. Hollins called Paavo into the meeting with Calderon, Benson and Markowitz's attorney, Ethan Keller. Keller told them that as they'd talked, all Markowitz's attention had been focused on stopping the ascension of the Dark Lord's Queen.

"Ah, yes, his mysterious Dark Lord." Calderon sneered. "And, did he happen to say who's been chosen as the Queen of this master demon?"

"Tell him," Hollins demanded of Keller.

Keller loosened his tie as he took in Paavo's scowl. "Markowitz said something I didn't understand. Well, one thing among many that I didn't understand. He said, the one who believed him must watch his woman to keep her safe. We... uh... Lt. Hollins thought you might have some idea what he's talking about."

Hollins eyes narrowed at Paavo. "Aren't you the one he thinks believes him?"

Paavo's breath came quickly. "It sounds like Angie could be in danger."

"No, no, no!" Calderon yelled. The others faced him. "None

of you get it. Angie was a part of it. She helped him escape. It's all part of the game that's going on with Markowitz. He says these outrageous things and gets gullible people to believe him."

"Wait a minute—" Paavo began.

"No, you wait. He's only saying this because Angie's friends helped him. That's how he knows her. The rest is all nonsense, scare talk to get everyone worked up."

"If you really think the man is a serial killer," Paavo said to Calderon, "I should think you'd be very worried about Angie and Scout both. Or, do you suddenly believe Markowitz is a lot less dangerous than you were saying?"

"Of course he's dangerous, but serial killers aren't dangerous to the ones who help him."

"You're wrong," Keller said. "I've been doing a lot of reading since I took this case. Serial killers have been known to turn on their own mothers."

"Angie had nothing to do with this!" Paavo insisted. "She was as shocked as anyone else by what happened. She's perfectly innocent."

"Let's see how helpful she is to us," Calderon said. "I want you, Paavo, to find out from Angie all you can about her two workers, where they live, everything else that might be useful. Don't bother about anything else. I'll handle it."

Paavo glanced at Hollins, who nodded in agreement with Calderon. Paavo left quickly before he said anything he'd regret, pulled up the information he already had found on Scout and Rysk, and transferred the files to Calderon.

Inspector Pamela James was at her desk in the Missing Persons bureau. "Pam, I need help," Paavo said, then went on to explain what he was looking for.

She did the search as he'd asked. Location, Chicago or San Francisco. Sex, female. Age, 16-18. Name, Greta Vannix.

A school picture came onto the screen of a smiling teenager.

As he studied at the picture, his shoulders sagged as if with the weight of it all. Scout had told him she was in the city looking for her missing sister, and she also said her sister went to the Baron's club.

Now, that he was looking for it, he could see the resemblance between the two sisters. If Scout's hair hadn't been dyed black, and if she didn't wear all that dark Goth make-up, she would look a great deal like her sister.

And he would have seen the resemblance between her and the first victim, the young woman killed in Sausalito, the one who had called herself Mina Harker.

Paavo went back to Homicide to show Calderon and Benson this latest piece of the puzzle. Scout clearly didn't know her sister was dead, and may have thought Markowitz would lead her to Greta. Or that he could give her an answer to Greta's disappearance.

Connie stood up from his desk as Paavo entered the bureau. He was stunned to see her and quickly looked around for Angie. She wasn't there.

A sense of dread filled him. "What are you doing here?" he asked Connie. "Where's Angie?"

"I don't know," she said eyeing his expression. "What's wrong? I heard she would be here serving cake, and I thought I'd come to see her, to talk and set our foolish problems aside. But when I got to the reception, it had already ended. I thought she'd be here with you."

"I'll try to reach her on her cell phone," Paavo said,

punching in her number. "She went to your apartment, hoping to find you there. If she's not with you, where is she?"

Again, Angie didn't answer. He scowled at the phone and tried Connie's gift shop. Maybe she was there waiting for Connie to return.

Bo Benson sauntered over to Connie. "Hi, there, you a friend of Paavo's?"

"Yes. And Angie's my best friend. Or was."

"Was?" Benson asked as he put the Markowitz folder on Paavo's desk. "I'm sorry to hear that. I'm sure she'll come around. Have you two known each other long?"

"Not very long. But we hit it off right away." She smiled at him.

He pushed the folder to the side and sat on the corner of the desk. "If you and she run around together, does that mean you're also single?" he asked, smiling back.

Angie was no longer at the gift shop, so Paavo decided to try her number once more.

"Well, does divorced count?" Connie asked coyly. She reached for the cup of coffee she'd gotten earlier while waiting for Paavo, and as she did, she bumped Benson's folder. It toppled to the floor and several papers and photos slid out of it.

She bent over to help him pick them up. Suddenly, she let loose a screech of shock and fear.

Everyone jumped. Calderon pulled out his gun and Bill Sutter dived under his desk.

Paavo jumped to his feet while Benson grabbed her arm.

"What's wrong?" Paavo asked.

"There." A wildly shaking finger pointed at a picture taken inside the Baron's club. "It's him! It's my stalker!"

"Stalker?" Paavo asked. "The guy you mentioned near your house?"

Connie nodded. "I'd had an eerie feeling of being watched, but I tried to ignore it. Then, one night, I got home a little later than usual and he was already across the street looking up at my apartment. He was under the streetlamp so I saw his face. When he noticed me, I glared at him. He scared me half to death, but he hurried away. So far, he hasn't returned, I don't think. But now, you've got his picture. That's him!"

"Tonight," Markowitz rocked back and forth in the backseat of the minivan. "We've got to stop him tonight."

"I know, already!" Scout shouted nervously. She had parked Angie's minivan in front of the old church just a bit past the Baron's house. Now, while Rysk sneaked around to check out the house, she sat behind the wheel, ready to drive off as soon as he returned. "We will, as soon as Rysk comes back and tells us what he found."

"I can't wait. If he gets the Dark Queen, he will be too powerful to fight. I must go now." He tugged on the door handle. Luckily, the minivan had a child's safety lock, and Scout had used it. Markowitz wasn't going anywhere.

She needed him to find Greta. He'd promised he would do it as soon as he took care of this Dark Queen business. In his confrontation with the Baron—or, Baalberith, as he always called him—he would somehow force the man to tell him where Greta had gone.

Now that Scout had been barred from the Crypt Macabre for some unknown reason, she had no one but Markowitz to help her. If only the man didn't talk in riddles, his instructions would be a lot easier to follow.

All she knew was that Greta seemed farther and farther away from her with each passing day.

"*Saint Michael the Archangel, defend us in battle,*" Markowitz prayed. "*Be our safeguard against the wickedness and snares of the devil—*"

"Damn it, stop already!" He was spooking her, just like the Baron's quiet house. With its Gothic tower piercing the night sky, and a half-moon with wispy black clouds looming overhead, it could have been part of a Wes Craven movie.

Rysk had snuck into the back of it over ten minutes ago and hadn't returned. Where was he? "Rysk should be back by now," she said. "I don't like this."

Markowitz seemed so much crazier to her now than he had before being imprisoned, it scared her and made her wonder why she'd ever listened to his cockeyed scheme about breaking out of jail and confronting the Baron to learn about the Dark Queen as well as Greta. So far, to her amazement, his plan had worked, but Rysk's prolonged absence was making her very nervous.

"*May God rebuke him, we humbly pray--*"

"Hey, cool it!" She twisted in the seat and faced him. "What do you think is happening inside? Do you think the Baron's hurt Rysk?"

Markowitz stopped his prayer and looked at her strangely. "The Baron? Why should the Baron hurt Rysk?"

Scout froze. "What do you mean? The one you call Baalberith. Isn't--"

Before she could finish, shots rang out.

CHAPTER THIRTY-SEVEN

Paavo parked a half-block from the Baron's house. The street was empty and quiet. A light shone in the front window of the house. Connie was with him, her eyes wide with fright as Paavo began to make calls on his cell phone.

Yosh had just entered Angie's apartment using Paavo's key. No one was there. Rebecca and Bill Sutter went to Paavo's house. Angie wasn't there either. Calderon and Benson went to Connie's. They'd found the apartment door unlocked.

Inside, Officer Crossen had been knocked unconscious and tied up. All he could say was that there was more than one person involved. As he'd followed Angie into the apartment, someone struck him from behind, and when he stumbled forward, he felt another blow from the front. After that, nothing until he saw Calderon's ugly face yelling at him to wake up.

Angie still wasn't answering her phone, and Paavo was beyond frantic. "Time to visit the Baron," he said to Connie. "You might want to wait here."

"No way," she said, following him up to the door to Baron Severus's house. There was no answer to his loud knock. Along the edges of the drapery-covered windows, he was able to see that some lights were on inside.

"The hell with it," he said, and took out a lock pick. In a moment, the door sprang open. He turned to Connie. "Go sit in the car. Be ready to call for help if needed."

Connie backed onto the street, her eyes wide as she took in the aged, gaudy furnishings in the house.

Paavo unsnapped the strap over his gun holster and went in, leaving the door open, calling out that he was the police and had entered the home. Immediately, he sensed something cold squeezing his lungs, trying to steal his very breath. He gasped, fighting it, and continued toward the parlor.

Candles lit the room. Hundreds of votive candles, all reeking with the familiar smell of camphor—the same as the candles found at the ritual murders. In the shadows, near the window, sat Severus. His back was toward Paavo, his head dropped forward.

Gun in hand, Paavo crept closer. "Baron?" Was the man asleep?

Paavo lightly touched his shoulder. "Baron Severus?" A cold prickle went through him as he whirled in front of the man. His eyes were open but sightless, his mouth, too, hung open and a bead of blood dribbled from it onto his shirt.

The Baron was dead.

Angie opened her eyes, then quickly shut them again. She was sitting on a wooden chair, her wrists bound to its arms. She heard the sound of footsteps, shuffling footsteps, around her.

She remained still, not making a sound.

But then she peeked and saw a skinny young man in a black robe silently walk around the windowless chamber lighting candles. Floor and walls seemed to be made of stone. When he finished, he climbed a staircase built flush against a wall. At the top of the stairs was a small landing and a door that must lead out of this deep dungeon. No railing protected the stairs or the landing, and the young fellow stayed close to the wall as he walked.

In the chamber, on one side stood a long table, a wooden chest beside it. Against the opposite wall, on the floor, their arms and legs tied, were Scout and an old man. Mason Markowitz, Angie thought. But the three of them had been left alone in the cold, dank room. Where was Rysk?

Whatever was happening here didn't make sense to Angie. She remembered the Baron's talk of rituals and Paavo telling her about Markowitz and a Dark Queen... and her. The Baron had to be the one behind this. But wasn't Scout his friend? Why had he tied up Scout? And Markowitz? Had Rysk, for some reason, double-crossed them?

Her eyes caught Scout's, and the fear in the other woman's made her blood run cold. Angie could tell by the bruises on her face she'd been beaten. Dried blood was caked at her mouth. She'd put up a fight and lost. The old man looked dazed.

Maybe, somehow, Rysk had escaped. Angie knew he cared for Scout. He couldn't have allowed the Baron to do this to her, unless... No! He was out there. He would call Paavo, she was sure he had enough sense to do that. But how would Paavo know where to find her?

Somehow, if she and Scout and, possibly, Markowitz, hoped to get out of here alive, she had to take care of this herself.

Mason Markowitz was muttering. She understood the words. She, too, had learned to say the rosary in Latin. Hearing him shook her. His were not the words or demeanor of a serial killer.

"What's going on?" she asked in a whisper.

"He's going to kill us," Scout whispered in return. Even so,

Angie could tell her voice was hoarse, perhaps from yelling for help.

"He is the demon Baalberith. With his Dark Queen, he will rule the world," Markowitz said. "She will make him stronger than he's ever been. Through the centuries he's searched for her, and now, finally, the hour is near. He's killed four women, and now, he plans to kill his fifth. His Dark Queen."

"You're talking about the ritual killer?" Angie asked, her voice tiny.

Scout nodded.

"Where's Rysk?" Angie asked, hoping against hope they'd tell her he was rounding up the police as they spoke.

Scout's tears began to fall again. "I don't know. He was casing the Baron's house when we heard shots. He's got to be all right, Angie, he's just got to be."

"The fifth victim will be the Dark Queen." Markowitz's pronouncement cut through Scout's sobs.

"After she's dead?" Angie asked.

Markowitz nodded.

Just then, the door at the top of the staircase opened.

***

Paavo heard a stifled scream and turned around to see Connie standing in the doorway, gawking at the body. She had pressed her back to the wall, her hand covering her mouth. "I thought it would be okay to follow," she said. "I had no idea. Who is he?"

"Baron Severus. Stay back." Gun drawn, he continued down the hall. She followed.

He glanced back and frowned at her.

"I'm afraid to stay alone," she whispered. "What if the murderer is still here?"

His experience with Angie told him it was easier not to argue. The two continued through the house, Connie watching the hallway as he searched one room after the other for more people or victims.

At the back of the house, beyond the kitchen, he opened the door to a room whose only furniture was a table set up as a sort of altar with candles, incense, rocks and goat horns atop a black cloth.

In the back corner of the room was a door, and in front of the door, face down, lay another body.

Angie stared, wide-eyed, scarcely able to breathe for the fear that filled her as a man wearing a heavy black robe and full black face mask came down the stairs. He didn't look at any of them, but went straight to the large table.

He lifted a wooden chest onto it and drew a key from the pocket of the black trousers he wore under his cape. Opening the chest, he took out a syringe and a bottle of serum.

"By the power of God," Markowitz shouted, "thrust down to hell Satan and all wicked spirits who wander through the world for the ruin of souls."

Behind the mask, Angie could hear the man's laughter. Her head felt light, her heart pounded as she watched him. What was the serum? And who was he going after? She had to know. "Why am I here?"

He didn't answer, but continued to mutter and set up an old book and candles in what resembled a makeshift altar.

"I don't know either," Scout said. "Unless..."

The Dark Queen? "Not me," Angie cried. "I haven't done anything. I've minded my own business! It's not even Paavo's case. All I've done is bake and bake and bake until I'm sick of it." As the so-called demon prepared the syringe, her hysteria grew. "Isn't it bad enough that my business is ruined, that I have no friends, that my boyfriend doesn't even think about getting married? I tried to be a good person, I really did. Is it my fault that I screwed up? I don't want to end this way!"

He whirled on her. "Shut up!" he demanded.

"Please, Baron," she said on the verge of tears. "I don't want to be your Dark Queen."

"You're mistaken, young lady," Markowitz called. "That's not the Baron."

"He's not?" Angie asked, stunned.

"And," Markowitz continued, "you're not the Dark Queen."

Paavo hurried to the body and turned it over. It was Rysk. Bullets holes pierced his shirt and leg, and blood puddled on the floor.

Paavo felt a light pulse, and used his cell phone to call for an ambulance even as he tore open Rysk's shirt to see the damage and found a bulletproof vest. The kind cops wear. The vest had protected him from the heart shots he'd taken and had saved his life.

The leg wound looked bad. He'd lost a lot of blood. "I'll get a rag or sheet for a tourniquet," Connie said and ran toward a bedroom.

As Paavo checked him over, Rysk opened his eyes. He looked startled, dazed, then shifted as if he wanted to sit up. Paavo put a hand on his shoulder, stopping him.

"Who did this?" Paavo asked as he ripped the sheet Connie gave him.

"There were several, all wearing robes, masks," Rysk replied, his voice weak, his eyes dazed. "I think they were from the club. I'm pretty sure I recognized the way a couple of them moved. The shooter was older, bigger."

"He also wore a mask?"

In a voice scarcely a whisper, Rysk answered, "Black. Shiny. Full face."

Paavo bound the leg and tied the tourniquet tight as he quickly called in the Baron's murder. The M.E. and crime scene investigators would soon arrive.

Connie helped Rysk drink some water, which seemed to help a bit.

"You saw the Baron dead?" Paavo asked.

"Yes, at the same time as I heard the others. I pulled out my gun, headed for the back door. Two moved closer, acting like they didn't even care if I shot them, I hesitated, and that's when the shooter got me. I went soft." His eyes wanted to shot, but he forced them to stay open. "Stupid of me!"

"Did you see Angie?"

"Angie? No." Blinking helped his eyes clear a bit. "Where's Scout? Is she here?"

"No. Neither is Markowitz."

Rysk tried to sit up. "Damn! I've got to find them."

Paavo held him down and asked Connie for blankets and a pillow. "You aren't going anywhere. What's this about? Why did you spring Markowitz?"

Rysk refused to lie flat. Connie brought blankets to cover Rysk, then went outside to direct the ambulance as soon as they arrived. Paavo used pillows to help Rysk sit up.

Rysk put his head back against the wall and shut his eyes to gather strength a moment. "I'm DEA. We got a tip about a dealer—the Baron. I was elected for undercover, to build a case against him and his suppliers. Met Scout at The Crypt, and tagged her as a fraud. She interested me—I couldn't figure her out, especially when she got a job with Angie. I followed her, knew her story was phony, so I kept after her. Big mistake."

"Tell me."

"I fell for her, hook, line and sinker. She's strange, but good-hearted." He needed to pause a moment. "She thought Baron

Severus was behind her sister's becoming a junkie and disappearing. She wanted to find the girl and wanted revenge. Markowitz was supposed to help her, but he got arrested."

"Markowitz kept talking about the full moon and Friday the thirteenth—today. He had to get out of jail to stop some demon. Scout believed him. I went along to make sure she didn't get herself killed. But also, I came to believe that Markowitz was innocent. And you know what?"

"What?"

"I think there are demons here."

Paavo flinched.

Rysk shut his eyes again. "Forget I said that. I'd like to keep my job."

Paavo nodded. "You have any idea where they might be?"

Risk shipped his head. "The only place I ever heard the Baron mention was some abandoned Catholic Church he used for ceremonies."

The medics showed up, and Paavo backed away from Rysk ready to run to the church right next door. At first, he had to ask, "You were the one who called in the tip about Lolly Firenghetti weren't you?"

Rysk nodded. "Find Scout for me," he whispered as the paramedics began to work on him. "Please find her."

"I'll find them both," Paavo said as Connie led the EMTs to Rysk.

The Dark Lord turned from the altar with a sneer. "You? You thought you were my Queen!"

"I'm not the Queen?" Angie could scarcely believe her good fortune, for once thankful she wasn't the one "selected."

"You're too pushy, and not even a virgin." His voice was tinged with disgust. He placed his hand lovingly over the book.

"My Queen is beautiful, and pure. Twenty minutes before midnight tonight she will become mine, and the commandment of the *Ars Diabolus* shall be met."

"Midnight where?" Angie asked, not understanding who or what he was talking about. "Your book sounds like Latin. If it's from Italy, midnight is long past. You lose." She hoped she'd bought them all some time, and hadn't just signed their death warrants.

He laughed. "You are clever. Perhaps, you will tell me where my Queen has gone tonight."

"Me?"

"Once we find her, you and your friends will be let go. If we don't, you will all die."

"Don't listen to him," Markowitz shrieked in a shrill, quavering voice. "If he finds her and gains her power, everything will be lost. Sacrifice us, but don't give her to him." He stared at the masked man and sounding more forceful, cried out, "I exorcise you, Most Unclean Spirit! Be uprooted and expelled from this Creature of God."

"You filth!" The masked man roared at him. "Vomit-eating pestilence! Abandoned by your own wife, flesh of your flesh, you have no one! How does that make you feel? You are nothing! And I... I am the Dark Lord!"

Angie stared at them both, wondering which was craziest. "Who am I looking for?" she asked the Dark Lord, hoping to stop him and Markowitz from going after each other.

The Dark Lord spun toward her. "Your friend, damn it!"

"*What friend?*"

His chest heaved. "The beautiful one. The most perfect being on the planet. My other half, my love, my completion."

"You've got the wrong person," Angie insisted. "I don't know anybody like that."

"I saw her with you in your car, in the graveyard next to this church."

"Connie?" She was flabbergasted. "You want Connie to be your Queen? *My* Connie?"

"She should have been home tonight!" He pounded his fist against his hand. "She's always home, every evening. I've watched her, night after night. I don't know where she's gone, but you should know—you're her friend. Or were. You *will* find her for me."

Angie thought quickly. If she convinced him not to go look for Connie, then he might choose... someone close by... already captured... oh, dear! "Okay," she said. "She's a fine choice. Excellent. In fact, I always could see an aura of royalty about her."

"Connie—so that's her name," Markowitz murmured to Scout. "I'm sorry. I never could see her clearly." Then he faced Angie and said, "She really does value your friendship very much."

Angie's spine tingled with his words at the same time as realization struck. She faced Scout. "Your questions about my friends, looking at my address book—you were trying to find Connie, weren't you? All this time, it was all about Connie."

"No. I had no idea. I was looking to see if any names jumped out at me, nothing more," Scout said.

"Quiet!" the Dark Lord demanded. "We don't have much time."

"Let me use my phone to call Connie," Angie suggested. "She's probably got it with her." She'd try to put in the call to Paavo, and if that didn't work, somehow she'd get a message to him or Connie that she was in terrible danger.

"Your cellphone is in your handbag?" he asked.

"Yes." She glanced at the wrist bindings. "But I can't use the phone with these. I need them untied I always use both thumbs."

He slashed through them, freeing her. "Don't try anything. I have a knife and a gun."

Angie shrank back. "I'm sure I'll find her."

He tossed her handbag at her. "Good. I already have my four consorts, but perhaps I will allow you to be one of her handmaidens."

As she reached into the handbag for her phone, she had to wonder how all this had come about. All she'd wanted to do was have a sweet little business baking comical cakes. And now she was looking at creating her own handmaiden's tale.

CHAPTER THIRTY-EIGHT

Paavo called Yosh and Calderon to let them know what was happening, and to send backup quick to St. Michael the Archangel Church.

"She'll be all right, won't she?" Connie asked, her voice cracking.

Paavo forced himself to a place where no emotion could reach him. He couldn't allow himself to think about that now—couldn't think about what that mad men might be doing to Angie.

"She'll be fine," he said firmly.

The statue of St. Michael the Archangel on the church roof was visible against the night sky as he ran to the main doors of the church. They were locked. With Connie close by—she again refused to sit alone in his car—he searched for another entry.

Despite the warmth of the night, he was suddenly freezing, so cold, he could see his breath with each exhale.

Angie found her phone, unlocked it and was about to put her finger on Paavo's contact number when the Dark Lord snatched it from her.

"First things first," he said. "I want everything ready for her. But if you move, I will punish you in a very painful way."

Angie froze with fear.

Holding the knife in one hand, from the wooden chest, the masked man lifted a flask, a scissor and pliers, and placed all on the table. Beside them, from his pocket he took the syringe he'd prepared earlier. Looking at all that, Angie felt faint.

He lifted the glass top from the flask. "This is the oil of purification," he said. "We will bathe my Queen and her hand-maiden in this oil, to make her ready to receive me."

"I don't think so," she murmured, even as her heart pounded. "People are looking for me right now. They'll find me."

"The cop won't be helping anyone, ever again," he said.

No! Her mind screamed as the world tipped. "Paavo?" she whispered, unable to breathe from what he was suggesting.

"Not him. The other one. The one who hung around and pretended to be one of us. Did he think I was so stupid I couldn't tell? I could smell it on him."

"Rysk?" Scout cried, her eyes betraying her pain. "Oh, my God, no..."

Angie stared at him, holding back tears close to the surface, her mind whirring between relief over Paavo and horror over Rysk. Rysk... a cop? Strangely, it made sense to her. His questions, his watchfulness, his always hovering near ready to help, his bravery... much like Paavo, in fact. But she wouldn't believe he was dead. She couldn't. He was too young, too full of life and laughter. Please, God, she prayed, let him live.

In the background, Markowitz continued to speak the rite of exorcism.

A plastic sheet lay folded in a corner of the basement.

Finally, the Dark Lord put the knife down as he spread it on the floor and placed a stack of towels beside it. The once-white towels had a rust-colored stain, the color that appears when blood is imperfectly washed from cotton.

He drew aside a cloth that covered a portion of a wall. Painted in silver on the wall was a five-pointed star, with the fifth point facing straight up. Nailed to each of the other four points was a human heart.

Angie stared in horror. "Here are my Queen's consorts. The empty space is hers. Here are Julie, and Lucy, and Tashanda, and Mina, my first." He ran a finger over the desiccated heart, then faced Scout. "She preferred that name to Greta."

Oh, no! Angie felt sick. Scout sister. And this bastard had known who she was; all this time, he'd known she was dead.

Scout screamed hysterically and in her fury and despair, managed to pull her hands free from their bindings, stripping away her skin as she did so. Bloodied, she lunged at him.

He knocked her to the floor, but she was beyond caring.

Still shrieking, she clawed at his legs, his stomach, crawling up him. He put his hands to her throat. She tried to pull his hands off her, but he squeezed harder.

Angie hurled herself at him, breaking his hold. She tried to punch him, but he let Scout fall, and turned toward her. She jumped back, away from him.

Even through the round holes for his eyes, she could see that they burned red. As he moved toward her, she attacked again, hoping to catch him off-guard, and reached for his mask.

The mask came off in her hand. She looked up, and the pallid, fleshy face of Wilbur Fieldren, the Baron's assistant, stared back at her.

This was no demon, no "Dark Lord," just a weak, homely man trying to make himself into something important at the expense of women like Scout and her sister, Rysk, and her own dear Connie.

Fieldren grabbed Angie's arms. "Look at my eyes, and be lost to God."

Paavo shouted a warning as a Goth-looking woman leaped from the shadows of the unlocked back entry to St. Michael's church where she had been standing guard and grabbed a handful of Connie's hair. Connie reared back her fist and smashed the woman in the jaw, knocking her out cold.

At the same time Fredrick Limore, dressed in a long, black robe, flew at Paavo, hands fisted and skinny arms outstretched. Paavo made quick work of Limore, but two other Goth teens, the ones Limore had named as Taylor Walters' friends, attacked, each swinging heavy four-by-fours of wood, and aiming at his head.

Connie leaped on one's back and stuck her thumb in his eye.

Fieldren! That this cretin, this very human cretin, had inflicted so much destruction and pain was more than Angie could stand. She'd pay him back with her tongue if nothing else. "You think you can control people with those piggy-little eyes? Look in your eyes? Only if I want to throw up!"

"Quiet!" he ordered.

"You're so pathetic! A disgusting blowhard who needs a Thigh Master and a serious diet—"

"I said—"

"You're a ball-less, fat lump of gristle, not worth the water to flush away. "

"Damn you!" Momentarily stricken at her assault, Fieldren shoved her away from him. His face turned crimson. He almost tripped on his long black robe, and tore it off, revealing a black shirt and trousers. He picked up a wooden chair. "I'll crush you! You are not worthy to be anything for my Queen! I'll beat you until there's nothing left."

"Oh, I'm so scared! Lord of the Stupid and Craven, that's what you are. Put down that chair and leave us alone before you find yourself being strapped to a different chair. An electric chair."

"You will rue today for eternity!" He lunged at her, trying to jab her with the legs of the chair. She stepped between them, two chair legs on one side of her body and two on the other. She grabbed hold of the stretcher between the legs and tried to yank the chair out of his hands.

He pulled it back, but she wouldn't let go. He jerked it toward her again, then swung the chair from side to side, but no matter what he did, she held on, preventing him from getting enough leverage to hit her with it.

Finally, he pressed forward with determination, pushing the chair with Angie trapped inside toward the wall.

"Begone, Most Evil Serpent!" Markowitz thrust his foot in Fieldren's path. Fieldren tripped on it, falling hard onto the cement floor.

Angie let the chair drop.

Furious, Fieldren grabbed it and hit Markowitz with such force the chair cracked into several pieces. Markowitz lay in a bloody heap. Fieldren tossed aside the chair and turned toward Angie.

She wasn't there.

He slowly turned in a circle. One of her shoes lay on the stone steps leading out of the basement, and the door at the top was partially ajar. Had he left it that way? Or had she gone up there?

After a quick sweep of the cellar he picked up the shoe and

ran up the stairs to the top landing. There, he stopped and made another search of the cellar.

Suddenly, he gave a sharp laugh and pointed.

By the sound and the direction he was pointing, Angie knew he'd spotted her. She looked down at herself and saw that the shoeless toes of one foot were jutting out from beneath the discarded robe she'd burrowed under.

His laughter turned hollow, and then into a roar. Unmindful of hiding any longer, she tossed aside the robe and looked up at him. He stood at the top landing, bending forward, toward her, his face contorted, his eyes slanted into those of a serpent, his nostrils flared, and his mouth and jaw protruded with sharp, uneven teeth. He reminded her of a drawing of a demon she'd seen as a child in a Classics Comic book of Milton's *Paradise Lost*. She stared, unable to move, expecting fire to spew from his mouth at any moment.

"You are mine." A deep voice reverberated through the cellar, the most chilling, unearthly and unholy sound she had ever heard.

Petrified, she screamed, pulling the remains of the broken chair in front of her as a meager protection.

Behind Fieldren, the door at the top of the stairs suddenly swung open, hitting him in the backside as he bent on the edge of the landing yelling at Angie. He lost his balance, his arms gyrating like windmills as the door knocked him from the landing and he fell straight downward... to land atop a broken chair leg sticking straight up. The leg impaled his stomach and came out his back.

He jerked once, twice, and then collapsed. Angie stared at Fieldren's face. In death, it was again the flabby, nerdish face she'd known. She must have just imagined the strange transformation at the top of the stairs—a hysterical reaction on her part, nothing more. Of course, nothing more.

Angie then glanced up to the landing where Fieldren had stood and saw her dear sweet Connie standing there.

"Angie!" Connie shrieked and bounded down the steps. The door had blocked her view of Fieldren's fall, so the would-be Dark Queen had no idea what she had wrought.

Next, how both stepped to the landing, followed by you and what seemed to be a whole squadron of blue uniforms. Although they hurried down the stairs, Paavo remained on the landing. She saw his astonished gaze go to Scout and Markowitz, both bloody and unconscious, to Fieldren, who now looked very dead, and to her, standing amidst it all.

She held his gaze, smiling tearfully, until she was swooped into a bear hug from Connie. "I was so scared for you!" Connie burst into tears. "Did he hurt you?"

Angie hugged her friend hard. "I'm fine. Now."

They both began to laugh through their tears, all the while hugging, and patting each other.

Yosh was checking out the very dead Fieldren, while police officers were administering first aid to Scout and Markowitz, who were both stirring.

"Are you all right, Angie?" Paavo asked, embracing her as much as he could with Connie still holding onto her. He'd retrieved her shoe and handed it over. "Do you need a medic?"

"I'm fine. I don't need anyone now that you're here," she said, one arm still around Connie. "Thank God you got here when you did. Both of you."

"I'm so sorry I ever doubted our friendship," Connie said, tears in her eyes. "Thinking you were in danger told me how important you are to me. I love you, girlfriend. I'm sorry I've been such a pill."

"You were out looking for me with Paavo?" Angie asked.

"Absolutely," Connie said.

"Thank God!" Angie realized that was why Fieldren

couldn't find her. In that same instant she decided never to tell Connie how close she came to becoming royalty... dead royalty.

"I didn't know you could take out three people all by yourself," Connie said with awe.

"Oh, I didn't--"

"Good work, Angelina," Calderon said, as he and Benson marched into the chamber, trying to see what was going on with *their* case. "You caught the escapee, the woman who helped him, and this nutcase who captured all of you."

"No, that's not—"

"Wow, you are some babe," Benson said. "You got a cool woman, Paavo. You ever get tired of her, give me time to line up." Despite his words to Angie, he smiled at Connie and winked.

"I don't know if I'd want a woman who could do all this," Calderon said with a chuckle, looking at the chaos around her. "What if she got mad at me?"

He and Benson laughed and then moved in to begin the preliminary steps for a homicide investigation. At the same time, the medics arrived and took over the care of Scout and Markowitz.

Angie watched over both while the cops told the paramedics of her bravery.

She finally got a chance to explain to Calderon and Benson that Markowitz wasn't the serial killer after all, that Fieldren was, and Connie actually was the one who'd knocked him off the stairs. Also, Scout, the sister of one of Fieldren's victims, was also in a sense, a victim herself.

She then drew aside the cloth that covered the wall holding a pentagram with the hearts of the four women.

This caused even more of a stir as the cops realized that she had stood up to a serial killer, and a deranged one at that.

That didn't stop her knees from shaking as she realized just how close to dying she had come. She wasn't really courageous; she simply had no choice. Yet, as the compliments continued, she couldn't help but stand a little straighter.

CHAPTER THIRTY-NINE

Paavo looked at Angie with pride throughout all this, even though at the moment he felt about as useful as a potted plant. But at least he was a warm potted plant. From the time Fieldren died, the aching chill he had struggled against vanished. It had to be a bizarre coincidence. Surely, nothing more.

None of that mattered as he grew increasingly agitated watching one after the other of the homicide inspectors, uniformed cops, paramedics, medical examiner assistants, and even the crime scene inspectors stop and tell Angie how incredible it was that she not only found the serial killer, but managed to keep her cool long enough to give them time to get there and prevent any more murders. There were all sorts of brotherly and sisterly pats on her shoulder as cops and paramedics circled around her, and Krazy Glue couldn't have stuck Connie more firmly to her side.

The way they were talking, she sounded like some Superwoman or something. Xena, move over, he thought, not to mention Buffy. But she wasn't any of those things. She was just Angie—the woman he loved and wanted to marry.

The woman he could never seem to find the right time or place to tell those words to. And now, with this madman, he'd nearly lost her.

What the hell was he waiting for?

"Angie, let's get out of here," he said, taking her arm.

She pulled back. "Get out? But my friends. I can't leave Scout. I'll have to go the hospital."

He didn't want to wait. No more delays. No more nonsense —just him and her so that he could tell her all he'd wanted to say, and hadn't, for far too long. "We'll go later. She'll be under doctor's care for a while. As will Rysk. She'll have his company there, whether she wants it or not."

"Rysk is alive? Thank God!" Angie smiled down at Scout. "She'll want his company, that's for sure."

"Let's go, then," Paavo said once more as he reached for her.

She turned away, scanning the room, gazing with affection again at Connie. "Calderon wants my statements. He said for me to wait right here."

"He can get them later."

"Later, we're going to the hospital, remember?"

"Angie—"

Just then, Officer Crossen ran down the steps and stopped in front of her, a huge bandage on his forehead. "I was sent home from the hospital, but when word came over the police band about the action here, I had to make sure you were all right."

"I'm fine. Thank you for coming." Stepping away from Paavo, Angie kissed Crossen's cheek, then hugged him. He hugged back.

Paavo couldn't stand another minute of this. "Angie," he called.

"This woman should win the bravery award for the year. Maybe for the decade," Crossen said to another blue uniform as Angie beamed.

"Angie, let's go."

She glanced at Paavo, confusion in her eyes. "Go? Why? Whatever could be so important?"

It was on the tip of Paavo's tongue to blurt out the words, but after all this waiting, he wasn't about to ruin everything. All he knew was from the time he realized how close he'd come to losing her again, he knew he wasn't about to waste another minute.

"It's time to get away from all this, *and for us to be alone!*"

All eyes turned toward him in stunned silence. He hadn't meant to say those last few words so loudly, but obviously he had.

He also had Angie's attention now, along with everyone else's. "Okay," she said, looking at him with more confusion than ever.

Paavo told Calderon and Benson she would give her statements the next day. No one argued with him.

He'd blown it, he realized. All his plans for moonlight and roses and a romantic setting had fizzled, and he'd ended up practically ordering her and everyone else around. A first-class idiot would have shown more sense.

But when she looked up at him with those big, brown eyes he loved, he could see that she wanted to be with him, just as he wanted to be with her. Wordlessly he led her from the old church to his car and drove her to his home.

Once there, he took her cell phone and his, and turned them off. "What are you doing? You never turn off your phone," Angie said.

"I know," he murmured, then he got her some water after her ordeal and gave her time to freshen up and unwind. He poured them both some chilled white wine and waited in the living room where he lit a small fire in the fireplace.

After a short time, looking refreshed, she joined him and

sat beside him on the sofa. "Okay, what's this all about?" she again asked.

He studied the fire along moment. "This isn't the way I planned it at all," he confessed. "I wanted a fancy restaurant, and we've gone to several recently. I would get dressed up, and ask you to do the same." He gazed at her. "But despite my plans, it never worked out."

Her brow furrowed.

"But then," he continued, his gaze holding hers, "as I wondered why, I thought of how this is the spot I first realized I was in love with you. This is where we first kissed, and where we first made love."

She smiled. "Yes, so it is," she whispered, still a bit puzzled. "And you know I've always loved being here."

"I know. So, what better place to do this than here?" He got down on one knee. "Don't laugh."

Laughter, he quickly realized, was the last thing on her mind. She put a hand to her mouth and her eyes sparkled with tears he hoped were happy ones.

Seeing her reaction, his throat tightened, and he felt pressure behind his own eyes. All the flowery words of the speeches he had practiced time and again flew from his mind and he spoke only the few words he knew must be said. "I want to spend my life with. I love you." He then took the ring box from his pocket and, his heart in his throat, opened it. "Will you marry me?"

"Oh my! Yes! Of course, yes." She threw her arms around him, kissing and hugging him tight. He felt as if he could breathe again as relief and love fill him. Finally, he'd done it. And she said yes!

She then drew back from him, quickly wiping away a tear. "And this ring! It's so beautiful! I love it."

He joined her again on the sofa and watched as she put the

ring on and held out her hand. "It's perfect, and it fits perfectly. How did you know?"

"I am a detective, after all," he said with a grin.

She put her hands on the sides of his face and then brushed her fingers against his hair, caressing him. "What did I ever do to deserve you?"

As he drew her close for their first kiss as an engaged couple, he whispered, "Well, after all, you are a demon slayer."

THE END

Dear Reader,

I hope you've enjoyed this latest "Cook and Inspector Mystery." The next mystery is **Blind Date's Bitter End** *in which Angie's best friend Connie has decided to get serious about finding herself a boyfriend, to the extent of going out on a blind date. Of course, Angie is trying to help, but nothing works out as either of them expect.*

ABOUT THE AUTHOR

Joanne Pence was born and raised in northern California and now lives in Idaho. She has been an award-winning, *USA Today* best-selling author of mysteries for many years, but she has also written historical fiction, contemporary romance, romantic suspense, a fantasy, and supernatural suspense. All of her books are now available as ebooks and in print, and most are also offered in special large print editions. Joanne hopes you'll enjoy her books, which present a variety of times, places, and reading experiences, from mysterious to thrilling, emotional to lightly humorous, as well as powerful tales of times long past.

Visit her at www.joannepence.com and be sure to sign up for Joanne's mailing list to hear about new books.